Heartache. Betrayal. Forgiveness. Redemption. It's time to head back to Magdalena, New York, and spend a little time with the people we love to love and even a few we love to hate.

Eight years ago, tragedy struck the town's perfect couple, Daniel "Cash" Casherdon and Tess Carrick, days before their wedding. That tragedy shredded their dreams of a life together and sent them fleeing Magdalena. Now, destiny has brought them back and the town is determined to see this couple mend their differences.

Angelo "Pop" Benito will lead the crusade to march Cash and Tess down the aisle with the help of The Bleeding Hearts Society, a garden group more interested in healing people's hearts than helping a sick basil plant. But they're not the only ones cheering for this couple's second chance.

Who would have thought Nate Desantro would be giving advice on relationships, love, and marriage? But when a man finds the right woman, anything is possible. Add a baby to the mix; well, that's pure "hero" material. Christine will offer her share of support and wisdom to Tess and stand up to an old troublemaker in the name of family and friendship.

From the fifty-something widow who is afraid to open her heart again to the pregnant friend who believes everyone has a soul mate, to Lily Desantro, the shining light who makes others believe anything is possible, Magdalena's finest will rally to give Tess and Cash that second chance. But all the prayers and contrivances in the world won't help until Tess reveals the secret she's carried for too many years, a secret that could destroy her chance with Cash forever...

And if you're wondering about Harry Blacksworth and his brood, you'll glimpse a snippet of what he's up to, but he'll be back in full force in *A Family Affair: Fall*. Not only that—he's moving to Magdalena with Greta and the kids! Can you imagine Harry maneuvering a lawnmower or carrying out the trash? Oh, but his past is going to catch up with him and then...Sorry... Harry has to wait for *A Family Affair: Fall* to share his misery *and* his story.

For now, enjoy the journey as you catch up on the lives of the residents of Magdalena. They're waiting for you!

Truth In Lies Series:

Book Thirteen: *A Family Affair: The Return*

If you love to read about second chances, don't miss:

That Second Chance Series:

Book One: *Pulling Home* – (Also prequel to *A Family Affair: The Promise*)

Book Two: *The Way They Were* – (Also prequel to *A Family Affair: The Secret*)

Book Three: *Simple Riches* – (Also prequel to *A Family Affair: Winter*)

Book Four: *Paradise Found* – (Also prequel to *A Family Affair: The Wish*)

Book Five: *Not Your Everyday Housewife* – (Also prequel to *A Family Affair: The Gift*)

Book Six: *The Butterfly Garden* – (Also prequel to *A Family Affair: The Return*)

To my husband: my very own Mr. Darcy—on a Harley!

1

Magdalena, New York

IF SHE KNEW her life were about to shatter into a million bits of unrecognizable tragedy, Tess Carrick would have kissed Daniel "Cash" Casherdon with greater urgency that afternoon, savored the taste of his naked flesh, dug her nails into his back. She would have ignored Magdalena's raised brows and clung to him with the desperation of one taking a last breath.

Because in the end, that's exactly what it was—one last pure breath of the most consuming love she'd ever known. After, despite the town's honest attempt at comfort, there was only pain. Lies. Betrayal. Too much guilt. Fate killed the memories of loving him with one shocking act, so concise, so final, there would be no retracing steps to an earlier time, no recapturing innocence or second chances. There would be nothing left but survival.

But, of course, she knew none of this that night.

Twenty-two minutes before the event that changed Tess Carrick's life forever, she was just another jittery bride, counting the seventy-two hours until she could write Mrs. D. Casherdon sixty-two times on something other than a legal pad. The waiting had all been worth it: the four years of college to complete her nursing degree, the money-pinching to afford an apartment in Philly, Cash's moonlighting as a security guard two towns over, the restless nights in an empty bed. The constant wanting. Soon, they'd pledge themselves in St. Gertrude's Church just as her parents had, in the presence of God, friends, and family. Some of those very same friends and family who had attended her parents' wedding would be in the pews. They might look a bit different: thicker middles, wrinkles, and whiter, thinner, or less hair; but the joy and teary well-wishes they'd offer would be the same.

For now, there were the lists to get through, organized on a spreadsheet with six columns, compliments of Gina Servetti, Tess's maid of honor. *Stuff silk daisies into tiny vases for centerpieces at each table, tie Jordan almonds in pink netting, pack for honeymoon to Niagara Falls, remind JJ to pick up his tux.* Seeing her kid brother in a tux instead of baggy jeans would definitely be a photo moment. Maybe Cash would even convince him to shave off the ten strands of fuzz sprouting from his chin. Tess had always thought her dad would be the one walking her down the aisle, the one who would brush away her tears through the father-daughter dance. One giant heart attack had squeezed the life out of him last year and now it was just JJ, Mom, and Riki, though no one had heard from Riki in five months.

And there was Cash, of course. He consumed her world, and maybe, depending on what time he got off work tonight, he'd sneak over in his squad car and she'd show him just how lucky he was to be marrying her. Of course, *that* detail wasn't on Gina's spreadsheet.

"Tess, can you hand me the scissors?"

There was no way Gina knew what Tess had been thinking just now, though Gina had a way of acting like she did. It made Tess wonder if her friend possessed a sixth *and* seventh sense about people—or maybe just about sex. Of course, Gina didn't like to talk about sex or lack thereof...or men, or lack thereof. Bree said she thought it had more to do with making sure the town didn't compare her to her "Sex oozes from my pores" cousin, Natalie Servetti, than the fact that Gina wasn't a size 2. Or a size 12. Gina worked awfully hard convincing herself and her prospects that she was undesirable. She was studying to become a physical therapist, and when Tess and Bree asked how that was going to work, seeing as she'd have to actually touch a male patient's body, Gina responded that men and women consisted of muscles, bones, tendons, and joints, and that was her focus. Apparently Gina really did think she could separate body parts and people in that overly compartmentalized brain of hers.

Unlike Bree, Tess's matron of honor, who was ninety-nine percent emotion and one-percent logic. "I absolutely cannot wait until Saturday. You are undoubtedly the hottest couple this side of the Mississippi." Bree Kinkaid spoke with a hint of southern drawl, though she'd never been south of Baltimore. Gina said it was all affected, ever since Bree watched *Gone with the Wind*. But there was something about Bree, with her long legs and model figure, even seven months pregnant, that could make a person think about elegance and femininity. And sex, of course.

Seven months ago, they'd been tying baby's breath and lace for Bree's wedding to Brody Kinkaid. Big, broad, and bronzed, Brody had been all-county tight end for the Magdalena Mustangs, and even played in college until he busted a knee during spring ball, came home, rehabbed, and got cut from the team. Angelo "Pop" Benito, who followed Brody's career, said it had more to do with the boy's inability to get past freshman math and English, though how a man like Pop, who had never graduated ninth grade, would know about college was the bigger question. Or maybe it wasn't. Pop Benito was the Godfather of Magdalena, and he possessed a wisdom and common sense that could not be learned in the classroom.

Of course, Bree had insisted that Brody's early exit from college was due to financial issues and not his skills, academic or otherwise. Whatever the reason, it bothered Bree more than it did Brody, who had found his niche with the Magdalena Volunteer Fire Department, chasing flames, climbing ladders, saving lives—a new way to funnel the charged-up adrenaline and testosterone soaring through his body. Unfortunately for him, he also had to bring home a paycheck and that's where Bree's father came in. Rex MacGregor owned MacGregor's Cabinets and was not going to let his baby girl go without, so he hired Brody as his sales manager, even though the young man didn't know the difference between a hinge and a handle.

Gina nicknamed him "Testosterone Brody" because he got his honeybee pregnant on their honeymoon. Not a surprise, considering Brody did everything with an all-or-nothing attitude—climbing ladders, eating massive amounts of red meat, making love to his wife. The man was a gentle giant who loved his country, his town, his wife, and his future children. He planned on six: five boys and one girl. A regular front line.

Tess placed three miniature silk daisies in a vase and worked a pink ribbon around the mouth. Six more to go and she could put a check under column six on the spreadsheet.

"Mimi's got the bridal suite all ready for you," Bree said, her expression wistful and dreamy. "Just wait until you see it. Pure Heaven."

Gina let out an annoyed sigh. "Not everyone wants to do it on a bed of rose petals. Kind of messy."

Bree closed her eyes and smiled. "Every time I smell a rose I think of that night and I hunt down my man."

Sixty-six-year-old Mimi Pendergrass, descendant of John and Harriet Pendergrass, Magdalena's founding family, owned and operated Heart Sent, one of the town's two bed and breakfasts. The other, Rusty's B&B, provided no competition once a visitor met Rusty Clemens, a bearded former logger who had yet to connect with soap and running water on a daily basis. Mimi pretty much ran the town as mayor and president of The Bleeding Hearts Society, the latter providing more leadership than the former. Despite losing a husband and a son, Mimi believed in love and opened her bridal suite, which was an over-sized room with a heart-shaped tub, velvet draperies, three-inch-thick carpeting, and a king-size bed strewn with rose petals, to Magdalena's newly married couples. And she invited them back on their first anniversary.

"Then stay away from my place," Gina said, scrunching her nose. "I don't want you procreating in my flower beds."

"Oh pooh." Bree laughed. "I said I hunted him down; I didn't say I stripped him naked and had my way with him." The Southern drawl licked her words like a child's tongue on a melting ice cream cone. "I do have some self-control where my husband is concerned, though admittedly, not much. But I'm not going to give this town one more tidbit to gossip about than they already have. That dang Bleeding Hearts Society is worse than a tabloid and the only thing they grow is gossip."

Surprisingly, Gina was the one to defend the club. "You know they do a lot of good for people aside from the obvious."

Bree let out a delicate snort. "Such as?"

"They're like the town cheerleaders. When my aunt lost my uncle, they sent a whole chicken dinner, and the stuffing

was real, not boxed. Pumpkin pie, too. And they brought inspi-
rational books and vases filled with lilacs and hyacinth. They
were there for her when the rest of the town moved on." Gina
shrugged. "If that's being a busybody, then maybe they are,
but they really care, not just a quick how-do-you do?" She
looked away and said, "I was thinking about going to a
meeting."

"Really?" This caught Bree's interest. "You think they'll let
you in?"

Gina shot her a look that would have been taken for disgust
if she hadn't added a smile to it. "Pop Benito belongs. You think
they won't let me in?"

Tess pictured Pop in his football jersey and high-top sneak-
ers, singing Sinatra's "My Way." "Good point. Now, can we get
back to business? I'm getting married in three days and there's a
whole spreadsheet left to cross off."

"To the sexiest man in Magdalena," Bree cooed. "Next to
Brody, that is. I'd add Nate Desantro to the list if he ever smiled."

"Would you smile if your mother took up with a guy who
visited her a couple times a month, then left for who knows
where, only to come back again? And had a kid with her?" Gina's
dark eyes turned darker. "You know he's got to be married."

Bree sighed. "It's so sad. I like Mrs. Desantro and I met
Charlie Blacksworth once. He was a real gentleman. And he had
the bluest eyes…"

"Give the blue-eyed man a star for being a real gentleman
while he's two-timing his wife and leaving his Down syndrome
daughter behind every month."

"Oh, Gina. That's pure tragedy." Bree swiped at her eyes.
"And you don't know that he's married. There could be a very
logical explanation for his monthly comings and goings."

Gina rolled her eyes and looked at Tess. "Well? What do you
think?"

Tess had never met the man, but she wasn't naïve. "I think he's married."

Bree wanted to find the gray between the black and white of right and wrong. "What does Cash say?" she asked. "Does Nate ever talk to him about it?"

"Only to say they aren't going to talk about it."

"Oh." Bree's lips pulled into a frown. "How sad." She leaned back, rubbed her protruding belly. "I can't imagine not being with the one you love." More rubbing as her voice dipped to a whisper. "There's nothing sadder than that."

THE FIRST TIME Tess set eyes on Daniel Casherdon, he was, unfortunately, in the back of her Uncle Will's police cruiser. Not a good place for an almost eighteen-year-old with long hair and a reckless streak. Uncle Will made it his personal mission to "deal with those hoodlum types," as he called them, and the punk kid from Artisdale Street was no different. Only Cash *was* different, as they would all soon discover...

When Cash stared at her from the back seat of the cruiser, the warnings about hanging around with boys who got in trouble with the law melted under that intense gaze, and by the time her uncle realized what was going on, it was too late. Tess had fallen under Daniel Casherdon's spell, just like all the other fifteen-year-olds at Magdalena High.

It would be another year before Cash actually talked to her, and she later learned it had to do with the lecture or rather, threat, Uncle Will gave him in regard to his niece. Pretty much a "Leave her alone or find yourself in the back of the squad car every time you don't." The threat fell apart one sweltering July afternoon outside MacGregor's Cabinets. Bree's father, Rex, owned the place, and Cash was one of the new hires. Bree had gotten her driver's license six weeks before, and she and Tess stopped at the cabinet factory to deliver a tuna on rye, courtesy of Bree's mother in her continual attempt to get her husband to lose that spare tire. When they stepped out of the car dressed in cut-offs and halter tops and smelling of suntan oil, Tess spotted Cash eating lunch at an old picnic table with several other workers. His gaze unsettled her and she tripped going up the steps, a fact that humiliated as much as angered her. Daniel Casherdon was a nobody, even if he had eyes that made a girl lose her balance and a mouth that said, "Kiss me" without uttering a word. He was too good-looking, too daring, too...too everything. And that meant danger.

Cash found her that night, standing outside Lina's Café with a group of her girlfriends, and when he spoke her name, his voice sent shivers straight to her brain, erasing her earlier thoughts about him. She got in his Chevelle and drove to The Lookout where they sat and listened to the night sounds of Magdalena: crickets, owls, rustling leaves. She'd grown up with the familiar sounds, but they were intensified by the presence of Daniel Casherdon. For all of his supposed bad boy history, he didn't try to kiss her or make a move, even though she later realized she would have let him.

There were a lot of things Tess would have let him do, and many which he eventually did. Wasn't that what love was all about? A giving and sharing, stretching emotions to a point where it was impossible to determine where one stopped and another started? She and Cash spent six years preparing for a life together, one that included venturing outside Magdalena to build careers, travel and explore, and eventually make their way back to start a family and take their place in the community as Mr. and Mrs. Daniel Casherdon.

And in three days they were going to start their journey.

2

C ash fiddled with the radio station until he located his favorite. Aerosmith's "Sweet Emotion" sifted through the speakers, perking him up as much as the coffee he'd just finished. He glanced at the clock on the cruiser. Two more hours. Tonight he was glad to be policing Magdalena where nothing more critical happened than escorting Howard Singletary out of O'Reilly's after one too many beers or listening to Gladys Blinten complain because the "hoodlums" behind her were listening to "sacrilegious" music. If the band heard that, they'd probably hire Gladys as their spokesperson.

The town did have its charm in a backward, sit-down-and-stretch-your legs kind of way. A person couldn't live in this place without warming to at least a few of the locals like Pop and Lucy Benito with their stories that taught as well as entertained, and their endless collection of herbs, flowers, and wisdom. And that garden group, doling out flowers and advice like Dear Abby in garden gloves. He and Tess would come back here one day, but that was way down the road. Right now, too many years and too much opportunity stretched in front of them: nursing for her, more police work for him. In a big city. With real hospitals and real crime. It didn't matter where they ended up as long as they were together, a truth Tess's mother struggled with even now. Olivia Carrick loved to control things, especially her family.

When the second song finished, he figured he'd listen to one more and then take a walk down Main Street, glance in the darkened windows of the shops, and show his presence like Tess's uncle had taught him. *Control through presence*, Will Carrick instructed. *Works every time*. Will had been right about a lot of things, especially Tess.

Cash yawned and eased back in the cruiser, letting Journey's melody drift over him as he thought of Tess. Will could have ended it all when he caught them making out in the back seat of Cash's car. Olivia Carrick would have grounded her daughter until she was twenty-five and Tess's father would have bent to his wife's will and agreed. Of course, Thomas Carrick would have escaped right after the punishment, just as he'd done for too many years before his death, heading out on the road to peddle dog food.

But Will said nothing to his brother and sister-in-law. He did say plenty to Cash, though, like *Cut your hair, stop sneaking around, and pick her up at the front door*—which meant, *Meet the parents*. Cash hadn't liked authority and didn't appreciate the ultimatum, but he was all twisted up in Tess; her silky skin, her throaty laugh, her lily-of-the-valley scent. So he did it. That step had turned into another, and eventually, with Will's guidance, Cash enrolled in the police academy.

And now he'd taken it upon himself to do the same with Tess's kid brother, JJ. He wasn't a bad kid, just easily influenced and desperate for acceptance, something that happened when a father either dies or disappears. Cash knew all the signs— shoplifting on a dare, scribbling profanity on public property, drinking in the back seat of a car. The kid listened to Cash even if he ignored his mother and conned his sister, but that was something they were going to work on. Respect was the next step to turn JJ Carrick into a normal human being. If Cash could make the conversion, so could the boy. And though Cash was moving away, JJ knew he'd be checking in on him, which meant accountability. It also didn't hurt that the boy was just a little afraid of Cash's kick-ass attitude.

It would all work out fine. Will even had a job for JJ clearing brush and building a barn on his eighteen-acre tract of land, two miles outside Magdalena. As Ramona said, *Busy hands leave no room for mischief.* His aunt had lots of sayings and if you tempered them to modern-day lingo and threw in a cuss word or two, most made sense. Practical living for the twenty-first century.

Speaking of practical and living, in three days, Tess would sleep in his bed every night—naked. He could touch her and taste her any time he wanted. Now that was damn practical. It sure was living, too. Visions of Tess floated through his brain, settled in his groin...

After, he could never say if it was the sound of the music's drums or intuition that jerked him to full alert as he spotted the masked figure in baggy clothes running from Oscar's convenience store. The rush of the implausible kicked in as Cash flung open the squad car door, drew his weapon, and zeroed in on his target. The dead night air clamped the breath in his throat. This didn't happen in Magdalena, and yet the events spilled out in full-blown action like a police training session. "Police! Stop!"

Officer training couldn't have scripted the next scene any better. The suspect stopped and Cash advanced, gun drawn. "Hands behind your head." He called for backup as he assessed the situation, taking in the low-slung jeans and black tennis shoes. *He's just a kid, probably 130 soaking wet.* The thought ticked him. No respect for people or property; he belonged in a scared-straight program. That would settle him down. He relaxed his gun. Ten bucks said he knew the kid. JJ probably knew him, too.

Four feet separated Cash from the kid, who stood there, hands at his side. The kid was drunk, high, or bent on being antagonistic because he still hadn't put his hands behind his head. Fine. He wanted to act like a punk; he'd get treated like a punk. Cash holstered his gun and reached behind his back for his cuffs. A night in jail would sober the kid up; maybe smarten him up, too. "Let's go, hands behind your head." He'd cuff him first, then pull off the mask. Cash had half a mind to send JJ to his uncle's farm in case the boy ever got any ideas about pulling a stunt like this. Manual labor never killed a soul and it damn well saved quite a few. Cash heaved a sigh. There'd be reams of paperwork to deal with, which meant no Tess tonight.

Even in a sleepy town like Magdalena, all good cops lived in the moment, never stretching or considering past real time. Real time got the bad guy, garnered the promotion. Or busted it apart. Mistakes happened in real time, lives were ruined, people died. A cop could anticipate all he wanted, but reality stuck its ugly face in the mix every time: a twitchy gun finger, a moving target that stopped moving. Milliseconds separated the hero from the disgraced, and it was that millisecond that turned out to be Cash's undoing.

He could hit a moving target from one hundred yards away. Obliterate one from four feet. But he made one big mistake; he didn't consider the kid a threat and, therefore, he relaxed, which proved a true death knell in the police handbook.

Cash lifted the handcuffs, already planning his scared-straight talk with the kid, when the boy jerked to the right and yanked a gun from his hoodie. The action startled Cash but good cops reacted by instinct and instinct was Cash's strength. In a single motion, Cash drew his weapon, aimed, and fired. The aim proved dead-on. The suspect dropped the gun and crumpled to the ground in a gasp of air and pain.

"Ah, Christ." Cash fell to his knees and placed his hands on the boy's chest. A sticky wetness seeped through the sweatshirt and smeared Cash's hands. "Hold on, okay? Just hold on. We'll get you help." The kid tried to talk but it came out in a croak. "Don't say anything, okay? I'm going to take off your mask so you can breathe." His fingers shook as he eased the ski mask over the boy's chin, past the fine nubs of hair sprinkling his cheeks, the slender nose, the hollow cheekbones, the eyes.

Cash stared at the boy, fighting the sudden rush of nausea that clamped his gut, threatened to spew out chunks of disbelief and horror. "No."

It all started and ended then, the sirens in the background, the blood gurgling in the back of the kid's throat, the chill to his skin, the disappearing pulse. "Hang on, kid. Damn it, don't you leave me!" By the time the ambulance arrived, Cash had blood on his hands, his face, his shirt.

"We'll take over from here, Cash."

He knew that voice, had gone to school with the guy, played poker a few times at his house, but he couldn't find his name because his brain was saturated with blood.

"It's over, Cash." The man whose name he couldn't recall spoke again. "The boy's gone."

"I KNOW we're not supposed to talk about it, but I will absolutely miss you to death." Bree sighed and absently rubbed her belly. Pizza boxes stacked the corner of the room, with an empty salad container sitting daintily on top. Rolls of tulle and ribbon covered the table in shades of cream, lavender, and pink, all signs of a productive pre-wedding event.

"It won't be forever," Tess said. "And we'll come home to visit on holidays." She and Cash had talked about the opportunities waiting for them. The places they would visit, the travel, the areas they wanted to live in, the work, the new and different people they would meet. It had all sounded so wondrous and amazing and, of course, it was, but Tess hadn't stopped to consider all she was leaving behind, especially the people. Best friends like Bree and Gina, neighbors and townspeople like Pop and Lucy Benito and Mimi Pendergrass. Family like JJ and Mom. And Riki, wherever she was. A tiny hurt pinged her chest but she pushed it aside with visions of the hospital where she'd work and the apartment she and Cash would share. They were starting a family, just the two of them, and in a few years they'd add a dog. A few years after that, a baby, with dark eyes and long fingers, just like his daddy's. Picturing Cash as a father double-pinged her heart so hard she gasped.

"Too many hot peppers on the pizza, huh?" Bree tucked a chunk of strawberry-blond hair behind her ear with a knowing look. "Just wait until you're pregnant. You'll see what real heartburn is like." She rubbed her belly three more times. "Like fireworks exploding in your gut. *Bam, bam, bam!* Even plain old yogurt bothers me sometimes, but I'd suffer a volcano eruption for little Brody here."

Gina cast her a doubtful look and said, "All the positive thinking in the world won't put a stem on that orange."

"Don't jinx it. I've already got Brody's mother knitting blue and green booties." She fished in the Jordan almond bag and dug out three blue ones. "I am really not up to his mother's squawking about one thing or another. She's already told me her son doesn't like tomatoes. And I told Georgia, of course he does. He absolutely loves them. I didn't tell her I was wearing one of those cute little teddies from Nanette's Naughties when I served them to him." She rolled her eyes and giggled. "Creative Cooking 101 is what I call it."

"Maybe you should teach cooking class—with props," Gina said. "Wouldn't that turn Georgia's hair white?"

"Turn it white and stand it straight up like a porcupine," Bree said of the mother-in-law who prided herself on having virgin hair and less than a dozen of them white.

Tess laughed, picturing the prim, proper, plump Georgia Kinkaid with a spiky head of white hair.

"Oh, that woman will be the death of me," Bree said. She sniffed, grew quiet. "I'm really going to miss you, Tess. It was one thing when you were an hour away in school. I could drive up to see you, and you came home once a month. But Philly? It might as well be Pasadena."

Gina shook her head. "Not quite."

Tess clasped Bree's hand, squeezed. "It's not forever. Just for a few years, five tops." Then they would head back to Magdalena and start a family.

"It feels like forever, though, or a 'see you sometime, maybe when we're all in our thirties with stretch marks and minivans.'"

Gina glanced up from a mountain of pink netting and frowned. "Or just stretch marks. Not everyone has kids."

Bree considered this. "True. There's something to be said for a brain that's never been immersed in Play-Doh or stinky diapers."

That made Gina smile, which was good since she never smiled when they mentioned words like *men, dating, marriage,* or *babies.* "Good point. I might just enjoy my spinster days. I could play godmother or aunt to your sixteen children and by the time Tess and Cash get started, I'll have it figured out."

"Speaking of, when do you think you'll start expanding the Casherdon brigade?"

If it were up to Bree, she'd have everyone procreating until the universe was filled with playpens and sippy cups. Of course, Tess wanted children. Just not yet. There was so much newness surrounding them, gobs of it to absorb: a city, a marriage, travel —each other. They'd waited so long for this time together and now it was really almost here. Seventy-two hours away. She glanced at her watch. How many minutes was that?

"Answer her, Tess," Gina prodded. "If you don't, she'll start the grand inquisition and you'll be done."

"Huh?" She'd been calculating the minutes until she and Cash stood before half the town and exchanged vows.

"Babies?" Bree eyed her. "You and Cash?"

"Yes." He'd be off duty soon. He might sneak over here. He might even—

"When? How many?"

Gina blew out a disgusted sigh. "Really, Bree? You do not remember having this exact conversation two nights ago? Or the week before that? You've been on her since the day after Cash gave her the ring seven months ago."

"I just asked a simple question. Can't a person inquire or is it too mundane to talk about babies? Maybe the two of you would rather talk about what you plan to do once you blow out of Magdalena like it's a leper colony."

There it was again, Bree's insecurity resurfacing. No one but Tess and Gina knew how badly Bree had wanted to finish college before starting a family, but Brody had nixed the deal with his testosterone-crazed personality and gotten her pregnant on their honeymoon. Between the morning sickness, a calculating mother-in-law, and a husband who counted his masculinity based on number of "knock-ups," as he called them, Bree collapsed and gave up on the dream of getting a degree. Tess and Gina told her she could have a family and go to school, not that they knew that firsthand, but it didn't matter because

Bree vowed to devote every waking moment to her husband and growing family.

"Tess told you she was going to wait a few years to start a family. Like maybe five," Gina snapped.

Bree dug around for another blue almond and popped it in her mouth, crunching as she talked. "Which is more than a few. A few is two or three. But what do I know?" She crunched on two more almonds. "I'm only going to be a mother, not a nurse or a physical therapist."

Gina scowled. "Stop playing the drama queen. You're not auditioning for the high school play. You already hogged all the leads. Remember?"

Tess threw down a silk flower and stood. She hated being caught in the middle, which was where she always ended up when the three of them were together. Why did Bree and Gina always have to compete for favorite with her? Why couldn't they all just be friends—equally? She guessed that was like asking why dogs sniffed out patches of grass to do their business. "Can you two stop? This is ridiculous."

Bree folded her arms over her protruding tummy and stuck out her bottom lip. "I only asked a simple question."

Gina glared at her. "And I gave you a simple answer—which you didn't like."

Tess sighed. "I can't always slice things exactly down the middle. You're both my friends but this is exhausting. I've only been back in town three weeks and the whole time, it's been nothing but bickering and posturing. You're both in the wedding —maid *and* matron of honor—you're both giving toasts. Why can't we all share our friendship? Why do I have to pick a favorite?"

Gina pulled on a roll of pink tulle. Bree picked at a thread on her cotton shirt. Dead silence. The fighting had started in middle school and escalated with Bree's pregnancy and Gina's Dean's List announcement in the *Magdalena Press*.

Bree slid a glance in Gina's direction. "Sorry."

"Me, too." Gina met her gaze and shrugged. "I really do love you, Bree, but sometimes you bug the crap out of me with your passive-aggressive-helpless routine."

So much for peace. Tess prepared for Bree's backlash, but it didn't happen.

"I could blame it on hormones, but sometimes I'm just not a very nice person." Bree's voice filled with pain and self-recrimination. "Everybody thinks I am and it gets hard to always be so dang *nice*. You know? That's why I slip when I'm with you and Tess. Because you know I'm a pain, but you love me anyway."

"Why do you feel you have to be nice all the time?" Gina asked. "I never feel that way."

Obviously. *Please, Bree, let that pass.* She did, quite graciously, too.

"I don't know. Why do I? I've always been a people pleaser, even when I didn't want to be." She swiped at her eyes. "You know what I wanted to do? Run Daddy's company, but he pooh-poohed that away saying a woman had no business in a man's world, especially one that had machines and steel-toed shoes in it. And then I thought I'd study finance because I was always good with numbers in Mr. Spencer's class, but Brody said it wasn't feminine."

"So you quit and got knocked up?"

Gina could not put a compliment in her words if her life depended on it.

"I didn't quit," Bree insisted. "I love Brody and I want children. I'm just revising my goals. After I raise the children, I might think about going back to school." She said the words with about as much conviction as nothing.

"Uh-huh. I bet you'll go to school when I meet Prince

Charming and we ride off into the sunset together. Maybe I'll try to snag Nate Desantro; I'm sure he'd love the idea of marrying and settling down."

They all knew that was like saying the Pope wanted a wife and kids. Even so, Tess had heard enough. "Why are you both so hard on yourselves? Why can't you go back to school *and* find Prince Charming? Why does it have to be one or the other? And Cash says one of these days Nate Desantro is going to meet his match. That, I'd like to see, but it could happen. Anything can. We're twenty-two years old and we can have anything we want." Her voice gentled. "We can have it all; we just have to figure out what that means."

Their eyes filled with such sadness, Tess almost looked away. It was Gina who spoke, her words carrying the certainty of someone who has been disappointed too many times. "Nobody can have it all. One way or another, we all have to choose."

"Except you, Tess," Bree said, her eyes shining with tears. "You do have it all: the man, the job, the life you want. And it couldn't have happened to a more deserving couple. I mean, look how you and Cash watched out for JJ, especially after your daddy died, and your mom..." She paused, shook her head. "We all know she's had a hard time, even if she refuses to show it. But you got through it and now you're getting your reward." She sniffed. "These dang hormones make me so gushy. Hey, why don't we try on our dresses, huh? One last time while it's just us three?"

Tess eyed her mother's room. The dresses hung in Olivia Carrick's closet, altered, pressed, and waiting for Saturday morning like fresh bouquets of daisies. "I don't know." If her mother got an inkling she'd been fiddling with her wedding dress, she'd have something to say, and it wouldn't be, *How beautiful you look*.

"Oh, what the heck." Gina flung aside the pile of pink tulle and scooted off the rocking chair. "Get your camera, Bree. We're about to make a memory."

It took forever to slip Tess into her dress, but she had to be so very careful not to wrinkle it or smear the edges of the bodice with makeup. One wrong move and the telltale evidence would seep into the fabric and then all of Magdalena would hear Olivia Carrick's disapproving remarks.

But Olivia was at the library, sixteen minutes away if she made all the lights, which no one ever did. Tess thought she heard the faint wail of a siren. She'd always had a heightened awareness of sirens, first because Uncle Will was a policeman, and later, Cash. Sirens signaled warnings like, *Be careful* and *danger*. The sound disappeared as Tess stepped into a pair of ivory heels with clusters of tiny rhinestones attached to the tops.

"Tess." Bree covered her mouth with her hands and sighed. "Just look at you."

Tess glanced at the full-length mirror behind her mother's door. The ivory gown swished as she moved from side to side in a calming wave of tiny seed pearls and satin. She'd never considered herself beautiful; her eyes were a bit too wide apart, her mouth too full, her nose too long. But right now, she felt beautiful. Right now, she felt perfect.

Gina called her name and when Tess turned, she snapped a photo. Then another with Tess laughing and Bree dressed in her pink bridesmaid gown, patting a round tummy. "Let's get all three of us." Gina smoothed her dark hair, set the camera on top of Olivia's dresser, and hurried to her friends. They clung to one another, smiles fixed, eyes bright, waiting for the inevitable flash to capture their picture and create a lasting memory.

If only time could have stood still.

They didn't hear the knocking at first. Not until the sound morphed into a banging did they realize the noise was not part of the music blaring from the speakers in the living room. Gina unwound her arm from Tess's and said, "Hey, somebody's at the door."

"I'll see who it is. Tess, stay here." Bree scooted out of the bedroom, and seconds later the music ended, making the banging on the door reverberate through the house.

"Maybe I should get out of this dress," Tess whispered. "What if it's one of my mother's friends?" Of course they'd tell Olivia that her daughter had been cavorting around in her wedding gown, and then Tess would be subjected to the lectures that wouldn't end until her first anniversary.

"Shhh, wait a minute. I want to get one more picture of us. Bree will get rid of whoever it is."

"Cash!" Bree's voice seeped through the bedroom door in a decibel-deafening shriek. Tess didn't stop to consider the bad-luck omen for the groom to see the bride's gown before the wedding or how she'd explain why they were playing dress-up when they were supposed to be making wedding favors. Nothing mattered but getting to Cash. She kicked off her shoes and ran barefoot to the front door where her fiancé stood.

"Cash?" Blood smeared his shirt, his pants, his arms. A patch of red covered his chin. But it was the hollowed-out desperation in his eyes that spoke of unimaginable horror. Had he been in an accident? Had someone attacked him? Maybe tried to knife him? She couldn't see slashes or, God forbid, a bullet wound, but there was so much blood. She reached out to touch his cheek—a part of his body not smeared in red. "Talk to me."

His jaw twitched. Twice. He swayed to the left but managed to straighten himself. When he opened his mouth to speak, nothing came out. Not even a croak. The past few hours faded as fast as the flash on Gina's camera until nothing remained but Cash and the blood staining his body. She'd feared this moment from the first time he mentioned joining the police force. And now it was here, three days before their wedding. "Cash? What happened?"

Those beautiful lips, the very ones that had touched and tasted every inch of her, opened and spilled out the unthinkable. "JJ."

"JJ?"

Cash held out both hands, palms up, splattered with blood. "It was an accident."

Images flashed through her brain. JJ speeding down the winding back roads away from Magdalena. JJ laughing that 55 miles per hour wasn't on his speedometer. JJ being JJ: young, unafraid, reckless. "Did he hit something? Or someone?" He'd already almost lost his license twice and would have if Cash hadn't stepped in and seen that he took a driver improvement course. But he'd been doing so much better, had even talked about trade school to become a welder.

Cash's face turned ashen. "JJ," he said again.

Tess grasped his arm. "Tell me. What is it?"

He shook his head and stepped back, breaking contact. They'd tried so hard to get through to JJ, especially Cash, but there was a small piece of him that did not or would not grow up and be responsible. Why should he when his mother stepped in and rescued him from his mistakes, saying he had a learning disability or scars from losing a father?

And now, from the look on Cash's face, JJ was about to pay for his latest mess-up. Maybe he'd even go to jail. Tess leaned forward and kissed Cash on the cheek. Whatever had happened wasn't Cash's fault. He'd tried so hard with JJ and whatever her brother had done was on him, not Cash.

She stepped back to get a better look at his face and followed his gaze, which had settled low on her belly. A single spot of red smeared the middle of the ivory gown. Blood red. Dead red.

Hurt red. The color spread through the fabric, bleeding into the gown until it formed tiny fingers, like blood vessels.

Her brain disconnected as she studied the red spot. Olivia would be furious. They'd have to dab it with something? Hydrogen peroxide? Would that work? Possibilities skittered through her head, and all the while another part of her brain screamed, *JJ, what have you done now?*

"I have to see him. Now, before Mom gets home." She'd talk some sense into her brother and make him tell Cash about the pot she found in the back of his closet three days ago. Bags of it, a scale, too. JJ swore he was only holding it for a friend, though he wouldn't give a name, probably because he knew Tess would go straight to Cash. Well, JJ was going to tell Cash himself and the boy would take the consequences, whatever they were.

She hoped he hadn't hurt anyone. And if he'd been drinking and driving—again—he could say good-bye to driving until he was twenty-one. Maybe twenty-five. And if—

Cash sliced through her thoughts, hard, fast, and final, with a pain that seared her heart, ripping it to shreds of nothingness. "He's dead, Tess. I killed him."

3

Eight years later—Richmond, Virginia

MELANIE FLEMING PERCHED her tiny frame on the edge of the massive desk and studied Tess. "Haven't you ever wondered how the other half lives? You know, the normal half who date, get married, have children? Actually sleep in their own bed instead of a hotel room and don't hope for a transatlantic flight every twenty days?"

Tess forced a smile and shrugged. "Not really." That answer didn't appease her boss who never missed an opportunity to point out the numerous shortcomings in Tess's personal life. No boyfriend, no husband, no child. Always centering around a man, or lack thereof.

Melanie rubbed the tiny bulge in the midsection of her grape tunic dress. She was a perfect vision of thirty-something beauty with her glossy black hair, cream complexion, bright whites, and slender frame. Except for the bump, which if one didn't know her, might attribute to an excess of carbs and not a first-trimester bulge. Melanie Fleming, CEO of Her Lips du Jour, was in the throes of several firsts: first anniversary, first business, first child. Life was proceeding according to Melanie's ten-year plan.

But it was a life about which Tess knew nothing and in which she had no desire to participate, personally or vicariously. Unfortunately, Melanie believed everyone should share in this newfound-life-love-baby experience, and it was this faith that drove her to constantly solicit converts.

"Will you just listen for a minute?"

Even if Tess said *no,* Melanie would persist as any good sales-woman would. But Melanie was more than just a superb sales-woman. She was the owner of Her Lips du Jour, and Tess was the senior vice president of sales. They'd also been friends for almost six years, which probably made Melanie feel compelled to "help" Tess settle down into married and family life. Since there was no way to stop the inevitable barrage of well-inten-tioned suggestions, Tess settled back in her chair and sighed. "Okay, give me your monthly spiel and be quick. I'm hungry."

"Tuna on wheat? Your turn to buy?"

"Sure. Talk fast."

Melanie's perfect face turned serious. "I've been thinking a lot these past two weeks." She paused, placed a protective hand over her belly. "Since the bleeding."

She meant the bleeding that smeared her linen pants and ripped the office with panic until the ambulance could transport their boss to Hope Medical Center where an ultrasound revealed a placenta praevia and where Melanie spent four days praying she wouldn't lose the baby. Her lawyer husband, Judson, remained at her side the entire time, leaving only long enough to shower and shave and then returning, even spending the night beside her, his long frame crammed in a narrow cot.

Touching. Raw. Too exposed.

Tess had allowed that sort of exposure once and it had almost killed her.

"So, I've been thinking about things. You know, life, purpose," she paused. "Destiny."

Tess nodded. *Next will come the part where I'm falling short and missing out on life. Then she'll talk about men and their attributes. And then, she'll offer to introduce me to a friend, or a cousin, or maybe one of the partners in Judson's law firm. She tried that once, but there were three other partners...*

"We're selling the company."

...have fun...relax...slow down... "What did you say?"

Melanie worked her lower lip until she stripped off a section of lip protectant. "We're selling the company. Judson says I'm under too much stress and he's worried about the baby and my having a relapse." She leaned forward and grasped Tess's hand. "Try to understand. I started this company and I've loved every single minute of it. But we're talking about a life growing inside me, a flesh-and-blood life. I can't jeopardize that."

In the span of a few sentences, Tess's world shifted and landed on top of her. Everything she'd built these last six years —her identity, her reputation, her bank account—all if it was threatened by a life that hadn't even drawn its first breath outside its mother's womb.

"Isn't there a way to have both?"

Melanie's voice reached her, soft and knowing. "Spoken from one who has obviously never had to compromise. You can't have it all, no matter what the magazines tell us. Something always suffers, and it's not going to be my family." Her voice dipped lower, filled with sympathy. "It must be very difficult to be an only child, no brothers or sisters."

I have a sister, somewhere. And I had a brother. "You get used to it."

"And I know you aren't big on family."

Tess shrugged. "Sorry." Melanie knew nothing of Tess's life before she joined the company. It was much easier to manufacture a generic family minus two siblings and an ex-fiancé. There was no pain, no heart-on-the-sleeve sympathy from onlookers. No real feelings. Nothing. Some things should not be relived or revisited, but must be buried so deep, they could never be excavated—dead brothers, missing sisters, ex-fiancés, and a life that could have been—belonged in that category.

"What's going to happen to my job?" The job she'd created from nothing when Her Lips du Jour was showcased at mall kiosks and home parties. Tess had worked with Melanie to grow the company and when the opportunity to expand the market overseas came along, Tess jumped on it. She'd travel to different continents to spread the luscious lipsticks to consumers and malls and glossy advertising companies. She'd embraced back-to-back travel, plane hopping, sales meetings, transatlantic phone calls in the middle of the night. Along with that came money, recognition, and company growth, escalating to a level that kept Tess moving so she didn't have to think about *that* other life, *those* other choices.

"I'm going to take care of you, Tess. You'll have a huge severance package and the stock from the company. You can take time and think about what it is you really want to do with the rest of your life." Her blue eyes turned bluer. "You could do anything."

"I'm doing what I want to do." *I am. I am.*

"Eating in airport terminals? Sleeping on pillows with paper covers on them? Racking up so many frequent flyer miles you could probably fly to Australia for free?"

"Flying to Australia for free is a great idea."

"Right. As if you'd take time for something as extravagant as a vacation. You need a life, Tess. We're selling lipstick here, not a cure for old age."

"I disagree. Wearing lipstick makes women feel younger."
And lipstick is safe.

"Tess." Melanie's tone said she thought Tess had a few issues
that might be helped with therapy. Well, she'd had therapy and
it hadn't helped. Nothing had except denial—constant, merci-
less, gritty denial.

"What if I worked for the new owner? I could do that." She'd
worked too hard to let it slip away. "Nobody knows the products
better than I do. I could help with the transition, do whatever it
took." As long as she kept moving, she didn't have time to stop
and contemplate the emptiness in her life.

"They have their own people. And besides, they're looking at
a total revamp and transitioning to other products: face, hands,
feet, the usual. Online sales will be a big factor, at least for the
first year."

"But I can do all of that. I'm a great salesperson. You know
that." They'd met at a recruiting fair where Tess had just
completed a sales class and Melanie was looking for a rep. The
job was easy because it didn't require the emotional attachment
nursing did. How close did a person really get to her lipstick?

Melanie threw her a sympathetic look. "Everyone in the
industry knows you as Tess of Her Lips du Jour. The buyers want
a new look and a new name. You'll only remind them of this
company."

Well, there it was. Washed up at thirty.

"There is one more thing." Melanie slid off the edge of the
desk with the grace of a ballet dancer, which she'd been in her
younger years. She stood before Tess, glowing with pregnancy
hormones and happiness, the illumination so bright Tess had to
look away. "You signed a non-compete clause."

That brought Tess around—fast. "So?" She'd signed it as a
matter of course, back when she and Melanie had first met,
before they became friends. A non-compete could be treacher-

ous, but Tess had never felt threatened by its existence because she'd never considered leaving a job she loved. Then again, she'd never considered losing that job either.

Melanie cleared her throat. "Yes, well, I'm going to enforce it. You can't work for a competitor for six months."

"You can't be serious." This was her friend? The woman who had asked her to be her child's godmother?

"It's only because I care about you. It's for your own good. Don't look at me that way. I could have said a year, like the contract does, but I'm only enforcing six months."

"I can't believe you're doing this." Numbness settled in the middle of Tess's chest, spread through her body. Friends didn't do this. Friends looked out for one another. If she hadn't gotten close to Melanie, she might have seen this coming, might have been able to protect herself. But how? Maybe they weren't really friends at all. What kind of friend conjured up a make-believe family, like Tess did? As if the real ones had never lived, or breathed, or left their mark on her? Melanie kept talking, her glossy lips moving, her white teeth gleaming.

"I'm doing this for you, because if you don't step back and reassess your life, you'll be fifty and have no life." Her voice shifted to a soft plea. "Just give yourself six months. Okay?"

For what? To reassess a life she'd been running from for eight years? *No, thank you.* Melanie would never understand. How could she when she had a husband who loved her and a baby on the way?

"Tess? Please try to understand. You're on the fast track to burnout. I see it, even if you don't. Consider this a second chance. Go back to that quaint little hometown you once told me about. Rest. Relax. Watch the flowers grow."

Return to Magdalena? Hardly. It's not like she'd left on good terms. She'd been responsible for the animosity that split the town in two—one side supporting her, the other siding with

Cash. The town had been more than happy when she'd packed up and disappeared. Maybe they'd forgiven her over the years, but who knew? A semi-annual crate of lipstick for The Bleeding Hearts Society and a special package of "Poppy Perfect" to Lucy Benito until the year she passed were not exactly a peace treaty.

There were too many years and too many ill-spoken words to simply move on. Besides, Magdalena wasn't the kind of town that turned a page as though nothing had happened. Oh, they'd forgive, but not until they had their say, and the "say" would be brutal and demand the truth.

Why did Tess refuse to even talk to Cash when he was acting in accordance with police rules and regulations?

What if the gun in JJ's pocket had been loaded?

And what if JJ had fired it?

After all, he'd been high.

Should Cash have stood there and waited?

Gotten himself killed because the kid robbed the convenience store on a dare?

Well, should he?

No, she could not go back and face Ramona Casherdon who must despise her for accusing her nephew of cold-blooded murder and driving him from Magdalena. And Bree and Gina? She'd dodged the calls and visits from the two women she called best friends. And then there was Pop Benito, the Godfather of Magdalena. He would certainly have a lecture ready, stronger than the high-test coffee he drank every morning. She couldn't go back and face them because deep down, she knew she'd been worse than wrong, knew she'd driven Cash away, ruined their chance at happiness.

That was why she drove herself through work, why she didn't slow down until she was near exhaustion, and why she had no life. She didn't deserve one, not after what she'd done.

The town would agree and they didn't even know the whole truth.

"I don't think I'll be heading home anytime soon." Melanie grew up in San Diego. She wouldn't understand that people in Magdalena carried grudges as big as a warehouse filled with lipstick, especially when one of their own skipped town without so much as an apology. She'd been so confused and full of pain, she could think of nothing but getting away from Cash, who insisted they talk and deal with things.

And what had she done? Made a grand escape. Well, she'd escaped all right, straight into a self-imposed prison with invisible bars and no way out. Daniel "Cash" Casherdon lived in her soul, a constant reminder of what she'd thrown away.

"I'll bet everyone will be happy to see you," Melanie went on, creating Tess's backstory as though it were true. "They probably think you're some sort of celebrity, being a small town and all."

Hardly.

"You need to do this, Tess. Go home. Relax and regroup." She gave her a quick, strong hug. "And call me in six months."

Tess flipped through the travel brochure she'd picked up this morning. Blue skies. Blue ocean. A seven-day cruise to the Caribbean. It did look relaxing. It even sounded relaxing with descriptions of massages, saunas, poolside drinks. There was only one problem, but it was the same one that threw a roadblock at the other five brochures she'd perused the past ten days.

She couldn't relax. She'd tried, but the attempts were more stressful than a red-eye to Hong Kong. The very word *relax* signified a release of control, a giving up of carefully constructed defenses, like denial and self-preservation. Once that happened, then good old introspection snuck in, taking over her brain and her memory until all that remained was the truth and with that the by-products of that truth: remorse and guilt.

Relaxation gave a person too much time to think. It was as bad as analyzing oneself and one's motives, which she'd spent a full year doing. Books, lectures, classes, even three sessions with a therapist, had rendered the same answer, the one she ignored. What was the point of confronting something that couldn't be changed? The pain would still be there, the wounds newer, more severe. The regret, endless.

And the results would still be the same. JJ was dead. Cash was gone. Her choices could not be undone, no matter how many books she read or therapists she saw. The only way she could breathe day in, day out, was to obliterate the past and avoid as many situations as she could involving couples, families, and children. That wasn't always possible, but with enough practice, she'd gotten quite good at extricating emotion from situations, which earned her a reputation as cold and uncaring.

At least with a reputation like that she wasn't in danger of having her life crushed again. Tess threw the brochure aside and rifled through the others. The Grand Canyon. Australia. India. New Zealand. She pushed them all aside. She needed work. Long hours. Deadlines. Time zone changes. Damn Melanie and her six-month non-compete clause. Maybe she should call her mother and invite her to Virginia. They could head to D.C., tour the Capitol and the Smithsonian—but only for a few days.

She didn't like to surround herself with her mother's scrutiny, and though Olivia Carrick was never obvious about it, there were semitransparent cues during their monthly phone conversation: a long pause when Tess told her where she'd been, a hitched breath after the mention of someone's grandchild, a casual and recurring remark about family. Olivia had very specific opinions about her daughter's life and how she should be living it. Or rather, how she *shouldn't* be wasting it selling lipstick.

Tess chose to ignore the subtleties and limit the time she spent with her mother. Instead, she sent gifts: a watch, a mixer, a sweater. Money for a new washer. She was debating a slow cooker for her mother when the doorbell rang. She slid off the couch and made her way to the front door. Maybe Melanie had reconsidered her position on the non-compete clause and would—

"*Ramona?*"

Cash's aunt stood on the other side of the door, her dark eyes piercing Tess with determination and purpose. Eight years had streaked her black hair with gray, shifted her complexion to sallow, morphed her body from curvy to plump. Her clothes were still dark and severe, her bosom larger than Tess remembered, her middle larger, too. She moved her head and the gold hoops she always wore swayed against her neck, but it was her eyes that held Tess. Deep, dark, soul-searching eyes that spotted truth and lies.

"I've come about my nephew."

Cash.

Fear shot through Tess and crumbled years of denial. "Has something happened to him?" Ramona ignored the question and stepped inside, dominating the room with her presence. She would not travel hundreds of miles, or worse, breathe the same oxygen as Tess if she had a choice. Something *had* happened to him, and it was bad. But what could Ramona possibly want with her?

"Please. Have a seat." Tess tried to remain calm. *Don't let her see how much this news has upset you. Play it cool.* She cleared her throat and sat on the couch next to the rocking chair Ramona had chosen. When the woman's gaze landed on the scattered brochures, Tess gathered them up, muttering, "They're for a friend."

"Cash was shot. He wasn't even on duty, just pumping gas when he witnessed the robbery and...tried to intervene." She paused, her lips flattening before she pushed out the next words. "He was shot in the shoulder and chest. He lost a lot of blood." Another pause, a sharp intake of breath. "He's back in Magdalena. He's had therapy but he's very weak and...and not like the Cash I remember."

Tess clasped her hands in her lap so hard her fingers hurt. "Will he be all right?"

His aunt shrugged. "What does that really mean? The doctors say he'll recover, with minimal limitations. But he's different." She sucked in a breath, frowned. "He's not the same Cash."

"I'm sorry." That was the second reference Ramona made to Cash being different. What exactly did she mean by that?

"There's more. He says the incident is all a blur and refuses to talk about it. Thank God there were eyewitnesses who saw the whole thing and could get to him, or..." her voice trailed off. "He's refused counseling and is on leave from the force." She studied Tess, letting the silence fill the room. Tess fidgeted, clasped her hands tighter, and looked away. She had more questions about Cash, so many of them, but if she started asking, she wouldn't stop, and the pain of asking would take over and suffocate her.

"I was with him at the hospital and I stayed in that chair until I knew he was going to make it." Her eyes glistened, but she didn't cry. "He would wake in the middle of the night and cry out. Always the same thing. I tried to ignore it, but I couldn't." Her voice grew stronger, zeroing in on Tess. "The truth often reveals itself when we are weakest or most vulnerable. I didn't want it to be so, but there it was."

"There what was?" Cash used to say his aunt had a sixth sense about people and could often tell when something was about to happen before it did.

She sighed. "You. He called your name. Such pain and torment, and there was nothing I could do but hold his hand and listen. I witnessed a broken man and it tore at my soul as surely as if the crows had pecked it apart. I vowed if he lived, I would find a way to make him whole again, no matter what I had to do or how many bargains I had to make." Her dark gaze pierced Tess. "And I plan to keep that vow."

Cash had called her name. Perhaps she hadn't been the only one hurting all these years. Perhaps Cash had known his own pain, had wished things were different. Had missed her even though she'd pushed him away. The knowledge made her dizzy and nauseated. "I'm so sorry."

Ramona ignored her. "You need to come back to Magdalena and make him whole again."

"What? I can't—"

"You're responsible for that boy's pain and you're going to take it away."

"You can't be serious." *This* was why Ramona Casherdon had traveled hundreds of miles to see her? Did she think a personal visit could persuade Tess to agree to what would certainly be a disaster on so many levels?

The woman's lips tilted at the corners in what could almost be considered a smile. "I'm very serious. You'll return to Magdalena, make Cash believe you've had an 'awakening' after learning of his near-death experience. You'll stay by his side; you'll make him care about living again."

"I can't do that." *I can't see Cash, look in his eyes, remember how things were...*

Ramona lifted the latch on her purse and removed a folded piece of paper. "You sent Cash a letter a few months after he left." She paused, lifted a brow. "I know it was returned to you, but not before I read it. Here." She held the folded paper out to Tess. "Would you like to refresh your memory?"

Tess sipped in breaths of air, her eyes on the paper. The truth and the destruction she'd caused lay in the folds of that paper. She shook her head. "No."

Ramona returned the letter to her purse and continued. "I'll expect you back in Magdalena within the week. You can call your mother and I'm sure she'll tell you about Cash, since the whole town is buzzing about it. There's your opportunity to say you're coming home."

"Please don't do this."

"I'm saving my nephew. And if you don't want me to blast the contents of that letter all over town, you'll do as I say." Her voice dipped, softened. "Your poor mother would never recover." Pause. "Word has it she's not well."

"What do you mean?" She'd spoken with her mother last week and Olivia had sounded as matter-of-fact as always.

Cash's aunt shrugged. "She has to have some testing done. Could be nothing, or it could be something. Either way, do you want this on your conscience?"

"Of course not, but even if I agree, what makes you think Cash wants to see me or would consider giving us another chance?" *Another chance with Cash...* Just thinking the words made her queasy.

"Oh, he won't want to have anything to do with you, but you'll figure it out. He can say whatever he wants, but the truth was in those words he moaned while he was in pain. Your name." Her mouth pinched as she spit out the next words. "He's never gotten over you."

Ramona actually believed her plan would work. But to what end? "What happens if I do 'figure it out' and he recovers? Then what? Do you really think we could just pick up where we left off eight years ago?"

The woman did smile this time, but it was cold and brittle. "Of course not. We both know that's not possible, don't we? Once my nephew is strong again, you're going to tell him the truth so he can move on and find someone to share his life with and it won't be you. Cash deserves to know he was going to be a father, and he deserves to know why he wasn't. When you tell him, I think we both know what's going to happen."

4

Another day in hell. The hours ran together with nothing to pull him through but the next pill. People called this living? Right. His aunt might think Magdalena and a pain-in-the-ass physical therapist would heal him, but he was past healing, even if she refused to see it. And it had nothing to do with a beat-up body and two bullet holes.

He'd only come back because he couldn't stand to hurt his aunt. Again. The woman had endured enough grief these past years, and he was the cause of most of it. The least he could do was stay alive for her, but there was a lot more than a messed-up shoulder and a wound in the chest holding him down, threatening to screw him up for good.

He did not want to remember what happened that night, did not want to think about the kid in the baggy pants and hoodie who reminded him so much of JJ that for a split second, Cash thought it *was* JJ. And that's why he'd hesitated and ended up with two bullet holes in his body. The kid wasn't JJ and he wasn't robbing a convenience store with an unloaded gun. He'd nailed Cash and by the time the paramedics arrived, there'd been enough blood on the cement to fill a bucket.

But Cash wasn't going to tell anybody why he'd hesitated, or that he *had* hesitated. They wouldn't believe him anyway, not when he had the quickest reaction time and deadliest aim on the force. Saying he paused was like saying a sharpshooter had decided to get a bead on a field of flowers instead of his target. Never happen. Only it had. A cop was still a cop, on duty or off, so that was no excuse either.

What if it happened again? What if his partner took a bullet because of Cash's hesitation? Ben Reed was strong, agile, ex-military, but he deserved a partner who didn't let a screwed-up past threaten his safety. In the eight years since JJ's death, Cash had never been in a situation that so closely mimicked the one that night, but now that he had, how long would it be before the situation recreated itself? Would it never happen again, would it happen twice, five times?

He couldn't risk that and that's why he was so royally messed up right now, why the physical pain was nothing compared to the mental anguish and doubt tearing at his body.

By the time Gina Servetti arrived, the pill had smoothed things out just enough to pretend civility and execute a plan to get rid of her. He'd tried belligerence, moodiness, plain anger, and sulking, but none of those stopped the damn woman from her mission. He had not tried sexual banter.

"Nice shirt. Why don't you open the first three buttons?" Her dark head jerked up from the notes in her hand. Aha. He caught the faint pink slithering up her neck, across her chest. Now he was onto something. Ten minutes and a few crass remarks would send her flying out the door.

Cash worked a lopsided smiled through the drugged haze and patted his bed. Hospital issue, rolled into his old room, compliments of Ramona and Magdalena General Physical Therapy. "Unbutton your shirt. Come get cozy with me."

Her dark eyes narrowed the tiniest bit. She'd be a real looker if she'd get rid of the "He done me wrong" pissed-off attitude. Didn't she know relationships were screwed from the start?

"Gina?"

"Stop it, Cash." She eyed him with equal parts curiosity and something else. He couldn't quite make it out. Interest? Women couldn't resist his smile, or his charm. Even with a busted-up body and a screwed-up head, those nurses and therapists still wanted him. And once in a while, he'd relented and taken what they offered. That had been an acrobatic feat, especially in a hospital, but he'd complied and they'd pulled the curtains and got what they wanted, or said they did. The sex was never the question. It was the other they expected, and when they didn't get it, even though he'd told them it wasn't there, they'd gone away crying or mad.

Hadn't he told every single one of them it would never be about more than sex?

Thanks to his ex-fiancée. She'd taken his honor and his heart and crushed them. Just as well. Being unencumbered had made him a better policeman. And now, indirectly, she'd taken that from him, too. The pure fact that he'd lost the choice created a slow burn in his gut that spread and made him wish he could obliterate *her* from his brain—permanently.

Wham! Something smacked the side of his head. "Hey, what are you doing?"

Gina went all soft and innocent on him. "Sorry. I guess I was so caught up in your attempted seduction, I got carried away."

Sarcasm at its finest. Cash closed his eyes and sighed. Maybe if he pretended she wasn't here...

"Really, Cash? You're going to resort to childish pranks?"

He didn't answer.

"Fine. You tell your aunt she's wasting her hard-earned money on you."

One eye flew open. She knew how to get to him. His aunt

had insisted he continue his sessions in Magdalena even though the physical therapy department in Philly had discharged him. Ramona thought his despondent attitude and continual grogginess necessitated more therapy. What she didn't know was that the attitude and the grogginess had more to do with his mental state and the pills he'd been taking and less to do with his beat-up body. Still, he'd have to get himself straight and soon because he could not have Ramona shelling out money she didn't have for therapy he didn't need. "Okay. Confession time."

"Is this where you're going to tell me you don't really need therapy? I figured that out on the initial assessment, but what I didn't understand was why you couldn't navigate basic weights and exercises." Her gaze narrowed on the bedside stand and the bottle of pills resting there. "There's your problem, isn't it?"

He ran a hand through his hair and sighed. "I might have taken an extra pill now and again to help me along."

"Help you along? With what exactly? Life? Your moods?" Her voice escalated with uncharacteristic emotion. "Addiction creeps up on you; a pill here and there, to smooth out the rough spots and before you know it, there are more rough spots than smooth ones. Stop now. Get out of bed and start moving."

"Okay, stop yelling."

"I'm not yelling." Her voice quieted. "I just don't want to see you mess yourself up."

She spoke like she'd seen somebody get messed up. Had she? He wasn't about to ask, even if he wanted to know. "Let's at least finish up the next two sessions so my aunt doesn't get suspicious. But we have to have rules."

She eyed him. "Rules?"

"I don't want to hear about town chit-chat. No telling me about Pop Benito's new tennis shoes. Or how The Bleeding Hearts Society planted a pansy outside of Lina's Café. And I sure as hell don't want you gushing about how Nate Desantro has turned human now that he has a beautiful wife and a baby. I don't care. Got it? And I don't want to hear about it."

Gina shrugged. "I don't gush. Ever." She wrote a few things in her chart. "He even smiles now."

"Who?"

"Nate Desantro. Laughs, too. I wouldn't have believed it if I hadn't witnessed it myself."

"He deserves it."

"Yes, he does after carrying too much on his shoulders for so many years. And then that first wife." Gina Servetti scowled and helped him sit on the edge of the bed. "She was a piece of work. Patrice. The town was glad when she left. But Christine is perfect for him, though you know who she is, right? And how my cousin almost broke them up last year?"

Despite his desire to shut down Gina's tales, this last piece intrigued him. Nate had been married before? Patrice? Patrice who? And then some cousin tried to come between Nate and his new wife? That had to be Natalie Servetti, sex in stilettos." She was like that even in high school. What the hell had Nate done? And why should he know who Christine was? And...Damn it, she'd yanked him right in. Well, he'd yank himself right back out.

"Enough, or I swear to God, I'll boot you out of here."

She ignored him and handed him a weight. "Eight reps. Nice and slow."

Six months ago, he'd been able to curl fifty-pound dumb-bells, but apparently lying in bed decreased muscle tone, even in healthy body parts. Screw that. He increased his reps. He was not going to turn into a scrawny—

"Easy. You have to build up to it."

The doctors told him he'd lost a lot of blood and it would take time to heal, but for someone who demanded endurance and perfection from his body, struggling to lift a puny weight was pathetic.

"I know why you don't want to talk."

He shot her a look. "Good."

"It's because of Tess."

Finally. He knew it was coming from the first time she walked into his room six days ago. What he hadn't known was how she'd broach the subject, or if she'd mention it at all. She could gather information and fill Tess in on the sad state of her ex-fiancé. If Tess even cared, which she probably didn't. Still, he did not want Tess Carrick to know he'd been reduced to a mess of body parts that didn't work like they used to and a brain that couldn't forget.

"I definitely don't want to talk about her."

"Switch hands and repeat." She shrugged and met his gaze. "I don't want to talk about her either. Bree and I haven't seen or heard from her since the funeral."

He wanted to ignore that, but how could he? "You three were inseparable. Hell, I thought you were best friends."

Her voice dipped. "I thought so, too."

NATE BOUNDED up the steps and opened the front door. Christine sat in the rocking chair Harry had sent them, with Anna cradled in her arms. She smiled when she saw him and his chest squeezed with pure joy. Would he ever get used to watching his wife and daughter? He doubted it. God had given him a second chance and he'd spend the rest of his life being grateful for it.

"Hi." He leaned over and kissed his wife softly on the mouth. Then he planted a kiss on the baby's forehead.

"Hi. She just fell asleep. A full tummy does that to her every time."

Nate stroked Christine's cheek, trailed a finger to the opening of her unbuttoned shirt and pushed the fabric aside. He'd never thought breastfeeding was beautiful, even sexy, until he watched his wife feed their child. "I think she had a better lunch than I did." He kissed the satin skin above her left breast, and whispered, "Definitely."

"Busy day?"

He shrugged and dragged the ottoman closer so he could sit next to her. "I spent the morning at the shop and ran out to Will's after lunch. He had a few questions and I'm trying to finish up the cradle for Jack's daughter."

Two months ago, Will Carrick had offered his barn to Nate as a workshop. There was plenty of room, power, a toilet and fridge, and it negated the need to use Gino Servetti's workshop —and run into Natalie Servetti. Word had it she was back in town with a story and a tear about how she'd been coerced by Gloria Blacksworth to destroy Nate's marriage. Right. That woman had a story all right—big, bold, and packed with lies.

"No news about your friend?"

Nate stroked the dark, fine wisps on Anna's head. Soft, delicate, so very fragile. "I've called four times, but Ramona said he's not seeing anyone. Mom said Pop told her the only person who's gone in the house besides Ramona is Gina Servetti to do his therapy."

She smiled. "Pop would know."

"He gets his information directly from Ramona and she has to know he's going to spread the word. Maybe that's exactly what she wants him to do." He shrugged. "Cash can only play the hermit card so long before the town stampedes the house. One way or the other, I'm going to see him. We have a lot to talk about." Like why Cash had avoided him after the shooting and left town without a word. Or how eight years had passed with nothing but distance and dead silence between them. They'd been best friends, two angry young men trying to figure their way out of hurt and disillusionment. When Cash's parents took off and his aunt moved in, he started hanging around with older boys, like Nate, trying to prove himself. Those attempts got him a bloody nose and swollen lip more than once, but he kept coming back. The damn guy just never gave up.

Until JJ's shooting. He lost a fiancée, a home, a reason to believe he deserved better. Nate blamed Tess Carrick for pushing his friend away. What kind of person accuses the man she's about to marry of cold-blooded murder? It didn't matter that it wasn't true or that she'd most likely regretted it as soon as it was out of her mouth. She'd said it, Cash had heard it, and the town remembered it. End of story. There had been an investigation that turned up nothing and three hours after the announcement, Cash was gone.

"What will happen to him?"

"I don't know. He'll rest up here awhile, then maybe go back to Philly. It's really up to him." He lifted her hand to his lips and kissed the middle of her palm. "I'm betting he's as lost and angry as I was before you came along."

Her lips twitched. "No one was as lost or angry as you were, Nathan Desantro."

He smiled. "True."

"Can you help him?"

How to answer that? His wife was as bad as Lily in that area. They really thought he had superpowers and could dig people out of any and all situations, especially ones of their making, even if said individuals had no desire to dig out. Still, he did not want to disappoint his wife or his sister.

"I'll do my damnedest, but if he's going to get through this, he's going to have to talk about Tess Carrick. And that could be a big problem."

Olivia Carrick was starting to believe in miracles again, something she hadn't done in a long time. Eight years to be exact. She'd lost too much to think the world could be a gentler, kinder place where lives were spared, people given second and third chances.

But Tess was coming back to Magdalena! She even planned to stay for a while, from what she'd said on the phone. A much-needed vacation, she'd called it. And true miracle of miracles, Cash was here, too. Of course Tess didn't know that. If anyone breathed a word before she arrived, she'd never set foot here. But this town had a way of keeping secrets and sometimes letting just enough truth seep out to set the wheels in motion.

Most small towns were like that, but Magdalena had the distinction of being the only one that prided itself on its ability to match-make, feed a stomach, and listen to a sad tale, all at the same time. The town had been responsible for matching Olivia and Tom Carrick. Indeed they had. She'd grown up two towns over in Willowick and met Thomas John Carrick the summer between her junior and senior year of college. Tom recited Robert Frost and sold cleaning supplies out of the back of his station wagon. He stood six-foot-three with a barrel chest and a booming, contagious laugh. It was the laugh that stole her heart, promised a surefire recipe for a lifetime of happiness.

It might have worked, had Olivia been a bit more carefree, Tom, a bit less. She trusted results and wasn't willing to dip her big toe in the waters of uncertainty, while Tom preferred to dive in head first, no consideration for depth, climate, or contingencies.

The union proved volatile and grew quietly disastrous despite their love for each other. When Riki was born, Tom changed jobs, selling dog food from county to county despite the fact that he was allergic to the four-legged creatures. After Tess, the search to fulfill that elusive dream stretched past New York, into Pennsylvania, Ohio, and West Virginia. By the time JJ came along, Tom only made it home every three weeks. But, oh, that week he was home, well, it filled the children's hearts, and it filled Olivia's heart, too.

Years and seasons passed, and Olivia ran the household, paid the bills, repaired the garbage disposal, and began teaching English literature to juniors at Magdalena High. She feared Tom would die on the road and leave her a widow and begged him to find a job that kept him home at night. But Tom Carrick couldn't live in the day-to-day life of most people's worlds. He needed the change to propel him on his latest adventure, even though he always returned to Magdalena saying there was no place like home.

The truth about her husband surfaced when a young Tess's appendix burst and she needed emergency surgery. Tom refused to visit her in the hospital because he couldn't stand to see her in pain. And later, when JJ was caught shoplifting fishing lures from a tackle shop, Tom would not acknowledge the problem. This left Olivia and her brother-in-law, Will, the town's police chief, to deal with JJ and his misdeeds. But in the end, she could not see her son punished and Will talked to the shop owner, who dropped the charges.

When Riki was diagnosed with bipolar disorder, Tom insisted the doctor had misdiagnosed their daughter, and when JJ's misdeeds continued, he would not agree to send the boy to counseling because he said, *The boy will grow out of his shenanigans by the time he hits twenty.*

Sadly, their son never lived to see twenty. Maybe he'd still be alive if he'd gone to counseling or been made to suffer the consequences of shoplifting, vandalizing, and doing drugs. Cash had done all he could to mentor and protect JJ, but the boy could not be protected from his own poor choices and that was what ended his life, not Cash's service revolver. Tess hadn't seen it that way until it was too late.

Olivia wearied of being a mother, father, parent to them all, wishing just once that her husband would take a stand, which he never did. She lost her family, one by one, from death, disappointment, and disappearance. Tom died in his own bed the night Olivia went to see her students in the high school rendition of *The Music Man*. For all the years she'd worried about him dying on the road, she'd been the one who wasn't home, and he'd died alone.

Olivia mourned the dreams she thought they would share that never happened. She'd given up on Riki years ago from sheer hopelessness and exhaustion, and because she simply did not know what else to do. Year after year of traveling from specialist to specialist, trying to find the next "right fit" that was never a fit at all. The worry when her eldest disappeared, then reappeared, found a job, quit, found another job, and never deemed it necessary to inform her family where she was, if she were okay, if she needed help. Riki had inherited her mother's brain and her father's wanderlust—a surefire and inevitable disaster.

With JJ's death, a piece of Olivia fell in the grave with the first shovel of dirt. Tess was her only hope. She took her daughter's pending return as a sign, a miracle that was about to happen.

Olivia sat at the dressing table and wrapped a red scarf around her dark hair, tucking every strand under the fabric. The doctor said they'd have the results of the ultrasound and lab tests in a few days. She'd delivered three babies and never had female problems until the bleeding a few months ago. But if she thought about it, there'd been pelvic pressure, leg aches, even problems going to the bathroom, for several months.

How on earth was she to know these might be symptoms of a problem? Growing older created all manner of havoc to a woman's body, from sagging skin to excess belly fat to unwanted facial hair. She'd assumed the female issues were just one more change in a sea of unwelcome changes.

The doctor mentioned fibroids. Dolly Finnegan had fibroids and she ended up with a hysterectomy. That meant surgery. What an inconvenient time to deal with this. She supposed whatever it turned out to be, she'd have to tell Tess eventually, but not right away. There was too much to do, and she was putting all of her efforts, prayers, and hopes into seeing Cash and Tess together again. Where they belonged. Miracles were about to happen in Magdalena and Olivia Carrick was not going to miss them.

NATE STOOD in the doorway of Cash's bedroom, taking in the posters, plaques, stacks of CDs, an old-school stereo with vinyl albums, all a blend of the boy he'd been and the man he would become. The posters on the wall were sports cars: a Ferrari, a Maserati, and a Lamborghini. In his teens, Cash could tear apart a carburetor faster than an Indy pit crew and had known all about pistons and spark plugs. Ripping apart cars and rebuilding them was his passion until Tess Carrick came along and became his ultimate passion.

Nate moved into the room, glancing at the row of plaques on the dresser. He didn't have to study them to know they were all related to marksmanship, a sport that had become Cash's specialty. And music? The guy could name the tune in less than three notes *and* mouth the words. No singing, though, because Cash Casherdon was not a singing kind of guy.

Nate didn't know what kind of guy his old friend was

anymore. Hell, he doubted if anybody knew. He turned toward the bed and almost wished he could have postponed the inevitable a few seconds longer. Cash looked washed out and beat-up, his features drawn, his face a close match for the hospital-white sheets. His longish curly hair brushed his neck and was perhaps the only true reminder of the old Cash. The forearms were still large and much darker than his face, but Nate guessed they were not as toned as they'd once been. His gaze shot to Cash's shoulder and chest, covered by a navy T-shirt.

Would he be able to rejoin the force? Live a normal life? Nate yanked back the last thought because, hell, what was a normal life? Did anybody fall back to "normal" after something like this?

"You really don't understand what 'no visitors' means do you?"

Nate swung his gaze to Cash's and shrugged. "I'm not a visitor; I always kind of thought of myself as a friend."

Cash scowled. "As a friend, you damn well ought to know I mean what I say."

Nate eased into the recliner next to the bed and ignored the "I'm in charge" look and said, "You always did think you had answers for everything, even when you didn't know what the hell you were talking about."

"You're really going to try and pull that 'get him pissed, get him talking' routine on me? Not going to happen. I just want to be left alone."

"I'm sure you do. Unfortunately, you've got an aunt walking around with rosary beads in both hands and a frown that's etched on her face. Okay, maybe the frown isn't your fault, since your aunt doesn't know how to smile, but the town's starting to think there's a corpse in here instead of a breathing man."

"So tell them the truth; I'm a breathing corpse."

Who the hell was this guy in Cash Casherdon's body? The

guy that Nate had known would kick the crap out of this belly-aching one. "I'm sorry about what happened in Philly." He hesitated a second, almost adding, *And what happened between you and Tess*, but decided against it. "Sometimes life really sucks." And then, because he had no idea what else to say, he threw in a bit of personal commentary. "You know, I've had my share of off days."

That perked him up. "Off *days*? Off years is more like it."

Nate shrugged. "Yeah, well."

Cash shot him a look. "I hear that's all changed."

Nate's lips twitched and his voice took an involuntary dip when he thought of Christine and the baby. "You could say that."

"I hear she's Charlie Blacksworth's daughter."

Was that a glimmer of interest? Charles Blacksworth still had people talking, even from his grave. "Her name's Christine."

"You hated that guy's guts. Putrid, black, decimating hate. What happened to change all that?"

Christine happened. She'd walked into his life and, despite the fact that Nate had acted like a miserable sonofabitch to her, she'd seen something in him. She'd made him want to be a better person and for the first time in his whole life, he believed in love, believed, too, in second chances. How to explain that? He couldn't find the words for those feelings, so he simply said, "I met Christine."

"She must be a saint." Cash paused and added, "Or one hot babe."

Nate stared at his old buddy, his voice turning hard. "If you weren't already on your back, I'd put you there for that comment. *Christine is my wife*, not a babe."

"Fine. Sorry. I'm happy for you." He let out a ragged sigh. "Who would have thought?"

Nate knew exactly what he was thinking. Who would have

thought Nate would end up in marital bliss and Cash would be alone, separated from the woman he had planned his whole future around—Tess Carrick. She was the other reason he was here today.

"I'm going to leave in a minute so you can rest up before Gina Servetti comes to manipulate the crap out of you. But first, I've got a few things I want to say. Now you can ignore me, but you ought to know me well enough to remember I always do what I say."

"You mean, you're a hardass? Yeah, I remember that about you."

"Then remember I'm your friend and I'm telling you this as your friend."

Cash looked away, an obvious attempt to shut out Nate's words. Wasn't going to work. "Everyone's tiptoeing around the real issue, but I've never been a tiptoer, so here it is. I'll be checking up on you," he paused, "regularly, so get used to it. Second, we *are* going to talk about what happened eight years ago and how you blew out of here without a word to me, your supposed best friend. I get that you were torn up, but damn you, all those years and not a word but the tidbits Ramona shared?"

Cash turned, glared at him. "I had my reasons. You know I did."

"That is such bullshit."

"Are you done?"

"Not quite." Nate stood, moved closer to the bed, and stared at Cash. The man was weak and beaten and this next piece of information could plow him under, but Ramona had insisted Nate should be the one to tell him. "She's coming back, Cash. I expect she'll be here in the next day or two."

There was no need to say Tess Carrick's name. Nate expected the woman still lived and breathed in Cash's soul, a constant torment of a love gone wrong.

5

T ess was less than an hour from Magdalena, but the
dread had started the instant Ramona Casherdon
pulled the "nightmare" letter from her purse. Olivia
Carrick's children did not get pregnant unless they were
married. Period. That was the first of her mother's beliefs that
would get blown apart if she read the letter. The other belief
that would be disproved with greater harm and devastation was
that once pregnant, the contemplation of an abortion was not an
option. Repeat. Not. An. Option.

But Tess *had* gotten pregnant and she had considered an
abortion, not without Riki's prodding and support, but still, the
thought had trickled through Tess's brain and sprouted possibilities. In the end, she hadn't been able to do it, not even with
Riki's uncharacteristic support and the fact that Cash had just
put a bullet in her little brother. She'd come close, walking into
the clinic, clutching Riki's hand, but before the doctor entered
the room, Tess grabbed her purse and fled.

As she lay in bed that night, hands resting over her still-flat
belly, she knew she would have to tell Cash, knew, too, she'd
have to bury all emotion as she talked about visitation rights,

schedules, and birthing classes. They had talked about raising children in Magdalena—together. Fate intervened and took her choice away, but it took so much more...

And now she must drive into the town as though she'd been on a short vacation and not on the run from herself for eight years. She would do this for her mother; Olivia Carrick deserved it. Tess tried not to think about facing Cash, what he might say, what he might not say. What did any of it matter? Once he'd gained strength and purpose, Ramona would force her to tell him about the child they'd lost. Perhaps Tess would be lucky and the numbness that had claimed her soul for years would protect her from the pain of loving Cash Casherdon again.

Or perhaps the truth would seep out from layers of denial; she'd never stopped loving him.

She could not risk her mother learning the truth, and she didn't doubt Ramona Casherdon would expose Tess's dark secret if necessary. The woman had traveled hundreds of miles for a face-to-face meeting, which meant she was on a mission to save her nephew, no matter the collateral damage. At least she'd forewarned Tess about her mother's health.

Heaven knew, Olivia Carrick was not about to offer up information as to the nature, or even the existence, of a possible problem. How sad that her mother couldn't confide in her. Olivia always said she was of strong German stock, the kind that showed little fear and even less emotion. Such self-sufficiency must have made it difficult for Thomas Carrick to measure up, and maybe that had been the problem. Maybe after a while, he'd stopped trying.

Forty-three minutes later, Tess headed into Magdalena and down Main Street. Lina's Café, Barbara's Boutique and Bakery, Victor's Pharmacy. The years hadn't altered much. Maybe a coat of fresh paint or a fancier sign. How could so little have changed and yet so much be different? A lifetime ago, she'd been making wedding favors, laughing with Bree and Gina, and talking about her future. In a flash of blood and horror, it was over, all of it gone; JJ, Cash, nursing, her future. Everything.

Tess pulled into the driveway of the old two-story and turned off the engine. In some ways, the house looked exactly as it had every spring. Bursts of color surrounded the quiet place in a gathering of red, orange, yellow, and pink. Clusters of tulips lined the pathway to the front door or scattered in beds alongside purple balls her mother called allium. White and fuchsia azaleas blossomed against a backdrop of shiny leaves, and her father's favorite, giant daffodils guarded the mailbox like sentries. The bombardment of color and shape, and later, fragrance, began in late March and ended in November when the last rose bloom froze on its thorny branch.

Despite the camouflage of color, the house looked like a weary soldier on duty. There were lifts in the roof, a few shingles curled from wear and the elements. Thomas Carrick had never been much of a handyman and words like *routine maintenance* were foreign to him. Once again, the task fell to Olivia. The tan siding had been newly power-washed and the windows sparkled, no doubt Uncle Will's handiwork. Her mother said he'd been coming around to help out with this and that, adding more insulation in the attic, repairing a few door hinges, installing a programmable thermostat. Olivia said that losing Aunt Julia had been hard on him, even though they'd all known the multiple sclerosis would take her sooner rather than later, but still, being prepared was never really *being prepared*.

Tess dragged the suitcase from the trunk and made her way up the sidewalk. When she reached the front door, she hesitated. Should she knock? Eight years was a long time. Things changed. Maybe her mother locked the door these days, though probably not. Still, Olivia might prefer that her daughter knocked. After all, Tess had chosen to leave—no, practically run

away—at a time when, despite her mother's silence and assur-
ances that all was well, Tess had known all was not well, and
she'd left anyway.

She should have stayed and battled through the despair and
pain with her mother. Wasn't that what families did? Got
through it together? She should not have called Cash a
murderer in front of half the town and refused to see him. But
most of all, she should not have accepted Riki's offer to get away
and then to get rid of the baby. She'd kept these truths buried so
deep, they hadn't been able to surface for years and yet, less than
ten minutes back and they'd bubbled to the top, threatening to
spill over and into her. Threatening to suffocate her.

"Tess!" Olivia Carrick stood on the other side of the door,
arms open wide, a smile on her lips. "How wonderful to
see you!"

Tess dropped the suitcase and hugged her mother. She'd
always craved the rare moments when Olivia Carrick showed
her nurturing side and this was one of them. All too soon, Olivia
pulled away and said in her usual no-nonsense voice, "Well, let's
not make a spectacle of ourselves on the front stoop unless you
want your picture in tomorrow's paper."

And that was that. It had taken years for Tess to understand
her mother's reluctance or inability to show affection—the
touchy-feely kind. Fear was the cause. The woman could fight
city council and tell The Bleeding Hearts Society when they
were butting in where they had no business, but she was petrified to show her emotions. Tess finally understood that fear, had
learned the reality of it since leaving. Guarding emotions was
safe. It didn't hurt and closed down the pain. Sadly, it also
reduced the joy.

"Mom, you've lost weight." The extra middle padding Olivia
had carried since JJ's birth was noticeably gone. Was it a sign of
the illness, maybe cancer, eating through her body?

"A lot can happen in four months," her mother said, sliding just the tiniest hint of accusation into her words. "And it's amazing what happens when you cut out the midnight candy bars."

She said it with the nonchalance that might make Tess believe her, had she not heard differently from Ramona Casherdon. "You don't need to lose weight. I thought you were fine." *Tell me about it. Please.*

Olivia responded in typical fashion. "What woman is ever happy with her weight? Even you, toothpick that you are, could probably point out an ounce or two you'd like to shave."

"True." She'd try another angle. "So, just cutting out a candy bar at night did that?" Tess gestured to her mother's flattened middle.

Her mother smiled. "A *king*-sized candy bar. It was the heartburn that stopped me, though, not the weight. When you can't sleep because of it, you start looking at what you're putting in your mouth and when. Candy bars at midnight with my favorite book sounds wonderful, but it was an idiotic combination, and oh, the discomfort." She shrugged. "Of course, it took Doc Gentry to lay it all out for me so I could see the logic of it. Sometimes it takes another pair of eyes to state what's staring right at us. Don't you think so?"

"Sure. Yes." What *was* she talking about? They made their way to the living room, which looked exactly as it always had with the exception of the piano that her mother had moved from the sitting room and placed alongside the wall where Thomas Carrick's Barcalounger used to be. Memories bombarded Tess: her father's extra-long body stretched out on the chair, roast chicken and dumplings on Sunday afternoon, and Olivia Carrick's signature apple crumble. JJ's chin hairs sprouting like a chia pet. His skinny arms, his heavy metal T-shirts. His laughter. Cash standing in the doorway, talking to her father, watching every step she took and then later telling her what he—

"I've always loved this piano." Olivia's voice dipped, cut off Tess's wandering thoughts, and not a second too soon.

"Do you still play?" She fingered the keys. Riki had been the only one to inherit her mother's talent for the piano. Maybe Tess should take up the piano again. A gift to her mother.

"Every night."

"Maybe I'll give it another try. What do you think?"

"What I think is you're trying to please me and have no interest in the piano." She raised a brow and said, "That's the problem with a lot of us. We're so busy trying to please those we care about, that we lose track of what's important to *us*." She sounded like she might be talking about herself, but how could that be when she'd loved teaching? "And if you love selling lipstick around the world—" she swept a hand in the air "—then sell away."

I won't be selling lipstick anymore, at least not for six months. She was not going to tell her mother about her job, at least not yet.

"How do you like the kitchen? Quite a change isn't it?"

"Wow. It certainly is." She took in the bright yellow, a marked difference from the papered rooster deco she remembered. Thomas Carrick had said it reminded him of the farm he worked on when he lived in Idaho and for that reason, it remained long past its time.

Olivia pulled out a plastic container of egg salad and a loaf of rye bread. "Your uncle talked me into it," she said with a softness around the edge of her words that surprised Tess. "I told him the wallpaper just needed a good scrubbing, but Will insisted the kitchen needed brightening up."

"Well, it's definitely bright." Sunglasses bright.

She smiled. "Silly man. He thought it would perk me up in the morning and I'd cut down on my coffee."

"Did it work?" Why all the talk about Uncle Will? And the smile. What was that about? Olivia's smiles were as rare as a purple rose.

"Of course not." She concentrated on making Tess's sandwich, placed a pickle on the side, and handed the plate to her.

"Where's yours?" Enough of the idle chit-chat. Tess wanted to talk about whatever was going on with her mother and how Ramona Casherdon knew more than Tess did.

"I ate a little while ago." She turned toward the fridge, making it difficult to see if there was truth on her face. But soon, Tess would find out. When Olivia sat down, she cleared her throat and her eyes grew bright, her voice quiet, yet determined. "There's something I need to tell you, and there's no good way to do it but say it straight out."

"Yes?" *Here it comes. Now she'll tell me she's sick.*

"It's Cash. He's been injured." She reached across the table and clasped Tess's hand. "He needed a place to heal." She paused. "He's in Magdalena."

CASH FORCED his left shoulder to remain straight as he fought through the discomfort. He'd sworn to Gina that Tess would not see him lying in bed like a piece of degenerating muscle mass. He should have been working harder on his therapy, doing the exercises in the booklet the therapist in Philly gave him, hell, acting like he gave a damn about recuperating. Instead, he'd popped pills so he could live in a blur of denial and self-pity. And that was fine, except right now he needed to show Tess he was as strong as she remembered.

Gina tried to convince him the maroon-striped button-down shirt brought out the golden highlights in his hair and added fifteen pounds to his frame. He didn't give a damn about showing off his hair, but he'd take the weight so he didn't look weak and helpless.

Maybe he shouldn't have taken that last pill, but seeing Tess Carrick after eight years of thinking about her even when he *wasn't* thinking about her? Well, that wasn't a challenge a man undertook without pharmaceutical assistance.

Cash snatched the remote to the television and flipped through stations. Nothing interested him, so he clicked it off. Why the hell had he agreed to see her? It wasn't like they had anything to say to one another, not after all the hurt and too many years. Nate had done his job and informed him Tess was back in town. That was shock enough, but actually seeing her, especially in his debilitated state, well, that was worse than torture. But Ramona had all but begged him to see his ex-fiancée, said it was time for the town to know there was no ill will between the two of them.

As if anybody but his aunt would buy that story.

The doorbell rang at 10:52 A.M. Tess used to set her watch fifteen minutes ahead so she arrived on time, but even so, she was invariably ten minutes late. Looked like that had changed. He wondered what else had changed since the last time he saw her. Cash sucked in a deep breath and eased out of the chair. The pill made his steps slow, the effort forced. He tried to shut down his brain, but the damn thing wouldn't cooperate. Two more small steps and he opened the door.

The eyes grabbed him first, the color of dew-coated grass in the early morning. So clear, so true, he almost lost his balance.

"Hello, Cash."

Same voice, but deeper, sexier, if that were possible. Her hair was shorter, cut just below her chin, parted on the side. It looked blonder than he remembered. She still had a damn beautiful body, thinner he guessed from the looks of her arms and neck.

No belly, small breasts, and just enough curve to mold to his body.

Eight years changed more than a person's skin and hair. It changed things deep inside them, sometimes for better, many times for worse. In Cash's case, it was the latter, but she didn't need to know that unless she'd already figured it out.

"Come in," he said, amazed the words tumbled out in any form of coherence. She offered him a tentative smile, the kind she used to reserve for uncomfortable situations and people she didn't know. Never for him. The pill he'd taken earlier made him languid and stretched his muscles, which made it hard to maintain the posture he'd lived with since he became a policeman. Counting steps and the resolve she would not see him for the crumpled mess he'd become propelled him to his chair.

Tess took a seat next to him on the plaid couch, her long legs tanned, toned, glistening. His gaze remained on them a second too long as he remembered the way she used to wrap them around his waist...

"Thank you for seeing me."

So perfect. So proper. "No problem. Ramona said you had something to say to me." He'd agreed to see her, but he had not agreed to idle chit-chat. She could ask her questions and then get out. Besides, if she stayed too long, the smell of her lily-of-the-valley scent would invade his lungs and smother the oxygen in the room.

"This is really hard, for both of us," she stumbled, tried again, "but we need to talk about that night."

Why wouldn't she look at him, head on, eye to eye? Was she afraid of him? Afraid of what he might say? Or was she afraid of showing the pity she must feel for what he'd become? "Oh, you were pretty clear that night." *I hate you*, she'd said. *You're a murderer and I never want to see you again.*

She shook her head and her blond hair shimmied and

swung against her jaw. Very sexy. Did she know that? He guessed she did.

"I said horrible things to you, Cash. You didn't deserve that." Her eyes misted like they used to when she talked about things that really moved her; like how much she loved him. He did not want to see her pain. That would only be one more burden to carry and he was already sinking in his own misery. Knowing she hated him fueled his commitment to his job with an unrelenting fierceness he would not have possessed had a wife been waiting for him.

"You said what you felt at the time." When had he gotten so damn philosophical? Maybe too many days in a hospital did that to a person. "It's done and there's no going back." *Though I'd give a body part to undo what happened.*

Those green eyes settled on his mouth and made his groin jump. *That* was not a welcome response. Feeling anything for Tess Carrick was dangerous, futile, and stupid, especially stupid.

"After you left..." she started, stopped, looked away again.

Either she was damn good at lying or she really was hurting. The hell of it was, Cash couldn't tell. Ironic, considering there'd been a time when he could interpret what it meant when she twitched or scratched her nose.

Her voice dipped, smoothed out. "I did things that changed my life and—" she paused, cleared her throat "—I've regretted those choices. Many times."

"Stop." He held up a hand to still her confession. What had she done? Something tied to forgetting about him, no doubt? Had sex with his best friend? Nate was the closest person to a best friend he'd ever had, aside from Tess, and if she'd looked at Nate sideways, his friend would have hauled her to Cash and made her confess. Sex with a stranger then?

Now that could happen, and imagining another man's hands on Tess made Cash angry, another emotion he did not want to associate with his ex-fiancée. But there they were—lust and anger squashed into the same breath as her name.

Damn.

He could still get rid of her and deny whatever feelings were swirling in his gut, his brain, every part of him. Hadn't he been denying those feelings since the second she told him she hated him? Cash shifted in the chair and winced as pain stabbed his shoulder.

"Cash? Are you okay?"

Pity from Tess? Hardly. "I'm fine." He pushed past the pain and pasted a smile on his face. "But I don't want to hear about any of your misguided choices. I've got enough of my own to carry, so you're just going to have to deal with them yourself."

"But—"

"No, Tess." The years slipped away until they were kids again, about to be married, so much in love. And then it all crashed around them. "No," he said again.

She ignored him, her voice growing softer. "You deserve to know."

What the hell did that mean? He deserved to know exactly how she'd loaded a few more rounds of ammo in the chamber to destroy him. He couldn't take it. "Some things are better left alone. Take my advice on that."

She pulled her lower lip through her teeth and *zing,* he grew hard. Just like that. Now he was pissed. He had to get her out of here, out of Magdalena, too. As soon as possible. "So, when are you leaving town?"

She hesitated. "I'm not sure." Pause. "I'm thinking a few weeks; it depends."

A few weeks as in fourteen days or was a few weeks twenty-one? Or longer? That was too much time. He couldn't risk it. "That long? Why?" He wanted her gone and out of his life before

Pop Benito and his garden club crusaders tried to play matchmaker.

He must have sounded harsher than he intended because those eyes filled with something awfully close to hurt. "I have some things to take care of and I wanted to spend a little time with my mother."

"I doubt Olivia needs you to babysit her."

A splash of pink climbed her neck, settled on her cheeks. "I didn't know my presence would offend you so much."

Offend him? That wasn't exactly the word that came to mind. Bother him? Make him remember things he'd fought years to forget? Now that was a hell of a lot closer to the truth. Tess Carrick's presence in the universe bothered him because no matter how hard he tried, he couldn't forget her—the softness of her hair brushing against his belly, the taste of her skin after they made love, the greenness of her eyes when she told him she loved him, the— *No!* If he didn't stop now, he'd say something stupid, like how he wished things could have turned out differently, and if he were really crazy, he might even admit, once in a while, usually after several whiskeys, he wished they could have tried again.

Admitting any of those tragic truths would be no better than a gun without bullets. So, Cash did what he did best when face to face with himself. He lied. He looked her straight in the eye and said, "Now you know."

6

H e was so thin. *Gaunt* would be a better word. All angles and slashes. He'd cinched his belt an extra notch but his jeans, at least a size too big, hung on his tall frame. The button-down shirt bunched at the belly, like there was too much material, or not enough man to fill it. Cash had always been lean, but he'd been a muscled lean. Now he looked weathered and sinewy, like skin with all the fat sucked out.

And still, he'd snatched her breath away.

She tried to convince herself the skittering heartbeat that kicked into gear the second she saw him—and didn't leave until she'd pulled out of the driveway—was nothing more than shock mixed with sympathy. But that was such a lie. Beneath the ill-fitting clothes and opaque gaze, he was still Cash and *that* was dangerous. When he spoke, his voice had seeped into the tiny cracks of despair to the loneliness that lived in the center of her soul. Ramona had told Tess she was the only one who could save Cash. What the woman didn't know was that Cash might be the only one who could save Tess.

Of course, that wasn't going to happen, not once he knew the truth about the baby and what happened afterward that had stolen her chance for a normal life. She would live with that pain forever and even if Cash grew to desire her, want a life and a second chance with her, she knew there would be none. Once she told him the truth, all of it, he'd discard her. There would be no more calling her name in delirious longing. There would be nothing but disdain. He would be done with her for good, and then he would move on, find a wife, have a family.

And that was exactly what Ramona Casherdon was counting on.

PEOPLE CAME to Pop Benito with their problems. He listened. He counseled in a roundabout manner that dropped insight into a person's lap. He never divulged conversations or names. The town referred to him as "The Godfather of Magdalena" and that was fine by him.

He'd called a special meeting of The Bleeding Hearts Society because there was serious business that needed tending to, and it had to do with little Tess Carrick, who wasn't so little anymore, and Daniel "Cash" Casherdon, one of Pop's favorites. Even if the boy hadn't chosen a profession as a policeman, Pop would still put him on the keeper shelf beside his Sinatra albums. The boy had zing. He wasn't zinging much right now, not with a bum shoulder, a bad attitude, and a "she done me wrong" heartache a mile long. But things would get better. Those two tragic love-birds belonged together, and Pop vowed on his dear Lucy's favorite Chianti that he would see it happened.

And that was the reason for the meeting. Christine Desantro, bless her heart, had made the phone calls for him, read Pop's "classified" letter to them, and driven Pop to the meeting. She was a member of the group, too, but between the baby and helping the town with budgets, loans, and overall money sense, she didn't get to a lot of meetings. Pop could have made the two-mile trek because his hip was all healed up and he had new tennis shoes with extra bounce—but he liked spending time with Christine, and she'd probably bring Anna with her. That baby was the spitting image of her mama and dang but if Nate didn't puff up proud whenever he saw her. Or maybe he was looking at his wife when he was puffing up. Or both. Didn't matter. The boy was happy, and for a person who hugged doom and gloom for too many years, that was saying something.

With a little help, Cash could end up just as happy as Nate. They used to be best buddies, until the horrible event that ripped a hole in the town and tore Cash Casherdon and Tess Carrick apart. But now, Cash was back in town, and maybe he was a bit banged up, but destiny often showed her face in times of adversity. That's what his Lucy always told him. And a sprinkle or two of holy water helped ward off the bad times, too.

Pop sipped Mimi Pendergrass's specialty hibiscus tea and picked up a slice of Miriam Desantro's pumpkin roll. Ramona Casherdon was the go-to person for refreshments, but since she wasn't invited for soon-to-be-revealed obvious reasons, Christine had asked her mother-in-law to fill in. That was big of Miriam because she didn't exactly condone The Bleeding Hearts, saying they were too busy poking in people's lives and not busy enough tending their own. True, to a point.

Pop munched on the pumpkin roll, savored the cream cheese filling. Miriam had Lily and Nate, and now Christine and Anna. Many of the group only had memories and each other, which made the goings-on of the townsfolk more compelling, kind of like watching a real-life soap opera. And the kick of it was that every now and again, The Society could tweak the outcome a bit and get a "happily ever after."

That's what they were all here for today: figuring out the "happily ever after" for Cash and Tess, but before they could do that, there was the business of how Tess just so happened to drive into Magdalena when she hadn't set foot here in eight years. It did make a person wonder if there'd been a snitch among them, but who?

"Pop?" Mimi Pendergrass saluted him with her mug of hibiscus tea. "We're ready to start."

Pop cleared his throat and scanned the table, taking in the familiar faces of the group. Of particular interest were Will Carrick and Bree Kinkaid. Will was Tess's uncle and had been Cash's boss and mentor. The man also had close ties to his sister-in-law, Olivia Carrick, Tess's mother, and the ever-pregnant Bree Kinkaid had been best friends with Tess and was still friends with Gina Servetti, one of the only people allowed in the Cash-erdon home. Maybe Gina was there for physical therapy sessions, but maybe she'd been there for something else, too. Gathering and sharing information, which she'd passed on to Bree, who took it upon herself to contact her once-best friend. Somehow, that didn't quite wash. Maybe Will had been the one to make the call to Tess. Poor man had always regretted what happened and even said he should have stepped in when JJ was out of line, but with a sick wife, he'd been tapped out in the energy department. Was this his way of tossing Cash and Tess together again? If it were, the attempt was about as lame as one of his jokes.

But Will wasn't the type to mix in other people's business, necessary or not. So who was it?

"Pop?"

"Huh? What? Oh, excuse me." He wiped his mouth with a napkin and nodded. "I been gnawing on a predicament for two days and I can't seem to work my way to an answer. That's why I called the meeting. Somebody here's got to know something about how two people who haven't set foot in the same state in eight years can both end up here in Magdalena at the same time."

"You mean Cash and Tess, don't you, Pop?"

Bree Kinkaid looked at him with those amber eyes and he wasn't sure if she was just being movie-star dramatic or was too dim-witted to put the puzzle together. Hard to say with a husband who wanted her to pop out babies like a popcorn machine.

"That's right, Bree. I'm talking about Cash Casherdon and Tess Carrick." He adjusted his glasses and peered at the faces of the group. "That's too close to be called a coincidence. I want to know who did it and why."

Bree's face lit up and she burst out, "So that's why Ramona isn't here! You didn't invite her because you don't want her to know." Her voice dipped and she added, "Tess's name is dirt to her."

Mimi Pendergrass cleared her throat and shook her head with enough gusto to bounce the shiny ball earrings she wore. "I still can't think about that sad event without tearing up. I could hardly take down the decorations for their wedding reception, and when I had to scoop up the rose petals off the honeymoon bed," she paused and blinked hard, "well, it was plain torture."

"The cake was good, though, wasn't it?" Wanda Cummings piped in. "Glad we convinced Ramona not to throw it in the trash can."

"And I was eating Jordan almonds for weeks," Bree said. "Even though the blue ones didn't help in the baby department." Her voice turned soft, wistful. "But Ella Blue sure is a daddy's girl."

"There's no sense reliving bad memories. Best to let them lie and move on." This from Will Carrick, who rubbed a work-roughened hand over his jaw and frowned. "I've been wondering the same thing as you, Pop. How did Tess end up here after too many years of pretending we don't exist?"

Will had a bead on that niece of his, and Pop would bet his new crop of parsley the man had a bead on his sister-in-law, too. Olivia Carrick was a tough bird but she had to be with a daydreamer like Thomas Carrick. The dang man could tell a good story fluffed with terms like *gonna do* and *want to do* but he never quite grasped the idea of *did*.

Will, on the other hand, was a man of action, duty, and his word. When MS finally took his dear Julia two years ago, Will mourned her something fierce, but eventually, he realized he had to move on or smother in his own misery. That's when he'd started hanging around Olivia Carrick's, fixing a door for her, painting the mailbox. Didn't fool Pop. He could spot a dog on the hunt from across town. Not that either one of those two recognized the ritual for what it was, but maybe now with Olivia having some sort of health issue (according to Wanda whose daughter spotted Olivia in the waiting room of the imaging center at Magdalena General two weeks ago), the two might get closer.

Pop scratched his jaw, considered the possibilities. "I can't picture Olivia calling up Tess and telling her about the tests she had done."

"Tests?" Bree glanced around the table, clearly confused.

Mimi waved a hand in the air, dismissing Pop's comment. "Some female tests. And Olivia's too practical to call her daughter home to hold her hand because of a test or two."

"Unless," Bree Kinkaid said in a swoosh of secrecy, "it's bad news."

"Stop it, Bree." Will Carrick threw her a stern look, another mark in Pop's book that said something was brewing between that man and his sister-in-law.

Pop would think about those two later. For now, he had to get to the bottom of Tess's sudden arrival in Magdalena, so he could start working on a way to get the two lovelorn birds together again. "Show of hands. Did anybody at this table contact Tess Carrick about her mother or," he paused, "her ex-fiancé?" They all shook their heads. "Okay, then we'll chalk Tess's return to destiny and go from there."

"And where exactly would you be heading?"

"Will, you know the boy better than most of us. He's had his hide beaten, been shot at and shot up. I hear he's got a bum shoulder and a disposition that makes the old Nate Desantro look like a charmer. Remember Nate a few years back, miserable and wanting the rest of the world to share in his misery? Lily was the only good thing in his life, the only person he cared about other than his mother." His voice softened and he said, "And then Christine drove into Magdalena, unannounced and unwelcome, kind of like Tess. Look what happened to them? They're so in love they could do ads for one of those match-maker places."

Mimi coughed. "Not exactly, Pop, but we get the idea."

"Good, because I want you all to think about that picture and remember how Nate was not exactly keen on poor Christine, and how Christine didn't want nothin' to do with any of us. But then things changed and that's my point. Tragedy can pull even the most unlikely people together and give them a second chance if they let it. I say Cash and Tess have never stopped loving each other and it's up to us to make them realize it."

"That is just so sweet." Bree sniffed and rubbed her big belly. "I don't know if it's hormones or the story, but I think I'm going to cry."

Mimi reached across the table and patted her hand. "There,

there, dear. Pop's right. Cash and Tess belong together and this town's got to help make that happen."

CHRISTINE TOSSED a handful of twigs and leaves in an old red wheelbarrow. She'd spent the last hour cleaning up the backyard from the debris that winter had left behind. Clumps of wet leaves, twigs, skinny branches, even wispy balls of paper-thin hydrangea flowers lay scattered on the wet ground. Nate hadn't wanted her to slop around in the mess, had said he'd take care of it this weekend, but the fresh air cleared her lungs and her head, and it was good for the baby, too.

Anna sat propped in her stroller, bundled from the chilly spring air. This yard was so different from the one in Chicago that was dressed and adorned with manicured shrubberies and hand-selected flowers. Gloria had always insisted on gardeners who could match the color and tone of the season to the shutters and brick on the house. How exactly did one do that? Christine often wondered if her mother interviewed the candidates and made them submit sample portfolios. Of course, the yard was beautiful and wonderfully accessorized, but no one ever visited it. All that color and beauty wasted. How sad was that?

Nate and Jack Finnegan had planted four bags of bulbs in the backyard last fall. Hyacinth, daffodils, tulips, and allium. She'd wanted to help, but Nate absolutely would not hear of it, as though a pregnant woman had never dug in the soil before. Apparently, he thought his wife should be relegated to supervisor in a "point and plant" capacity. Christine had let him fuss over her, because what pregnant woman doesn't like to be fussed over? The fussing hadn't stopped after the baby, though. Nate respected her need for independence but he took every opportunity to make her feel special and loved: fresh-brewed coffee and croissants in bed, lavender soap made by Jack Finnegan's youngest daughter, special-order winter gloves for the sub-zero weather. And then there was the way he cherished her body, with a tender fierceness that stole her heart *and* her breath...

This world they'd made with their baby was magical and holy, and Christine vowed to never take it for granted. When Nate played the piano for her after dinner, his long fingers stroking the keys with grace and passion, she sat beside him, their shoulders and thighs touching, the baby cradled in her arms. It was as close to a "perfect" life as she could imagine.

Before her father's death, she would not have envisioned living in brushed cotton and flannel with a fireplace and a giant of a man to keep her warm. She'd thought a fast-paced life of constant challenge and noteworthy accomplishments were the marks of success, and with that success would come the by-product—happiness. But nothing compared to this life and if not for the tragic loss of her father, she might never have known it, and that would have been the real tragedy. In a roundabout way, her father had given her a chance to live life on her own terms, and despite what he'd done and why he'd done it, she would always be grateful for that.

Pop said people who found their soul mates had a duty to help others find theirs. She didn't quite know about that, but Pop had pretty firm ideas on the matter, even a three-ringed binder with plans of execution that could make a plotted-out meeting between a couple appear as nothing more than chance. The more time she spent with Angelo Benito, the more she learned he left little to chance, depending instead on the guidance of his dead wife, Lucy, an hour of daily prayer, and the ideas that came to him minutes before he slipped into his afternoon nap.

His latest efforts had to do with the couple the whole town was buzzing about: Cash Casherdon and Tess Carrick.

Christine didn't believe in butting into other people's business, but after hearing their sad story, she wanted to see them together and would be willing, in small doses, to enlist in the effort. She was certain Pop would be more than happy to provide detailed instructions, similar to what he'd done this afternoon at the emergency Bleeding Hearts meeting.

He might need four binders stacked with play-by-plays of chance encounters to get this couple past eight years of hurt and—

"Hey."

She turned and spotted Nate standing on the deck, jacket open, dressed in his usual jeans and flannel. "I told you I'd take care of the yard this weekend."

Christine smiled as he bounded down the steps and made his way toward her and Anna. "We needed the fresh air. And look," she held up both hands, "I even wore the gloves you got me."

"So you did." He grinned and pulled her into his arms, planting a kiss on her lips. "I have my very own little gardener."

"Yes, you do." She brushed her lips over his, breathed in his scent. If they were married sixty years, it would not be enough. "And besides, Anna loves to watch the birds."

Nate released her and walked to the carriage. He leaned down, kissed his daughter's forehead, and said in a gentle voice, "Did you tell Mommy that? Or did you tell her you were watching the big hawk that keeps the backyard nice and clean?" He leaned closer. "What? Oh, I think she's pretty, too."

Christine shook her head and laughed. The first time she met Nate Desantro she would have bet her retirement fund he didn't know how to smile, and certainly not make a joke. But she'd been so very wrong. "Lily called a little while ago. She said you promised to cook hot dogs and burgers on the grill tonight."

He lifted Anna from the carriage and straightened. "That

little conniver. I did not say that. She asked if I would make hot dogs and burgers on the grill *sometime*, not today."

"You know she's looking for any reason to visit Anna."

Nate sighed. "Oh, I know. Like how she offered to come and dust the house for us and vacuum?" He laughed and slung an arm over her shoulder as they headed toward the house. "Next time I'm going to take her up on it and make her do it."

"She's just excited to be an aunt." How could they fault her for loving Anna?

"I know, but if she wants to visit, she has to clear it with Mom and not make up a bunch of excuses about how we need her to do work."

"She is getting pretty creative."

"And she was coming to cook dinner because you were too tired?" He looked at her and shook his head. "That's wrong on so many levels, but the main one is her assumption that you do the cooking."

"Nate Desantro." She smacked his arm. "I do too cook." Her voice dipped. "Just not as well or as often as you do."

His lips twitched but he tried for a serious expression when he said, "But you have so many other qualities that far surpass a simple meal. Trust me on that."

The intensity of his gaze heated her insides, swirled to her gut. "And don't forget it either."

"Oh, I won't, don't worry about that."

He opened the door and she stepped inside. "So, Lily and your mom will be here at six. Burgers and hot dogs are in the fridge and Miriam is bringing antipasto salad and a pineapple upside-down cake. Lily is making lemonade."

"Lemonade?"

"Fresh-squeezed. Miriam said not to ask."

Nate shrugged out of his jacket and eased into the rocker with Anna, who had begun to coo. He stroked her dark hair and nuzzled his face against hers, whispering into her ear. Christine watched them and thought about Cash and Tess. Would they get a second chance together, maybe eventually share a child?

"The mail's on the table," Nate said, eyes closed, rocking back and forth with Anna resting on his chest, her tiny fists balled against the flannel of his shirt.

"Thanks." She made her way to the kitchen table and rifled through the stack. The mail service didn't deliver to rural locations in Magdalena, so once every day or two, Nate or Christine stopped by the post office to collect their mail. Quite a bit different from Chicago, where the mail arrived in the box at the end of the driveway every morning by 10:00 A.M. and special delivery trucks dropped off packages several times a week. She set aside the catalogues and flyers and put the bills in another stack. The only remaining item was a half-inch padded manila envelope with a Chicago delivery stamp on it.

"Looks like my mother sent Anna another book." Gloria had sent five fairytale books and *Aesop's Fables*—how appropriate— at Christmas. Nate hadn't been pleased and Uncle Harry claimed she was merely trying to weasel her way back in, using Anna. Christine had listened to her gut and also to Miriam, who believed Gloria was truly sorry for what she'd done and sent a brief, impersonal thank-you note. When January arrived, so did more books. Nate kept quiet this time, but his scowl said more than any words could. She didn't tell Uncle Harry, but apparently Nate had, because he'd called with a long list of reasons not to trust her mother, beginning and ending with Natalie Servetti.

She hadn't forgotten how her mother orchestrated a set-up that almost destroyed their marriage. But she'd moved past that; she and Nate were solid and happy. Gloria couldn't touch them now, and while Christine accepted a random book here and there for Anna, she did not plan to let Gloria back into her life.

The absence of books in February and March made Christine think her mother's goodwill and kindness toward her grand-daughter had dried up. But now it was April and another package had arrived.

"Maybe Gloria forgot to pay her Book Club bill and they refused to send more books."

"Nate. Please."

"Just saying, you never know the truth or the motives of that woman."

She carried the package into the living room and sat on the couch, working a finger under the tape. "The other books came in a box, and there were more of them."

"Money could be tight. One too many salon visits and poof, the fortune's gone."

Obviously, her husband had not forgiven Gloria for her plot against him. It's not that Christine had quite let go of the hurt or sadness that her own mother had plotted against her, but years of living with Gloria Blacksworth had taught her that some things and some people didn't change and it was easier and much healthier to move on. That didn't mean you let them hurt you again; it just meant you didn't waste energy on an impos-sible cause. She lifted the tape and opened the envelope, wishing for a second that things could have been different with her mother.

"Whatever's in here is for Anna. Thinking of it that way makes everything much easier."

Nate's voice turned cold, his words harsh. "I'm not that generous with my forgiveness."

That was certainly true. Nate Desantro protected what was his. Period. "Well." She stared at the green cover of the slim book. It was Shel Silverstein's *The Giving Tree*. How interesting that her mother would send a book about the circle of life where child becomes caretaker to parent. Was there a hidden message here, a code between the pages?

She eased open the cover and there on the whiteness of the page, she found her answer, though it was not an answer at all. Gloria's scrawl read, *To Christine, my darling and most beloved daughter. Love, Mother.*

7

W ill Carrick was not the kind of man a person said *no* to. He'd done two tours of duty in the marines, been awarded a Medal of Honor, and come back to Magdalena to protect the town as police chief until he retired three years ago. He knew the ins and outs of everyone's backstory, on both sides of the law, and pretty much got along with all of them, using reason and common sense and sometimes a night in jail.

He stood in Ramona Casherdon's living room, arms crossed over his chest, telling—not asking—Cash to get his butt out of the chair and come for a ride.

"I'm really not in the mood right now, Will." Once he set foot out of the house, half of Magdalena would pounce on him with questions, well-wishes, and enough food to feed six families. He couldn't handle that right now. And he sure as hell couldn't run the risk of seeing Tess again. It hadn't even been twenty-four hours since she'd sat in this very room, and he needed time to get his head straight.

"In the mood?" Will's long, lean body towered over Cash. He

might be a civilian now but he still had that battle aura about him. "Would you like a tampon, too?"

"Go to hell."

"You plan on rotting in this house? Because the way I see it, you need to get out. Look at something other than a TV and these four walls. Now, I've given you your space, didn't make a fuss when you refused to see me, but enough is enough. Let's get in the truck so I can take you to the house and show you what I've been working on." He grinned. "Mighty impressive if I say so myself."

What the hell, he couldn't hide in this house forever while his aunt doted on him and Gina Servetti forced "range of motion" exercises on him. She'd told him in that no-nonsense way of hers that he didn't need a physical therapist; what he needed was to do his exercises, eat right, lay off the pills, and stop feeling sorry for himself. Yeah, she was a real bleeding heart.

"What do you say?" Will asked. "Ready for a little fresh air?"

"Your niece isn't going to be there, is she?"

Will threw him a look as if he wasn't quite sure what Cash meant. Bull. The man was already seven steps ahead of Cash in the plotting department. "Tess? Not that I know of." His blue eyes sparkled and he added, "But I can ask her up if you'd like."

Cash's lips twitched and his gaze narrowed on the man who had been mentor, boss, and friend. "Like I said, go to hell."

Will laughed and headed toward the front door and the pickup in the driveway. "Take your time. I'll see you outside."

Cash eased out of the chair and grabbed his sunglasses. The doctors said it would take time to regain his strength, but they couldn't say how much. Time was always that elusive factor— too much or never enough. The afternoon sun and the scent of Ramona's hyacinths hit him square in the face, reminding him of the lazy spring days he and Tess used to enjoy when they were too young to realize nothing lasted forever—especially them. She'd monopolized his thoughts since her visit, a fact that royally annoyed him. It was one thing to imagine what she looked like all these years later, imagine conversations and gestures...but to actually see her, hear her? Well, that was like standing empty-handed in front of a guy who had a gun pointed at you.

"You okay?" Will eyed him as Cash settled in the truck. "You're looking kind of squeamish."

Squeamish? Cash would bet a hundred bucks that any man who had to face his ex-fiancée after an eight-year absence would get squeamish when he recalled the meeting. And he might actually puke if he thought about the inevitability of seeing her again. He opened the window, sucked in a deep breath. "I'm good." And then, because he sensed Will was watching him a bit too closely, he said, "Do you use this truck for hauling?" He casually glanced down the street in the direction of the Carrick house. They lived four streets away and thankfully, there were no cars or people coming from that direction.

Her eyes were even greener than he remembered, and her hair, though shorter, had the same shininess to it...and her skin...

"I have been, as a matter of fact." Will flipped on the radio and one of those honky-tonk country songs he loved twanged over the air. "Building a house uses a lot of material." He hummed a few bars of the tune and headed toward the outskirts of town and the road leading to his house.

That got Cash's attention. "You're building a house?" Will had always tinkered in his workshop and even converted the old barn to a grand-scale shop with heat, a bathroom, even an old recliner. But a house? That required a bit more attention than constructing a bookcase.

Will laughed. "You sound surprised. Just because I don't

walk around town with a résumé of qualifications doesn't mean there aren't a lot of things I can't do."

"But a house?"

He shrugged. "I did most of it myself except for the drywall and plumbing. Nate's been a big help with the plans and bouncing ideas back and forth." He shot a quick glance at Cash and said, "It helps to have someone listen when you're trying to work out a problem."

What did he mean by that? Was he talking about Tess? What problem? They didn't have a problem. Did they? She was in town to visit her mother and he was here recuperating. End of story. The tragic tale that had consumed their lives was over, and neither one of them had a desire to rework the past.

Did they?

When Cash didn't respond to the "trying to work out a problem" comment, Will went on, "This house has been occupying most of my life for the past several months. After I lost Julia, I had to find a way to fill my days."

"I'm sorry about your wife. She was a nice lady."

"Yes." Will's voice dipped. "She was."

Cash scratched his jaw and decided to do a little information scavenging of his own. "Ramona said you've been spending a lot of time at Olivia Carrick's." When his aunt mentioned that, she'd given him the raised eyebrow that said there was a whole lot more to that story, if a person were so inclined to do a little digging.

"Your aunt should have been a judge or a spy, not sure which she's more suited to, but I'm thinking she'd like the judge part better."

Cash slid a glance in Will's direction, kept his voice even. "She was merely commenting."

Will laughed. "Your aunt doesn't comment on anything for the sake of commenting."

"Okay, so what's up with you and Olivia?"

"We're friends. I did some painting for her, oiled a few doors, fixed an electrical outlet. Basic stuff." He paused. "My brother never was much of a handyman."

They turned off the main road and headed down the long driveway of Will's homestead. He'd named it Blue Moon, and Cash had loved it from the first time he saw it. Will's family had owned the place and when Will returned from the war, he'd married Julia Artemis and together they fixed up the place and got ready for the kids that never came. Two days before their second wedding anniversary, Julia learned she had multiple sclerosis. That's when she'd formed The Bleeding Hearts Society, and while the main requirement for this invitation-only club was a love of perennials, most people shared something else: heartache.

"Would you like to see the house?"

Cash nodded. "Absolutely."

It almost felt like the old days when they rode in the squad car together. But this wasn't the old days and they weren't cops anymore—at least, not officially. That was another story, one that Cash wasn't ready or able to deal with right now. Will eased the truck past the sprawling house and barn and drove a half-mile further back to an opening that held a two-story log cabin with a front porch.

Cash stared at the log cabin, thinking it sure looked a helluva lot like the one he and Tess designed for their dream house, the one he'd pictured in his head for the last eight years. And now, here it was, a living, breathing reminder of what he'd lost.

"Your aunt found the plans," Will said in a soft, knowing voice. "She gave them to me a while back, but I just kind of hung onto them. When Julia died, I needed a way to fill my days, so I started working on them, but it wasn't until we heard about your accident that I became hell-bent on it."

The pitched roof. The front porch. The skylights. It was exactly as they'd envisioned it. Cash cleared his throat and asked, "What are you going to do with it?" It was almost too painful to look at. He'd dreamed of the memories they would make in this house, the children they would have, the love they would share...

"Give it to you."

Cash tore his gaze from the house and stared at Will. "Me? Why?"

"You're the son I never had. I always planned to offer you the land when you and—" he caught himself, corrected, "—when the time came to build. And I would have helped you build it, so I just gave you a jump start. There'll be plenty more to add: a barn, a garage, a workshop. Why don't you take a look inside? There are a couple of cold ones in the fridge." He paused. "Take your time."

His dream home. The thought was bittersweet. He'd designed it with Tess in mind. And the children they'd have. And the dog. Shit, the whole damn enchilada. And now it was just him, a beaten-up ex-cop with a hole in his heart. He turned to Will and asked, "You coming?"

"You go on alone. You should be by yourself the first time. I'll swing by in an hour and pick you up."

Will knew what it was like to lose your dream. For the first time since he'd been shot, Cash felt like somebody understood him. "Make it two hours," he said and turned toward the house.

For too many years, Cash had refused to think about Tess. That in itself was a flashing beacon that kept her right below his subconscious. When he saw a woman with long blond hair and green eyes the color of a dew-coated lawn, he thought of Tess. When he kissed a woman with full lips that tasted like honey and berries, he thought of Tess. And when he touched a woman with golden skin and small breasts, again, he thought of Tess. It was a curse, one he detested yet refused to give up.

The only time he permitted himself to think of the real Tess Carrick was when his defenses slipped in the early stages of sleep or exhaustion. Then, he let his mind wander through the dangerous field of "what if" scenarios. What if Tess were waiting for him in Magdalena? What if she wanted another chance? What would he do? He knew the answer before his brain did. He'd move back, marry her as soon as possible, and they'd get pregnant—as soon as possible. They'd get a dog, build their dream home somewhere in Magdalena. Maybe Will would sell them a lot. They'd have three children, maybe four, and they'd lie in each other's arms every night and wake up together every morning. And Tess's smile would warm his heart, make it beat for her alone...

Those pre-sleep scenarios worked until they started to seep into his waking hours, demanding to be analyzed and acknowledged, maybe even acted upon. It was the last that put him over the edge. A life with Tess Carrick was never going to happen. That realization made him fearless in his job, and why wouldn't it? What does a man have left when he's lost everything?

Cash made his way through the house, devouring every detail, from the hardwood floors and stone fireplace to the leaded glass on the kitchen cabinets. He paused when he reached the room directly across from the master bedroom. They'd intended it for the nursery. Their baby. A son or daughter with blond hair or brown curls.

He turned away, cursing as he made his way down the front stairs. Gina would harass him for not stretching or doing his exercises today but he had bigger things to deal with right now. Like how to get his life back and avoid his ex-fiancée until she left town.

TESS STEPPED out of the car and made her way to Will's house. She intended to visit him to discuss her mother. The man possessed both logic and a keen if not uncanny ability to understand Olivia Carrick. Chances were he knew about her medical issues and Tess wanted to know what they were. If she could help her mother, it would give her something to think about other than Daniel Casherdon.

She'd been thinking of him since Ramona's visit, but she hadn't been prepared for what it would feel like to be three feet from him. There hadn't been enough oxygen in the room for both of them and when he looked at her, oh, but she truly could not breathe. How could feelings so long buried and denied resurface like a wildfire? Had he felt them, too?

Tess knocked on the door again, but it looked like Uncle Will wasn't home. She headed down the steps and breathed in the mountain air. Clean. Refreshing. Virginia humidity stole the crispness from a person's brain and summer suns scorched. But this, she inhaled again, this was revitalizing.

Uncle Will had planted clusters of daffodils and naturalized them with the help of the squirrels, in the woods and along the trails. Off to the left of the rambling farm house was the renovated barn that Nate Desantro used for his furniture-building business. She still couldn't picture Nate Desantro married, with a baby. What kind of woman had come along to calm his restless soul? Oh, but Tess wanted to meet her.

She followed the path to the barn and peered through one of the windows. There were several machines lined up in the middle of the barn, ready and waiting for the next board. Long shelves held stacks of lumber, labeled and organized according to type of wood: maple, cherry, ash, walnut. Resting in the far section of the barn were finished and half-finished rocking chairs, chests, and tables. Her gaze landed on a cradle, pulled her in, held her, until she blinked and turned away.

A gravel road ran behind the barn, surrounded by pine trees, oak, and spruce. Had Uncle Will built another barn, maybe one for The Bleeding Hearts Society to harvest and dry their flowers? When Aunt Julia was active in the group, he'd opened the barn for that very activity, though word had it The Society spent as much time devising plans to help heal broken hearts and fatten up thin wallets as it did sorting flowers. Tess walked along the graveled road, curious to see what her uncle had been constructing.

But when she reached the clearing, she wished she'd ignored her curiosity and never gone down this path. The log cabin she and Cash had so carefully designed stood in front of her, a two-story reminder of what could have been.

Tess turned and ran.

It had never been a question of *if* Tess would see Bree and Gina again but rather *when*. She'd been back in Magdalena for three days and aside from the trip to visit Cash and then Uncle Will, she hadn't left the house. She'd refused her mother's invitations to the library: *They have the most wonderful selection of audiobooks*: and lunch: *Lina's Café has the best Turkey Reubens on Tuesdays and I know how much you always loved theirs*; and even Sal's grocery store: *You should see what he's done in the dairy section—six different brands of yogurt and tortilla wraps, too.*

Tess wanted to spare her mother the discomfort of running into those who might offer a comment or three about Tess's interesting and timely return that just so happened to coincide with her ex-fiancé's. What to say to that? There was nothing to say but smile and slip out a "thank you," which, of course, would never suffice. The residents of Magdalena were concerned but equally curious about the situation. Okay, some were downright nosy and weren't shy about poking around in off-limits territory.

On this third day, Tess waited until her mother headed to the library for an afternoon of tutoring sessions. Then she showered, dressed, and made her way downtown. Not much had changed in the eight years she'd been gone. Barbara's Boutique and Bakery had a fancy sign hanging overhead in pink and white surrounded by tiny lights. Victor's Pharmacy posted the same "Serving Customers One at a Time" sign in the window. It had to be twenty years old, maybe more. Was Mr. Winston still working or had his son, Raymond, taken over? He'd gone to school with Tess and had been in pharmacy school last she'd heard. She walked past the bank, the diner, and Miss Patty's Mentionables, an accessory store for women. There was the candle shop, the bakery, the post office, and O'Reilly's bar. Not much had changed, at least from the outside, but what could you really tell from appearances?

She crossed the street and worked her way from window to window. There were a few new stores that caught her interest: a hair salon, a pet groomer, and a consignment shop. Tess stopped in front of Lina's Café and peeked inside. Phyllis was thinner, her upswept hair a bit grayer, but she had the same laugh and crooked smile that customers loved. And Tess bet she still served up the best coconut cream pie in Magdalena.

Three doors down was an office sandwiched between the dry cleaners and the sub shop. The lettering etched on the door window read, *Christine Desantro, Finance & Investments*. Nate's wife? Now that was a woman she wanted to meet. Before she could talk herself out of it, she gripped the handle and entered.

The woman Tess guessed was Christine Desantro looked up from the paperwork on her desk and smiled. "May I help you?"

It was a genuine smile and the voice was cultured, well-bred, not filled with dialect and drawn-out vowels. She stood, ran a hand over the tiny wrinkles in her pink blouse, and moved toward Tess. This woman didn't need designer clothes or a stack of money to spell *class*. She had it, from the cut of her shimmering dark hair to the blueness of her eyes, and further still, to her walk: casual, elegant, natural.

"I was taking a walk around town, seeing what's changed since I've been gone." Tess offered Christine a smile, one of the first real ones since she returned to Magdalena. "This place is new."

"Tess? Tess Carrick?"

"That's me." She did not even want to think about what this woman had heard about her. Probably nothing good.

"Welcome back to Magdalena!" She clasped Tess's hands. "I'm Christine Desantro and I'm *so* happy to meet you."

Tess laughed. "Oh, I'm so sure you are one of three people who feel that way."

"That's not true. You've got a lot of people pulling for you, including my husband."

"Thank you." The woman was gracious even if she were fabricating. "It's nice to hear, even if 'a lot' means five."

Christine laughed and gestured toward her desk. "Come and sit down. I've been dying to meet you."

"I don't even want to ask what Nate's said about me."

She raised a brow. "If you know anything about my husband, then you know he hasn't said much." Christine sank into her chair and Tess sat in one on the other side of the desk. "Nate's got pretty strong opinions about things, but unless they affect him or his family, he keeps quiet." She leaned forward, eyes bright, and offered valuable information. "But he cares about Cash, and he's not going to sit back and let him feel sorry for himself. You know he went to see him, don't you?"

Tess shook her head. No, she hadn't known. "Not much news

is flowing to my mother's. This is the first day I've made it downtown."

"Ah. Well, let's see." She tapped her chin. "Cash refused to see Nate at first, but I'm sure that doesn't surprise you. Our men are both stubborn, though I'll bet mine gets the prize."

Tess wanted to interrupt Christine and tell her that Cash wasn't her man, not anymore, but that might prompt Nate's wife to begin a crusade to convince Tess just how much Cash was still hers. Some things really were better left unsaid for as long as possible.

"You know I haven't met Cash yet." She paused. "Nate said they'd been good friends."

"They were. I think they got along so well because they were both fighting their own battles. Cash's parents took off when he was very young and with Nate's dad dead and his mother—" She clamped a hand to her mouth to stop the rest of the words. She'd almost said something about Christine's father. "I am so sorry. Please forgive me."

"It's okay. Really." She picked up a pen and toyed with it. "If you think people don't want *you* here, can you imagine coming to this town as Charlie Blacksworth's daughter and facing Nate?"

"Umm, no I can't. I think I'd rather have the whole town after me."

Christine smiled. "It was an interesting several months, but in some ways it seems so long ago." She paused, met Tess's gaze, and said in a gentle voice, "As horrible as it was to find out my father had a secret family, one he probably considered his 'real' one, I've been gifted with a second chance and a life I never thought could be mine, with the kind of man I never knew existed."

"You're very lucky."

"I am, and I will never take this blessing for granted. But I think you can have a second chance too, Tess. We all believe that."

They did? "I'm not so sure."

"Pop Benito's already got The Bleeding Hearts Society on it," she paused, "Minus Ramona Casherdon. They're determined to get you two together. Even Bree," she caught herself and finished, "even the skeptics are having second thoughts."

She meant Bree Kinkaid, the friend Tess hadn't spoken with since she left Magdalena. "You know Bree?"

Christine nodded. "I do. We're friends."

"And Gina Servetti?"

"Yes." Her smile faded, flattened. "But not her cousin."

"Yeah, nobody's friends with Natalie, not even the guys."

"Not surprising."

Oh, that was a sore spot. What had Natalie done now? Still trying to steal other women's men, no doubt.

"Tess, I want to help you. Just let me know what I can do."

Christine Desantro had class *and* a golden heart. "Thank you."

"I've been on the outside," she said, her voice strong, her words filled with emotion. "I almost lost the man I love. I know that pain."

Tess wanted to ask her to expand on that last part but decided against it. Maybe when she got to know her better, Christine would share that story.

"Would you like to grab a cup of coffee at Lina's? She makes the best pecan rolls."

"I was just thinking about her coconut cream pie. Does she still have that on the menu?"

Before Christine could respond, the door opened and with it came two chattering, laughing female voices.

"Did you ever see such a sight? I thought I would pee my panties." More laughter. "He sure thought he was one hot body."

Tess froze. She'd recognize that affected Southern drawl anywhere and if she waited a few seconds, another voice would pipe in, lower, richer, more mature. She was not disappointed.

"My uncle is more of a lady's man than that guy and he's seventy-two with double knee replacements, a pacemaker, and a hearing aid."

Gina Servetti and the uncle she was talking about was Uncle Bruno, former trash collector for the city of Magdalena, primo polka dancer, and trumpet player.

"Hey, Christine. Ready for those pecan—" Bree rounded the desk and spotted Tess. She blinked hard, cleared her throat, and said, "Hello, Tess," as though she could sanitize the emotion from her words.

"Hi, Bree." Tess turned to face Gina, who made no effort to hide her stare or her distaste. "Gina."

"Hello, Tess." Her words slid through pursed lips, cold, biting.

Bree hadn't changed much since the last time Tess saw her: still tanned, blond, beautiful, and pregnant. Gina was curvier, her skin a healthy olive glow, eyes dark as charcoal, and the same ticked-off attitude. They hadn't forgotten how she'd run out on them without an explanation or a good-bye.

"Well, I think I'll get going." She glanced at Christine who was taking it all in. Bree and Gina must have filled her in on the whole sordid situation, beginning with the night JJ got shot and ending with Tess's refusal to see them.

"What about the pie?" Christine blurted out. "You can't turn down coconut cream." Before Tess had a chance to reply, she smiled at Bree and Gina and said, "Care to join us?"

"Uh..." Bree darted a glance at Gina who shrugged and shook her head.

So much for letting the past go.

"I think I would like a piece of Key lime pie," Bree said in a rush. "I've had a taste for it." She rubbed her protruding belly and added, "Since this little guy started doing somersaults."

Bree was still holding out for the boy.

"Great. Good." Christine shut down her computer and grabbed her purse. "Well then." When no one moved, she sighed and plunked her purse on the desk. "We are not going to Lina's and putting this all on display so we can read about it in tomorrow's *Press*. Let's get it all out so I can eat my pecan roll."

"It's not that easy," Bree said, darting a glance at Tess. "You don't know the pain we suffered. The not knowing, the worrying, the crying...it was awful."

"I'm sure Tess had her reasons."

"Which we have never been privy to." Bree faced Tess, her eyes bright, mouth quivering. "You just left us, and poor Cash, so distraught, we worried he'd try to hurt himself. Even Nate and your uncle couldn't calm him down. Do you know he was all set to drive to Riki's and see if you were there? Wouldn't that have been interesting? But no, your mother said you weren't there. She said Riki wasn't even there, and besides, wherever you were, you needed time alone. Imagine how we all felt when we learned that's *exactly* where you were." She paused, spat out, "Staying with the sister who had popped in and out of your life like a Ping-Pong ball. But you trusted her more than us."

"No. It wasn't that at all." She'd had to get away and there was nowhere to go except to her sister's. Riki would have been her last choice and it had turned out to be her worst.

"What was it then? Tell us, so we can understand?" Gina moved toward her, hands on her plump hips, dark eyes burning. She wanted answers Tess couldn't give. Not now. Maybe not ever.

"I don't think Tess is ready to talk about what drove her away," Christine said in a soft voice. "We have to respect that."

"Like she respected us?" Gina shot back. "I don't think so."

"I can't." They all looked at Tess, perhaps surprised by the pain in her words. "I can't," she repeated, blinking hard.

"And we're not going to pressure her," Christine said, her voice hard. "I know what it's like to have your world turned upside down; no answers, only a million questions. Bitterness takes over and you'll drown in it if you don't let it go. For months all I wanted to know was why? Why did my father do it? Why didn't he tell me? Why wasn't I enough? On and on it went until I was so torn I couldn't think." A faint smile hovered about her lips. "But by then I was in love with this town and the people: Miriam, Lily," she paused, her voice dipped, "Nate. The why didn't matter then; all that mattered was moving forward."

"I'm not sure Cash will feel the same," Gina said, her dark eyes hard.

"But he might," Bree piped in, "given time and a little hope." She turned to Tess and asked, "Are you going to give him that hope?"

"I...I don't know."

"It's not that complicated. I didn't even go to college and I figured it out." Bree touched Tess's arm and said, "Either you want to be with him or you don't. Which is it?"

Could she really have a second chance with Cash? Would he want one?

"Well?" Christine prodded. "The whole town is trying to get you two together, from Pop Benito and The Bleeding Hearts Society to your uncle."

"And your mother," Bree said.

"My mother?" Olivia had only mentioned Cash a few times and then only in regard to his injury, certainly not anything about having him for a son-in-law.

Bree laughed. "That's the rumor and I think it's true. So, do you want to get back with him?"

Tess tried to ignore the heat creeping from her neck to her cheeks. "It's not that simple."

"Nothing worthwhile ever is."

Bree really was a hopeless romantic.

"Gina said he got a funny look on his face when she mentioned your name."

Gina scowled at Bree. "Didn't I tell you not to tell anyone?"

Bree stuck her nose in the air and sniffed. "Tess isn't just anyone. She needs to know he still cares about her."

"I wouldn't say looking like you're going to throw up is exactly a profession of love."

"You probably misread his expression." Bree rubbed her belly and said, "You know you're not very good at that stuff."

And they were at it again, Bree and Gina sparring like the old days.

"Just because I'm not immersed in a man does not mean I can't read the signals."

Unless things had changed, Gina did not possess the ability to read or identify a man's interests, no matter how strong. Christine hid a smile. Tess looked away so she wouldn't laugh. But Bree was not going to let it go. "You just need practice, and we're here to help."

"One love story at a time, okay?" This from Christine. "Tess, I'm going to ask what the whole town wants to know. Do you want another chance with Cash?"

"And if you can't tell us the truth, then don't answer."

Christine shook her head. "Gina. Please."

"It's okay. I deserved that; I lost their trust and I've got to earn it back." Tess ignored the reason that landed her in Magdalena, the reason she and Cash could never work, and let her heart speak the truth. "Yes. I want another chance."

8

"So, what's with Cash and that Carrick girl?" Jack Finnegan pushed back his ball cap and leaned against the metal file cabinet.

Nate entered another number into the computer and shrugged. "No idea."

"Hmm."

That sound meant Jack didn't believe him and had his own opinion on the matter. If Nate waited, he'd hear it soon enough.

"Well, I heard she came back to take care of her mother." He gnawed on that for all of two seconds before commenting, "You know Olivia Carrick's got to have surgery, don't you?" He paused, lowered his voice, "Female problems."

No, he hadn't known, but he hadn't inquired either. "Hadn't heard."

"So, I guess that's a pretty noble gesture, coming from a daughter that ain't seen this part of the country in over eight years."

But Nate thought there was another reason for Tess Carrick's return.

"I think it has to do with the Casherdon boy."

Ah, so Jack thought so, too.

"They was crazy about each other. I used to see them up at the sawmill but I never told nobody about it. Young love is a powerful thing and I liked the boy. He was a good friend of yours, wasn't he?"

"Yup." Nate transferred another number from the spreadsheet.

"You gonna say anything longer than two syllables?"

Nate rubbed his jaw and kept his eyes on the spreadsheet in front of him. "Probably not."

Jack rolled right into his next thought as though Nate hadn't spoken. "'Cause I think you know a heck of a lot more than you're sayin'. Like how you visited Cash at his aunt's and gave him a talking-to, and how that little wife of yours has taken Tess Carrick under her wing. And I heard they were seen at Lina's Café with my niece, Bree, and Gina Servetti." He paused. "Chatting away and munching on pie and pecan rolls."

Nate threw down his pencil and looked up at Jack. "You sure are a busy reporter. Do you have sources all around town or is one person feeding you this valuable information?"

Jack shrugged. "I know people."

"Like Bree and your sister?"

"I don't talk to Edith. She's pure miserable and she might have a front seat next door to the Carricks', but I wouldn't believe a word out of her treacherous mouth." He blew out a long breath and muttered, "Mean woman."

"And Bree?"

"That girl's like a soda with too much fizz, bouncing around, wanting to see everybody matched up and spitting out babies. Thinks that's the key to happiness." He shook his head. "That girl could have done so much, but instead she settled on a baby-making machine with a peanut for a brain."

Nate's lips twitched. Brody Kinkaid was not Jack's favorite

person. The man wasn't even on his top 100 list, even though he could cook a mean chili, loved Bree more than sports, and knew how to fight a fire. Jack said a brain that couldn't think was a waste, and Brody Kinkaid did not know the first thing about using his brain, which was why Bree was pregnant again.

"Bree only gave me bits and pieces, and nothin' I didn't already figure out myself." He slid a sideways glance at Nate. "If I tell you my source, will you promise to keep it between us?"

"Sure." How had Nate gotten involved in this discussion in the first place? It was one thing to talk to his wife, but he didn't like gossip, had been the brunt of it for too many years in one way or another. And after that whole mess with Natalie Servetti, well, he'd just as soon keep his mouth shut. Period.

Jack leaned forward, so close Nate could see the stubble on his jaw, and said in a low voice, "It's Pop Benito. He's got people reporting to him right and left. Where did Tess go? What did she do? Did anyone go with her? What time did she come back? And what about Cash? Were they together? How long? Betty says he keeps a notebook of the findings. Don't ask me how she knows, but she does. And she says Pop's determined to get those two together, no matter what."

TESS HAD SPENT years hopping flights and time zones, always on the move, never pausing long enough to catch a real breath or consider another life—a different life. Since she'd returned to Magdalena, she'd hardly thought of Her Lips du Jour or lipstick, other than trying to guess the color on a woman's lips. How bizarre was that and why the sudden shift? Was it because she knew she couldn't rejoin the lipstick industry until the non-compete clause expired? Or did it have more to do with concern for her mother's health? Maybe the change had occurred because her mother appeared genuinely happy to see her and this was an opportunity to reconnect and strengthen their relationship. Of course, it could be her new friendship with Christine Desantro, whose quiet strength and compassion were helping to mend the fallout with Bree and Gina.

But there was no sense denying what had taken over her thoughts; it was hope. And the person behind the hope was Daniel Casherdon. She'd admitted as much the other day when Bree asked her point-blank about her desire for a second chance with her ex-fiancé. The truth had leaked out and filled her with hope that somehow she and Cash could find their way back to each other. But was that really possible? One day soon, she would have to tell him the truth she'd been hiding.

It was time to face her fears, starting with a trip to the dream home she and Cash had designed and which Uncle Will must have built. She'd called her uncle last night and asked if she could stop by and see it. There'd been a half-second delay on the other end of the line, and then he'd told her in a gentle voice that the door would be unlocked and she could visit whenever she liked.

Tess grabbed a quick cup of coffee and a bagel and was on her way to the cabin before Edith Finnegan opened the living room blinds. If she spotted Tess's car gone, that would send the woman into a frenzy wondering where and what Olivia Carrick's daughter was up to. She drove to Uncle Will's with the windows down, the smell of grass and late spring filling the air. Uncle Will's around-and-about-town truck was gone, but a beat-up one was parked behind the barn. She pulled up to the house and followed the gravel path to the log cabin where she and Cash had planned to eventually settle and raise a family.

Had Cash seen it yet? Had he walked from room to room,

remembering their dreams? Or had he refused to even think about it? There was so much pain between them, so many unanswered questions. *So many years apart.* How did two people go about rebuilding a damaged relationship, even if they wanted to?

She walked up the steps of the wraparound porch. There were two wicker rocking chairs set side by side and a pot of pansies by the railing. Tess glanced back at the gravel path. Once she entered the cabin, her brain would be smeared with memories she could never erase. They would come to her in the stillness of night and threaten to consume her. If she crossed the threshold, everything would be different, and real.

Tess drew in a deep breath, turned, and entered the cabin.

The small foyer spilled into a large family room with a stone fireplace on the far side of the wall and an open kitchen to the right. Tess had wanted to be able to keep an eye on the children as they played and she prepared dinners of roast chicken, pork chops, and Cash's favorite, chicken cordon bleu. They'd had it all figured out. Sadly, it had been for nothing.

She was surprised the place was furnished: a rocking chair, couch, table, television. Who had done it, and why? For that matter, who had built the house? Had Cash had it built when he was in Philly, with plans of returning one day? Maybe with a different woman, one who would prepare him his favorite meal while she kept an eye on their children? Tess tried to ignore the ache in her chest, but that was like trying to ignore a bleeding wound.

The master bedroom was on the first floor, on the opposite side of the kitchen. She stepped into the room, eyeing the skylight above the king-sized bed. *We'll make love at night, with the stars above us*, he'd told her. *And in the afternoon, with the sun heating our skin. Mornings, too.* He'd smiled then and she'd forgotten about the skylight, forgotten everything but the need pulsing through her body as he unbuttoned her shirt...

"What are you doing here?"

Tess spun around. Cash stood several feet away, bare-chested, a towel flung around his shoulders, jeans riding low on his hips. Barefoot. Wet hair slicked back. Memories simmered and boiled over in a croak of a response. "You live here?"

He shrugged, his expression unreadable. "For now."

Her gaze slid to his chest and the edge of scar peeking from beneath the towel: a reminder of the gunshot wound that could have killed him. He caught her looking and tossed the towel aside, snatched a shirt from the bed, and shrugged into it.

"Did you...did you build this?" His dark eyes narrowed and he studied her. What was he thinking? Was he remembering how they'd planned this whole house? How they'd dreamed about it and said it was the beginning of their legacy to their children?

"Your uncle did." He grabbed the towel and disappeared into the bathroom, emerging a few seconds later, minus the towel, still looking dangerously attractive. "Will didn't tell you about this?"

She shook her head. "No. I found it the other day when I stopped to see him. He wasn't home so I took a walk around." She paused. "That's when I found it, but I left." Her voice shifted, dipped. "I haven't been able to stop thinking about it...I had to see it."

"Will knows how to follow a plan, I'll give him that," he said, his lips firm, unsmiling.

Which meant her uncle had built their dream home *exactly* as they'd planned it.

"Might as well look around now that you're here. The bathroom is in there. Double sink, shower with two showerheads, private toilet." He motioned for her to take a look. "A little messy, but I didn't expect company."

Company. The word hurt, even though it shouldn't.

"Thank you. I'd like to see what he's done with it." She moved past him and into the bathroom, taking in the granite countertop, the brushed nickel hardware, the frosted glass on the shower door. Visions of water pelting their skin as they touched each other flitted through her brain, bodies slick with soap and desire...

"...the bedroom has two closets, one walk-in and the other enough for a normal person..."

Was that humor she'd just heard? He used to tease her about all of her clothes, items from high school she could never quite part with... What would he say if she told him she'd lived out of a suitcase for years and her whole wardrobe would fit into half of the smaller closet?

"You can look upstairs if you want, but it's unfinished," Cash said as he headed into the living room. "It's been roughed out for three bedrooms and a bathroom, but Will said the plans weren't detailed enough to determine which way to go." She didn't miss the strain in his voice, as though he struggled with the words, or maybe it was the meaning behind them that gave him trouble.

How many bedrooms do you think we need? She'd asked the question the first time he showed her the plans for the upstairs. He'd cupped her chin and kissed her long and slow before he replied, *How many can we fill up with little Casherdons?*

"I don't need to see it." He hadn't mentioned the room next to the master bedroom and neither did she. It would have been the nursery. Maybe it was better to pretend it didn't exist.

"Would you like a cup of coffee?"

"Sure." Beverages were safe topics that didn't tear at a person's heart.

"Light cream, one sugar?"

Unless the topic indicated a past intimacy. "Yes." Pause. "Thank you." He'd known everything about her eight years ago, from the way she drank her coffee to the brand of toothpaste she preferred. It had seemed natural and only the beginning of a lifetime of sharing and discovery.

Cash set her mug on the kitchen table and pulled out a chair for her. "I'd offer you something to eat but I'm not sure you'd go in for chicken wings and pizza at," he glanced at the clock above the sink, "10:18 A.M."

"Uh, no, but thanks."

His lips twitched. "Your loss." He sipped his coffee—black, no sugar—and toyed with the handle before settling his gaze on her. "So, what have you been up to these past eight years? Oh, too direct a question?" He shrugged and pierced her with eyes that had always seen too much. "Are we really going to be polite and pretend we've never done more than shake hands?"

"I..."

Her hesitancy annoyed him. "After all that's happened, why can't we just be honest for a few minutes? We planned a friggin' life together—a home, kids, a future. When it all blew up, I spent years trying to forget you." His jaw tensed, his gaze narrowed. "I never wanted to hear your name again and I certainly didn't want to see you. Or have you see me like this." He pointed to himself. "But then you showed up at Ramona's and, damn it, it all came back. Everything, and it's not going away."

So, she wasn't the only one who couldn't forget. "I know," she said softly.

He stared at her, as if that comment surprised him. Then his shoulders relaxed and he frowned. "It's a damn nuisance, isn't it?"

"If you mean the remembering what we want to forget, yes,

it's horribly inconvenient." Her pulse tripled. Maybe he'd wished for a second chance. Maybe he still did.

"I've never seen anyone with that same shade of blond," he said, studying her hair. "And I've looked."

Tess fingered a few strands of hair and murmured, "Genes, I guess."

"Yeah. I guess." He traced the handle of his coffee mug and said, "What have you been doing for eight years?"

She shifted in her chair and let out a small laugh. "Selling lipstick."

"Huh?"

"Selling lipstick." She slid him a smile. "I'm very good at it, too. Did you know the right shade can give a woman confidence and make her feel beautiful? It can change her life."

"Lipstick," he repeated as if she'd told him she sold farm equipment.

Tess shrugged. "It's the little things that can make a difference. I was the senior vice president of sales, in charge of the international division. I traveled the world, saw more places than I knew existed." Why was she trying to sell him on the idea of how great her job was? *It had been great.* "And the compensation was fantastic."

"What happened to nursing?"

There was no sense in avoiding the truth. "I couldn't do it, not after what happened."

"But you wanted to work with kids. How did what happened have anything to do with that?"

He meant JJ's death, but she meant something else altogether. Once she'd lost their baby, she couldn't be around children, and she certainly couldn't work in a place where they were a constant reminder of what she might never have, of what she'd lost. But it was more than that. After JJ's death, she could not work in an environment where she witnessed the fragility of life daily and the tragic, painful aftermath of those left behind.

"Tess? Answer me."

She couldn't tell him the whole truth, not yet. "When I was in school, I was so naïve. I only thought about the kids who survived. Oh, maybe they'd have a life-threatening condition that required treatment or surgery, but they'd get their happy ending. I'd be a part of that." She paused. "After JJ, I realized not all of them would, and no matter how good the care was or how hopeful the outcome, circumstances could change things in a single breath."

"That's called life."

"I couldn't do it."

"Look at me, Tess." She slid her gaze to his and wished she hadn't. There was anger in those eyes, and determination, and something that looked an awful lot like disappointment. "There are no guarantees. Do you think I haven't wished a million times that I hadn't been the one on patrol the night JJ died? Or picked up on some sign that he was slipping back?" His words pierced her, dug around until pain spurted through her like an open wound. "I should never have listened to everyone when you refused to see me and they said you needed time. I should have forced my way to you, broken down the damn door if I had to so we could deal with what happened. Maybe even get through it. But I didn't." He sighed, worked a hand through his damp hair. "I didn't listen to my gut and I've regretted that ever since."

She blinked hard, forced the tears to stay in place. "I'm not sure it would have changed anything."

"Maybe not, but we'll never know. When you took off, did you go to your sister's?"

She nodded. "That's how I ended up in Virginia. Riki left shortly after I moved to Richmond. I hear from her now and again. One year she's in San Francisco, six months later, Austin, then Charlotte. Same Riki."

"I knew it," he said under his breath. "Damn it, but I knew you were there."

"And you? You've been in Philly the whole time? On the police force?"

A thin smile stretched across his lips. "Yup. Living the life." He shrugged. "It gets old. You have to know when to get out and that's what I did."

"You resigned from the force?" Why hadn't anyone mentioned this?

He shot her a quick look. "I did. You're the only person in this town who knows that. I didn't even tell Ramona yet. Hell if I know why I told you."

"I won't say anything. Where will you go?"

"No idea. Just considering my options."

Was Magdalena an option? And if he said it was, what then? Would it matter?

"What about you?" There was an extra exchange of air before he finished in a casual manner. "When do you head back to Virginia?"

He picked up a pen and fiddled with it, as if her answer didn't matter to him. Years ago, he'd done the very same thing, but the feigned nonchalance was merely a way to hide deeper feelings. Shades of the old Cash crept through these actions and Tess found herself admitting the truth.

"Well, since we're sharing secrets, I'll tell you one nobody else knows. A few weeks ago, I got my walking papers and a six-month non-compete reminder. The company was sold and apparently my name is too closely associated with Her Lips du Jour to transition to the new firm."

"Her Lips du Jour? The women with the shiny red lips?"

She smiled. "Red is our signature color. Super sexy. Super shiny. Super pricey. That's us, or it was. Now it's just them."

His gaze slid to the pink stain on the rim of her coffee mug. "I've always been more of a pink man myself." His voice turned soft and sensual when he asked, "So, when exactly do you head back to Virginia?"

Tess looked at him, offered a hint of a smile, and said, "No idea. Just considering my options."

9

A t 2:15 P.M., Pop poured two glasses of lemonade and carried them onto the back deck, the very same spot where he'd had a sit-down with Tess just yesterday. What a sweet girl, but she had a hurting heart and a sadness in her soul that Pop figured had a lot to do with her ex-fiancé. If Pop had anything to say about it, and he usually had a lot to say about what went on in town, the *ex* in *ex-fiancé* would be erased soon enough, leaving only *fiancé* and then *husband*.

The reason behind the ache in Tess Carrick's heart was coming soon for a chit-chat and a glass of lemonade. Years ago, when the days were hot and sticky, Cash used to stop by on his way to work and Lucy would fill a thermos of lemonade for him. A baggie of pizzelles, too. She sure did have a soft spot for that boy, said he had eyes like a chocolate bar and a smile that could make a girl melt. When the tragedy occurred, Lucy prayed for Cash and Tess to reconcile and later, when it was obvious that would not happen, she'd simply prayed for the boy's safety and his eventual return.

Pop made his way back to the kitchen and arranged a few pizzelles on a paper plate. Word had it the boy was thin as a stick and Lucy would curse Pop to high heaven if he didn't do his part to fatten him up a bit. "I'll take care of him, Lucy. Don't you worry. I got lots cookin' and I don't mean food." He smiled at the portrait of his wife hanging over the mantel. Those blue eyes of hers smiled back at him. "I'll do you proud. You'll see. I'll get Cash and Tess back together, no matter what fancy footwork I have to use to do it." He tapped his high-top-sneakered feet twice and murmured, "You just wait and see."

When Cash arrived a short while later, Pop had to agree with the "thin as a stick" comment. The Cash from eight years ago had muscles that rippled under his T-shirt and along his fore-arms. This one looked like a lean piece of meat cut close to the bone. "We got to fatten you up, boy." He hugged Cash and shook his head. "You sure are a sight. All thin and rangy-looking." He grinned and said, "But you're still a looker. My Lucy always said you could melt a girl's britches with those eyes."

Cash coughed and turned the color of a beet. "Lucy said that?"

Pop shrugged. "What? You think senior citizens can't appre-ciate a fine-looking person?" He winked. "Sure can, and I'll do you one better." He leaned forward, whispered, "There's those that do more than appreciate. There's those that *act* on that appreciation." Oh, but the beet color turned deeper.

"Pop, please. Spare the visual."

Pop laughed and ushered Cash toward the deck and a rocking chair. "I'm just saying, it happens." He slid a look at the boy. "Even middle-aged widows who have been alone for a long time might catch an interest in an eligible widower." He paused. "Happens all the time; probably right under our noses. Don't you think?"

Cash sat down and rubbed his jaw. "You mean Will and Olivia Carrick?"

"Huh? I didn't say that, but now that you bring it up,

wouldn't that be convenient? No need to change out towels or last names." He plopped in his rocker and nodded. "Now that's what I call sensible."

"We'll see. I don't picture Olivia Carrick letting any man share much more than a meal."

"Hmm. I been breathing this air a lot longer than you, and I've seen things I never thought would happen, and then they did. Have some lemonade. Lucy's recipe." He gestured to one of the tall glasses, picked up the other, and took a healthy sip. "No one in this whole town would have ever pinned Nate and Christine Desantro as the perfect match." He slapped his knee and laughed. "Talk about fireworks. I thought somebody was gonna have to bring a fire extinguisher when those two got within forty feet of each other. But then, in between the anger and the hurt over Charlie Blacksworth, something happened." His voice dipped, softened. "Lily was a big part of it. Here she was, half-sister to Nate and Christine, and she loved them both so much her little heart burst open and shared that love. Lily made people see what was really important in life and she helped those two realize they didn't need to be enemies. And once that happened, well, there was another kind of fireworks—the kind that don't need extinguishing."

Cash bit into a pizzelle, chewed. "I know you didn't call me here to tell me about Nate and his bride. You've got a message tied up in there somewhere, just like you always do."

Smart boy. "You think so?" Pop sipped his lemonade and waited.

"Yup. This reminds me of the time you heard I was racing down Black Jack road. You told me to 'get my tail over here' before you called Will." Cash laughed. "I was scared you were going to tell him and then I wouldn't be allowed to see..."

Aha! "Tess."

"Right." The boy pushed her name out as if it weighed three hundred pounds. "Tess."

"She visited me yesterday."

Cash shot him a glance. "Did she now?"

Pop nodded. "Sure did. She looked about as queasy as you do right now when I mentioned your name." He lifted the plate of pizzelles and said, "Have another." Pop waited until Cash took one before he continued, "The heart is a strange creature. It loves, it hates, it hopes. It forgives. Nobody else is gonna serve this to you straight up, so here goes. No matter what happened in the past, what you did or she didn't do, nothing can change that. All you got is now and you don't know for how long. I see two broken souls, afraid to trust or care again, and sure as heck afraid to love again, but dang if they aren't hurting for each other. While you still got breath in you, there's a chance." His voice shifted as he thought of his dear Lucy. "No matter how hard it is or what you got to do, figure it out."

"It's not that easy."

Oh, there was some serious hurt in those words. "Never is. Maybe I got it all wrong; maybe you *can* walk away from Tess Carrick and never think about her again, never wonder what she's doing or wish you were doing it with her. My apologies if I was wrong." He nibbled on a pizzelle and nodded. "But if that girl lives in your soul and you're getting indigestion just thinking about being without her, then you got to do something about it. Talk. Talk again. Make her a batch of pizzelles; that always worked for Lucy." Pop leaned forward and placed a hand on Cash's arm. "You and Tess belong together and before I leave this earth, I aim to see you together."

Less than twenty-four hours after Pop Benito's "trust your

heart" talk, Nate called and extended a dinner invitation at his house. He casually mentioned that Tess had been invited, too. What he didn't say was whether or not Tess had accepted. Typical Nate. You had to pry information from the man and if it had to do with emotions, you better bring some heavy equipment to unearth that information.

Was the whole damn town orchestrating his reunion with Tess? Bad enough Pop had given Cash the soft lecture about going after the woman he couldn't forget, but who else was in on it? The Bleeding Hearts Society? Will Carrick? Christine Desantro and now, even Nate? At least he could count on Ramona to stay out of his business, though if she said anything on the subject, it would be an attempt to steer him away from Tess. His aunt blamed her for Cash's leaving and for the coldness in his heart. He guessed she'd been right on both accounts, but what would she think if she knew Tess Carrick might be the only one who could *warm* his heart? Maybe the only one who could make him stay in Magdalena, too?

Could he trust Tess again? Give her another chance like Pop said? Would Tess want that? He hated the indecision; it put him in a foul mood, and yet, whatever might or might not happen between them, could not be rushed. Not even for Pop Benito and his many followers.

Cash accepted the dinner invitation because he wanted to meet the woman who had made Nate Desantro human. She must be quite a woman to achieve that feat. People probably said the same thing about him, and no doubt, they inserted Tess's name in the "quite a woman" slot. He had another reason for accepting the dinner invitation; it was a chance to see Tess.

He could deny and complain and get angry, but he wanted to see her again. That thought didn't sit well, but so what? Nothing much in his life was sitting well at the moment; why not one more aggravation? And while he was making himself miserable, why not call Tess and offer to drive? If she were going, that was, and something told him she wanted to see the reformed Nate Desantro....and maybe she wanted to see Cash, too. Before he could overthink the situation, he picked up the phone and called her. There'd been a breathiness in her voice when she spoke, as if she were pleased to hear from him. The breathiness spread when he offered to pick her up and drive to the Desantros' if she were going, which she was.

And now, here they were, traveling in Will's new pickup toward Nate and Christine Desantros'. Cash had picked up a bottle of wine and Tess held a bouquet of flowers on her lap. He'd worn the new jeans Ramona had insisted on buying him and a navy polo. No worries about being underdressed with someone like Nate. The man was all about comfortable and casual, which made marriage to a Blacksworth such an unusual match. From what Cash remembered, Charlie Blacksworth was loaded. He guessed you just never knew...

"I'm curious to see what Nate cooked."

Tess's voice covered him with its soft silkiness, doing unwelcome things to his groin. "Nate?"

She laughed. "He's the cook in the house."

"Damn, the guy cooks and is crazy about his wife. Next you'll tell me he changes diapers, too."

"I think he does."

"Who would have thought it?"

"Is it really that hard to believe Nate's a good husband?"

Cash turned up the Desantro drive and said, "It's hard to believe the guy's a husband at all."

"Well, I think we're about to witness true marital bliss."

He parked the truck and grabbed the bottle of wine, then glanced at Tess. The sun filtered through the trees, casting a glow about her face that shimmered like an angel. His angel...

his beautiful angel... "Tess," he breathed and leaned toward her...

"Welcome!"

Cash jerked away and turned toward the door of the cabin. "Husband of the Year" stood on the porch, a smile on his face, and damn it, a baby on his shoulder. "Hey, Nate." Cash opened the truck door and moved toward Tess's side, but she hopped out before he could get to her, sending him a shy smile and then moving toward the cabin.

"Nate! It's so good to see you." She extended her hand and smiled up at him.

Nate grinned and pulled her against him in a quick hug, careful not to disrupt the sleeping baby in his left arm. "How are you, Tess?"

"I'm great. It's been a long time." She darted a glance at the baby. "Who's this?"

Nate's voice softened. "Anna."

"That's a beautiful name."

Cash thrust a hand toward Nate and said, "I heard some sick rumors about you cooking. Back in the day, you only made hot dogs and boxed mashed potatoes, and that was a challenge."

Nate raised a brow. "Don't tell my wife. She thinks I was born with a spatula in one hand and a frying pan in the other. Speaking of Christine, we better get inside before she burns the rolls."

Christine Blacksworth Desantro possessed a mix of beauty, intelligence, and class that made Cash wonder how the hell she'd fallen for Nate. But as he watched them together, the absent-minded touches, the lingering gazes, the compliments and smiles, he figured it out. Christine made Nate a better man, and he cherished the hell out of her. Cash guessed their relationship was built on a solid foundation of trust, respect, and forgiveness. And love, couldn't forget the obvious.

He glanced at Tess who was laughing at some story Christine and Nate had been telling her. Her blond hair shimmered under the soft lights just as it had in the truck, seconds before he leaned forward to kiss her...and didn't, thanks to Nate and his poor timing. It probably would have been a mistake to kiss her so soon anyway, because damn it, he couldn't get his head around what he felt for her or what was going on between them. *Or what he wanted to go on.*

And that was really screwing him up. He guessed the real question might be did he want a relationship like Nate and Christine's, which led to more questions. Was he willing to do what he needed to, as in open up and share what was going on his head? What guy willingly did that? None that Cash knew. But it sure as hell looked like that was part of the recipe. Damn.

When Tess looked at him, he almost felt like the man he'd been eight years ago: full of ambition and plans and a boatload of dreams. Could he ever feel that way again? And what about her? She'd done more than sell lipstick these past several years. He'd seen it in her eyes. There was something she wasn't telling him, something sad and lonely. Something she regretted. Well, he had regrets, too, and demons that visited him at night. If they were going to build anything, they had to pull out the demons and own up to them. That meant Cash would have to admit the real reason he left the force. He bolted down the rest of his wine and pushed away the thought. Not happening. Not now, maybe not ever.

"Nate, do you give cooking lessons?" Tess forked a piece of pork tenderloin. "Everything is delicious. What's in the mashed potatoes?"

"Garlic." He smiled. "I put that in just about everything but dessert. There's sour cream in there, too, but my wife prefers a heart-healthy version, so I substitute Greek yogurt."

Cash scowled and refilled his wine glass. "Aren't you just the little homemaker?"

Nate's lips twitched. "I can give you a few lessons, if you like. We'll start slow. Scrambled eggs and toast first, then we'll work up to hamburgers." There was no mistaking the humor in his words—at Cash's expense—when he added, "Anna will wake up soon and I can show you how to change a diaper, too."

"Yeah, well, I'll pass on that one. Ramona plans to keep my fridge *and* freezer stocked, so I'm good there, too."

"Huh."

That always meant something, even if there weren't any words attached. Nate had a way of attaching great significance to a sound, but Cash wasn't biting this time.

Unfortunately, Tess was.

"Nate? What are you thinking?"

Damn, here it comes.

"My mother's a good cook, too, but that doesn't mean I want to depend on her to eat. Or," he cast a glance at Christine and smiled, "have her intrude on my privacy. I wouldn't want her traipsing in with beef stew or a container of spaghetti sauce. Not that she would, but I like boundaries." He turned to Tess. "How are you in the kitchen?"

What the hell was he trying to do? Why not just ask if she planned to move in and make Cash his meals for the next thirty-two years because that's what he meant. Hell yes, that's exactly what Nate Desantro meant and that calm expression wasn't fooling anybody, certainly not Tess.

She blushed and stammered, "I'm not very skilled in the kitchen."

Thank God Christine jumped in. "Well, I'm horrible. Really bad." She laughed. "I did make the rolls and there's not a scorch on them." She laid a hand on her husband's forearm. "Of course, they came from the refrigerated section of Sal's, but I didn't have to use the back-up supply. That's a start, isn't it, Nate?"

His voice dipped, turned softer than the butter on one of his wife's rolls. "Yes, sweetheart, that's a start."

Cash looked away. Bad enough he had to hear what a great guy his old friend was; he did not have to witness it, too. Maybe he should just concentrate on the wine and block out the rest. A few more glasses should make him mellow enough that he wouldn't care what happened. Why did the sight and sound of a couple in love put him in such a foul mood? Nate and Christine deserved to be together, deserved to be happy. What was his issue?

Apparently Nate wondered the same thing because he grabbed a bottle of whiskey and two shot glasses and led Cash onto the deck while Tess and Christine cleared the table. The early evening sky had shifted to a pink-gray with the last rays of sunlight slipping behind the pine trees. Cash had missed the quietness of a small town. No sirens, no honking horns, no shouting. Nothing but crickets, birds, and his own thoughts.

Nate poured two shots, handed one to Cash, and saluted him before downing his drink. Cash threw back his shot, welcoming the burn as it traveled from his throat to his belly.

"Want to tell me what the hell that was about in there?"

Yup, Nate had noticed. Cash shrugged. "What?"

"Come on. You spent half the night practicing your sarcasm and the other half scowling into your wine glass. What's going on?"

Cash stared at the fire pit several feet away. He bet Nate and Christine sat out here at night, sharing conversation and dreams. "Nothing."

"You're jealous."

Cash swung around, stared at Nate in the semidarkness. "Of what?"

Nate shrugged, refilled their glasses. "Me and Christine. That we're happy, that we found each other."

"That is such a bunch of bullshit." Cash downed his shot and set the glass on the railing. "I'm glad you're not miserable anymore. And I'm glad she's the one for you. Hell, I'm friggin' glad you have a kid together and that you could get past the whole Charlie Blacksworth thing."

"Watch what you're saying." There was an edge to those words and Cash didn't doubt Nate could back them up with a left hook, and a right, if necessary. "You've been on a jag since you came back. None of us knew what to expect. But then we see you," he scowled, "when you *permit* us to see you, and hell, it's not your body that's messed up. It's your friggin' head."

"Shut up."

"Don't like the truth? You'd rather keep taking those pills you think I don't know about, or maybe getting shit-faced is more your style. I'm sick of it. People care about you. Tess cares about you, but you're so damn busy feeling sorry for yourself, you can't see that." He took a step closer. "Either you figure out what your problem is and let me help you, or stay away."

Nate grabbed the bottle and headed back inside, leaving Cash to think about what he'd said. Damn Nate Desantro and his self-righteousness to hell. He lifted his glass and caught the last few drops of whiskey.

Cash's mood didn't improve when he returned inside, though he suffered through Tess's ooohs and aahhs over "Chef Nate's" chocolate lava cake, before he mumbled a hasty "thank you" and escorted Tess to the truck. They didn't speak until he'd pulled into her driveway.

"What happened tonight?"

He gripped the steering wheel and looked straight ahead. "Nothing."

"Cash." Her voice slipped over him, into him, trying to coax the truth out. "Something was going on. Please tell me."

What could he possibly tell her? *I am so friggin' lost I don't know what to do?* Or, *You want to know the real reason I quit the force? It had nothing to do with being tired of police work. I loved my job. It had to do with JJ. Now do you want to hear the rest?* He wasn't prepared to tell her that, so he simply said, "It's nothing."

"I can't help you if you don't tell me what's wrong."

He turned to her and bit out, "Who said I wanted your help? Did I ask?" He should just shut up, but he couldn't. Anger and resentment burst from him, poured out in quiet rage. "When I needed you, you refused me. I begged you to listen and it didn't do one damn bit of good." He clenched his jaw, forced himself to remain calm. "I sure as hell am not going to play confession with you now." They stared at each other as Cash's words filled the truck, pulled them together, thrust them apart. Seconds passed with nothing but the sound of their breath between them.

"I never meant to hurt you," she said quietly.

That was the last thing he wanted to hear right now. Cash's gaze settled on her lips and before he could acknowledge the idiocy of his actions or the regret he'd suffer later, he leaned forward and pulled her to him, his lips harsh and possessive on hers. She opened her mouth and let his tongue claim hers. That surprised him, angered him even, because he did not want this kiss to be about need or desire. He wanted it to be about possession. His hand slid to the opening of her shirt, his fingers easing beneath the fabric, touching the soft flesh of her breast.

When she broke the kiss and pulled away, Cash expected to see disgust in those green eyes. Disgust he could handle. What he saw was desire, and that infuriated him. His voice turned cold and harsh. "Get out. Now."

10

The ringing jarred Christine awake. She eased out of Nate's grasp and reached for the phone. "Hello?"

"Christine, this is Tess."

"What's the matter? Are you crying?" Nate stirred beside her and she lowered her voice. "What's wrong?"

"I'm...sorry to bother you. I didn't know who else to call."

Christine slid out of bed and reached for her robe. "It's okay. Tell me what happened." She made her way to the living room and turned on the small lamp by the couch.

"Cash." Tears flooded the line. "He's at O'Reilly's. With Natalie Servetti."

Christine didn't need to hear more than that name to know the rest of the story. The woman was trouble and seemed bent on ruining other people's relationships any way she could, usually by throwing her over-sexed body at them. *Oh, Cash, don't do something you'll regret.* "Who told you?"

"Brody saw him there and he told Bree. She called me a few minutes ago." Sniff. "Why would he go with that woman?"

Why did any man go with *that* kind of woman? Of course, Christine wasn't going to put sound to her thoughts, so she simply said, "He's very confused right now. But don't you worry. I'll take care of it."

Sniff. "How?"

"As soon as I get dressed, I'm heading to O'Reilly's. Give me five minutes and I'll be on my way."

"*You're* going? Why?"

"Because you're my friend and somebody's got to stop that woman."

She left a note for Nate, telling him she had to help Tess immediately, and he could call her on her cell if he needed her. Then she threw on jeans and a shirt, stepped into a pair of scuffed loafers, checked on Anna, and grabbed her car keys. Maybe she should wake Nate and tell him exactly where she was going and why, but he might tell her to mind her own business and would most likely take it upon himself to get Cash out of there. That wasn't happening. She had a thing or two to say to Natalie Servetti and if she had to say it in front of the patrons of O'Reilly's, then she guessed the town would be reading about it in the *Magdalena Press*.

She didn't stop to think of the repercussions or how her husband might react when he learned about what she'd done. Natalie Servetti had almost destroyed Christine's marriage and while Gloria might have plotted the idea, *that woman* had implemented it. With great care. Layers of lies. And no doubt, exposed flesh—probably lots of it.

By the time she reached O'Reilly's, she had plenty to say to the woman, starting and ending with a warning to stay away from other women's men. Christine entered the bar, ignoring the curious looks from the patrons. She recognized a few; some of them even worked for Nate, others she'd met with to discuss financial needs. A handful nodded, but the rest turned back to their drinks, maybe out of respect for her, but more likely so they could tell Nate they hadn't seen or heard a thing when he asked them, and they'd be telling the truth.

Cash sat in a back corner booth, one hand on a bottle of beer, the other slung around a woman's shoulders, the woman being the tramp of Magdalena, Natalie Servetti. Tanned, toned, and glistening, she was sex poured into a low-cut white blouse and jeans. Her dark hair spilled over his shoulder as she nuzzled Cash's neck, ran her tongue along his jawline. If she got any closer, she'd be in his lap. For all of her attempts, Cash didn't look exactly happy. The tightness around his mouth, the eyes squeezed shut, spoke of misery and she'd bet that misery had to do with Tess. They needed to work things out, without the help of a troublemaking sex toy like the one fawning over him.

"Hello, Cash." Christine kept her voice even and didn't raise it above the music in the background. People would guess long enough at the reason for her visit without her providing the dialogue, too.

Cash Casherdon's eyes flew open and he blinked, blinked again. "Christine?"

Natalie lifted her head, spotted Christine, and edged closer to Cash, placing a hand on his belt buckle. "Well, hello, *Mrs. Desantro*." Natalie's dark gaze moved over Christine, assessing and dismissing her in the same breath.

Witch. "Why don't you find your own man instead of going after ones who are already taken?"

Cash squinted at her and said, "I'm not taken."

Christine pinned him with a look that said, "Oh, yes, you are definitely taken."

"You heard him." Natalie stroked Cash's jaw, leaned in close to press her breasts against his arm. "He's not taken." She paused and purred. "Yet."

Did men really fall for this ridiculousness? Obviously, they did and by the time they realized ninety-two percent of it was an act, it was much too late. But there was still time to extricate Cash from making a mistake he'd regret. "Come on, Cash, I came to take you home."

"Why?" He saluted her with his beer, took a long pull. "I'm getting acquainted with—" he scratched his head "—Natasha."

She stuck out her lower lip in a feigned pout. "Natalie."

"Natalie," he repeated, dragging out the vowels. "I'm getting acquainted with Natalie."

"Cash." Christine held out her hand and said, "We're leaving. Now. And if I have to go home and get Nate to drag you out of here, I will."

He blew out a long breath. "Nate is such a hardass some-times." He hiccupped, laughed. "But he's nuts about you. I can tell." He lifted a finger and wagged it at her. "Voice gets all gooey. You know what I mean?" His smile faded, his expression turned serious. "He's with the woman he loves."

"And you're with the woman who's going to make you *love* what she plans to do to you." Natalie's laughter spilled over him but he didn't seem to notice. His eyes were on the bottle in his hand, but Christine guessed Tess was the one he was thinking about.

"Yes, well, those plans will have to wait." Christine lifted the bottle from Cash's hand and took his arm. "Let's go." Cash shook Natalie off of him and slid out of the booth. No argument, no backward glance at the sex kitten, nothing but a stone-cold expression that made it hard to tell what he was thinking.

"Nate is not going to like this," he said as he followed her outside. "Bet he doesn't know, does he?"

She headed to the car and unlocked the doors, anxious to get him inside before Natalie Servetti came running from the bar in one last effort to seduce him. When she didn't answer, he rattled on. "Nope. Nate does not know."

"Fasten your seatbelt," she said as they pulled out of the

parking spot. Nate was home in bed, deep in a post-lovemaking sleep. What would have been the point to bother him ahead of time? He would have wanted to confront Cash, and "that woman" would have been there, so forget that. And she was quite capable of handling the situation with a calmer tone and no fists. Nate might not have been able to promise that. When men got together, the testosterone spiked and they had to play alpha dog, even if they were friends. It was ridiculous and unnecessary.

Cash blew out a long breath, closed his eyes, and leaned against the headrest. "If you weren't married, you could do whatever you wanted." He paused, went on. "Whenever, with whomever."

"True."

"You'd be freer than a bird."

"Right."

His voice turned rough. "Nobody could own you."

"Nope." She turned down the dark country road leading to Will Carrick's land where Cash's new house sat. If she kept him talking, even in a monosyllabic fashion, eventually his true feelings might spill out.

"No heartbreak. No love and happily ever after." He cursed under his breath. "Happily ever after," he repeated, then spat out, "That is such a bunch of bull."

"Is it?"

"Of course it is. *Nobody* lives happily ever after."

Oh, this man was in some serious pain. She'd love to spend a little time with him and gently pry, but if he was anything like Nate, she'd need a crowbar and a lot of persuasion to get him to admit anything. Men! Why did they always have to be so difficult? "There will always be ups and downs, but I like to think if Nate's beside me, we'll get through it."

"You mean if the muck gets deep, he'll put you on his back and wade through it."

Not exactly, but in a way, she guessed it could be construed in that manner. "What I mean is Nate and I are in this together. Period."

Cash rubbed his temples and muttered, "I'm getting a headache."

Code for I don't want to talk about it anymore.

She slowed the car when she spotted the sign for the Blue Moon. Nate thought Cash would find his place here, among the trees and the quiet, with Tess and their children by his side. That was a long way off and getting longer if tonight was an indication of Cash's willingness to admit he cared about and needed his ex-fiancée. Still, it wasn't hopeless, not with the town behind the effort.

She pulled up the winding driveway and turned left, past Will's house with the wraparound porch, past the barn where Nate did most of his furniture building, until she reached the two-story log cabin that had become Cash's home. Maybe it was only temporary, but maybe it would become permanent. She barely had time to put the car in Park before Cash opened the passenger door and stepped out.

He leaned forward and said in a quiet voice, "Thanks for the lift." He paused. "And stopping me before I did something stupid."

"You're welcome." She wanted to tell him to go to Tess and work things out, and to stay away from *that* woman. But Cash Casherdon was almost as stubborn as her husband, which meant he'd have to figure things out in his own time.

"I'm glad Nate found you," he said, then straightened and closed the car door.

~

CASH MADE his way up the steps of the cabin, wishing he'd stayed away from O'Reilly's and Natalie Servetti. Drinking and Natalie had been a poor excuse to blot out dinner with the Desantros in which he'd acted like a jerk and later, the kiss with Tess. Neither drinking nor Natalie would blot out that last one. Had he really thought they would? Eight years hadn't erased the taste and feel of his ex-fiancée; what had made him think a few drinks and a pass-around-the table woman would wipe the memories away? Sometimes he really was an idiot. He opened the door and stepped inside.

He did not expect to find Tess Carrick in his recliner, zeroing in on him with eyes that glittered and not in a good way.

"What are you doing here?" He should have listened to Will about locking his door against unwanted intruders, because right now he had one lounging in his recliner.

"Waiting for you." She slid out of the chair and moved toward him.

Those eyes pierced him, made him uneasy. He didn't like the set of her jaw either, like she was past pissed. And the mouth pulled into a straight line? Hard to do when a person had full lips like Tess's—unless anger had blasted the plump right out of them. Cash shoved his hands in his pockets and pretended nonchalance. "Why were you waiting for me?"

"How dare you!" She stopped when she was two feet away. He'd never been able to forget that mouth or what it could do to him. And he'd tried. Many times.

"*Natalie Servetti?*" She spat out the word like it was spoiled take-out and said again, "How could you?"

What? How could he what? Technically, he'd done nothing more than share a few drinks and let her kiss him...and touch him. It's not like he'd had sex with her. And if he had made that mistake, it would have been nothing more than another futile attempt to erase Tess Carrick from his soul. But he'd be damned if he'd admit that to her, so he opened his mouth and pretended. "What's wrong with Natalie? She's beautiful and not interested in ties."

She didn't like that question or his comment on Natalie's attributes, not one bit. Those green eyes that used to devour him with desire singed him with anger. "Hah! That woman's been stamped by half the men in this town and the next." Her nostrils flared. "And she'll tie you down so fast, you won't know what's happening until she's got you shackled." She lifted her chin and added, "With fifty-pound weights."

Fifty-pound weights? He shrugged, curious to see what else she had to say about Natalie Servetti and shackles and weights. "Maybe."

Tess opened her mouth, no doubt to spit out more venomous thoughts on the subject, but when she spoke, the venom was gone, replaced with what sounded an awful lot like hurt. "I called Christine because I didn't trust myself to show up at O'Reilly's, but I couldn't just sit at home, so I came here. When you walked through that door, I wanted to see your face when you told me you wanted that woman instead of me." She shrugged, and her voice grew softer, sadder. "But I see now that it doesn't really matter. It's not that you want Natalie Servetti; it's that you don't want *me*. You're never going to forgive me, are you? I've apologized for hurting you, told you how much I regretted it, tried to show you how sorry I am, but it's not enough." Her lips trembled, her eyes grew bright. "It's never going to be enough. I see that now. Good-bye, Cash."

She's leaving.

"I won't bother you again."

Don't leave.

"I told your aunt I'd stay, but I can't. Tell her to do what she needs to do."

"What does Ramona have to do with any of this, and what do you mean, 'do what she needs to do'?"

Tess blinked hard, cleared her throat, and centered her gaze on his chin. "She came to see me in Virginia, asked me to come back here." She shook her head and sighed. "Your aunt thought I could help you grab onto life, make you care again. Think about that. I tried to tell her I was the last person you'd want to see, but she insisted."

"Why would she ask you to do that?" *Why would she do that?* It made no sense.

"Desperate, I guess. She said when you were in the hospital you kept calling my name." Her lips flattened. "You were probably cursing me, but she didn't see it that way."

"So you came back." Why hadn't Tess simply refused the request?

She nodded, her blond hair swiping her chin. "I didn't want to." Her gaze inched up his face, settled on his eyes. "You are a dangerous man, Daniel Casherdon, even lying flat on your back."

His lips twitched. "I like to think I'm dangerous, especially when I'm on my back."

She did not appreciate his humor. "I meant because you were injured."

"Of course you did. And what about the other part, the 'do what you need to do'?"

"Ask your aunt what that means. I'm sure she'll be more than happy to tell you."

"I'm asking you."

"Don't. Please." She swiped at a tear and said, "This is not getting any easier. I have to go." She attempted a smile and held out her hand.

He stared at the delicate hand that belonged to the woman he could never forget. "You're kidding, right?"

Tess's smile wobbled, but she kept her hand extended. "I'd like to think we could at least part friends." Another tear fell but she didn't try to stop it.

"Friends?" He could barely get the word out.

She must have realized he wasn't accepting her damn handshake because she let her hand fall to her side. "Good-bye, Cash. I hope you find the life you're looking for."

She moved past him, her lily-of-the-valley scent suffocating him with too many memories of how things used to be with her. If she walked out that door right now, there'd be no hope for a second chance with her. Was that really what he wanted? Oh, he'd spent years cursing her for taking the life they should have had, but now that he might actually have it again, could he risk it? Could he open his heart and let her in? How could he not?

"Tess." She had her back to him and her hand on the doorknob. In seconds she would be gone from his life. He moved toward her, chest pounding with equal amounts fear and hope. "Don't go," he said in a hoarse voice. He touched her hair; soft, silky, pure Tess. "Look at me." Her shoulders shook and her hand fell away from the knob. Cash eased his hand to her neck, trailed it along her shoulder. "Look at me, Tess."

She did turn then, her eyes filled with tears and something else—hope, fear, love? Maybe all three? When she spoke, her lips trembled as if she had difficulty getting the words out. "I'll stay."

Cash let out a long breath, leaned down and kissed her, slow and deep. He pulled her to him, molding her body against his. It had been so damn long and yet he remembered the smell of her, the taste, the touch. "I want you," he murmured against her lips. "So damn much."

"Cash," she breathed, easing away so she could look at him. "We should talk. There are things you should know, things—"

"Shh." He pressed a finger to her lips. "Not now. Tonight it's just us. No past, no hurt, just you and me." He traced her lips and smiled. "We'll deal with the world tomorrow."

"But tonight will change everything." Her eyes glistened. "We won't be able to go back."

Tess was afraid. Well, so was he. "Then we'll move forward." He stroked her cheek and added, "Together." There was no talking after that as years of emptiness and denial fell away, pushed aside by the desperate need of two souls destined to be together. They made their way to the bedroom, unbuttoning, unzipping, kicking off shoes, shimmying out of jeans. Her bra landed on the chair sometime after her second shoe hit the floor. He'd planned a more leisurely reunion—when he allowed himself to consider a reunion with her at all, which was rare and mostly confined to pre-dawn dreams—but one touch of her naked flesh and he knew there would be nothing slow or casual about it. He wanted Tess. All of her. Now.

"I don't want to hurt your shoulder."

He cupped her left breast, sucked the nipple until she moaned. "I'm not thinking about my shoulder right now."

She sighed and held his head against her breast. "I can't think of anything."

"Good," he murmured. "Don't think." He slid a hand down her back, dipped his fingers inside her silk panties and slipped them off. Then he cupped her sex, feeling heat and desire—for him. That knowing made him harder, more desperate to have her. Tess was right; tonight would change everything. Thank God. She moaned into his mouth seconds before she eased his boxers down his legs and rubbed her belly against him, exciting the hell out of him. Much more of that and it would be over. Cash fell to the bed and pulled her on top of him. "This might be easier—" he lifted her hips and settled her over him "—the first time. After that," he smiled, "anything goes."

After, it would be hard to remember who the aggressor was.

Once she pressed her nakedness against him, welcomed his tongue into her mouth, the rest blurred in a frenzy of passion and need. Had she fallen onto him with a satisfied groan, or had that sound escaped his lips as he fitted her on his shaft? Who rode whom? Who began the stroking, the tantalizing thrusts? Whose moans? It all blended in a medley of heat, pleasure, and need. Sucking, stroking, thrusting, pleasuring...ah, *definitely* pleasuring, until their bodies convulsed against one another, slick, satisfied, spent.

Sex had always been this way with Tess. There'd never been another woman who could pull him from himself and take everything, even what he didn't know he had to offer. With Tess, it had always been about more than body parts and sensation. With her, it was a blending of body, spirit, soul. It had always been about love. And it always would be.

WILL Carrick was a good man who didn't gossip and kept what he knew to himself, unless he had something that needed saying. Like the phone call he'd made to Olivia early this morning, informing her of Cash and Tess's "sleepover." Heavens! The news was a relief as well as a delight, but that's where the story had to end. Details, comments, suppositions were more than Olivia cared to hear. She might have birthed three children and shared a bed with the same man for many years, but public displays of affection or discussions referring to the intimacies between a man and a woman were as unwelcome as eggshells in the omelet she planned to make for Will this morning. And that man didn't think he was going to get her talking about her own medical situation either, because she wasn't. She'd told him as much last week when he'd gently inquired about the testing she'd had done. As if she'd tell him she needed a hysterectomy!

Just because Will Carrick shared the same last name as hers did not mean they'd be sharing more, even if she did catch him watching her every now and again in a quiet way that made her insides percolate. That foolishness belonged to the young and that's exactly where it was staying.

Speaking of foolishness, if Cash and Tess planned to have regular sleepovers, they were going to have to be a bit more discreet unless they wanted the whole town knowing everything they did. Why hadn't Cash and Tess considered that? Well, they should have thought twice about sharing a bed in a place where the town knew what brand of toilet tissue a person used. Will had said he thought about moving Tess's car behind the barn, but he didn't have the keys and that meant going to the cabin to get them and considering what was probably going on in there, he'd decided against it. She'd heard the humor in his voice when he mentioned the part about what might be happening in the cabin, as if he found telling her quite entertaining. Oh, but she had not wanted to hear that speculation coming from her brother-in-law's lips.

The news would spread through Magdalena faster than a grease fire, but what she didn't know was who would be doing the spreading. There were any number of suspects, from the well-intentioned romantics like Pop Benito to the not-so-well-intentioned ones, like her next-door neighbor, Edith Finnegan. How a straight-shooting, honest man like Jack Finnegan could have a troublemaking, miserable sister like Edith was almost impossible to comprehend.

When Will's pickup pulled into the driveway, Olivia set aside the whisk, wiped her hands on the dishtowel, and hurried out the front door. "Thank goodness you're here." Will was tall, lean, and weathered with a take-charge air about him that his younger brother, Olivia's husband, had not possessed.

He stepped out of the truck, tipped his baseball cap at her, and said in a deep voice, "Morning, Olivia. Take a breath, it'll be—"

"Shhh. Do you want *her* to hear?"

No point putting a name to *her* because they both knew she meant Edith Finnegan. The woman was *not* to be trusted. Word had it she was behind the run on pumpkin pie filling a few years ago, when the town cleared out every shelf from Magdalena to Tristan for fear of a shortage, which, according to Edith, would "devastate" Thanksgiving pie bakers. Most bought ten and twelve cans or more, paying a solid forty percent above the usual price because they were *not* going to lose out on their pumpkin pie or pumpkin rolls at the Thanksgiving dinner table. Only thing was, the pumpkin pie filling never did run out, even with the increased number of purchases.

Some said Edith invented the tale to stir things up because she was bored and lonely, while others said she made a deal with store owners in the neighboring towns. Either way, nobody trusted her after that, especially not her brother, Jack. He pretty much disowned her for putting a move on the town like she did. Olivia glanced at Edith's house and swore she saw the kitchen curtain move. Will held the door to let her enter and Olivia was reminded yet again how Thomas had been so preoccupied with his plans, he'd forgotten about courtesy and courtship.

"How about a cup of coffee? Have you eaten yet?"

"Sure and no, I was just on my way to Lina's for an omelet."

"Hrmph. My omelets are every bit as good as hers. Would you like ham and cheese or a veggie omelet?"

He smiled. "You have to ask?"

"You just need to train your palate to try something new." She paused, raised an eyebrow. "Something that isn't loaded with fat and sodium."

Of course he ignored her and not only that, the man actually tormented her with, "Don't forget the sugar. You know I love my donuts."

She fixed his coffee, cream, one heaping teaspoon of sugar—she'd work on reducing his sugar intake later—and handed it to him. "Sit while I fix you breakfast."

Will sank onto the chair and placed his ball cap on the bench behind him. He'd painted the kitchen a sunflower yellow because he said it would cheer her up during the long, cold winter nights. When she'd first seen the color, she'd called it sunglass worthy and a bit too bright, but he'd convinced her it was exactly what she needed.

He said she needed sunshine in her life after living through so much darkness. He didn't need to provide names and a timeline. She knew he meant Tom and JJ's deaths, Riki's disappearance, Tess's broken wedding and subsequent departure from Magdalena. The paint was a symbol of hope and cheer, and now with Tess's return and the "sleepover," this might be the beginning of a whole lot of cheer.

Olivia whisked three eggs together with the casualness of one who's done it for years and met his gaze. "Just because she didn't come home last night doesn't mean they don't still have plenty of issues to work through. Like, where would they live? That's a big one. He'll probably head back to Philadelphia and she has a condo in Richmond, but she's never there. What kind of life would that be for them, with her on the road or in the air? Who would take care of the children? Day care is so expensive and even so, Tess is gone weeks at a time. That's no marriage." Her voice downshifted as she recalled her husband's many trips that took him everywhere but home. "It tears a couple apart."

Will set his coffee mug on the table and said in a gentle voice, "Is that last part something you picked up from experience?"

"What do you mean?" What *did* he mean?

"You and my brother. He spent more days on the road than at home." He pinned her with that blue gaze that saw more than it should. "It's a lonely life for the ones left behind."

She cleared her throat, looked away, and whisked the eggs harder. "I was referring to Cash and Tess."

"Sure." And then, "I think those eggs are...ready to cook."

She glanced down at the egg mixture she'd been attacking with the whisk. "Oh." She set the bowl aside and grabbed a cutting board and an onion. "Eight years is a long time to be apart. I do so want this to work, but I'm having reservations." She chopped bits of onion and tossed them in the frying pan next to her. "People change." She sighed. "Love changes."

"Don't you start putting doubts in Tess's head. She doesn't need that, not now. Those kids belong together and they're getting a second chance."

"I suppose. But it could all go so wrong," she said as much to herself as Will.

"Or it could go right. It could be the best damn thing that's ever happened to them. Look at Nate Desantro and his wife. Who would have ever thought he'd fall for the daughter of a man he despised? But look at them. They got past the mountain of hurt and accusations, and they're making a life together. I've never seen a happier couple but I'd have taken bets you'd never get them in the same room."

She had to agree. Nate and Christine Desantro had beaten all the odds, including a meddling mother. And Nate wasn't anything like the young, angry man he'd once been with a boulder of resentment weighing him down. She supposed love and the right person did that. Still. "They had Lily on their side." She glanced at him and smiled. "Can't forget her."

"So, we'll get Lily on Tess and Cash's side. Pop's already corralling The Bleeding Hearts to create situations and occasions for them to get together."

"I don't know…" She'd been so determined to get them together, but now all she saw were the pitfalls. Why couldn't she just be happy for them? Why did she always have to think there was trouble around every corner?

"Haven't you ever wished for a second chance?"

There was a rawness in his voice that pulled at her, made her heart ache for his sadness. Maybe even try to take away that sadness. She batted that last away faster than a fly on a spoonful of jelly. She had nothing to offer Will Carrick but the friendship of a sister-in-law.

"Well?" There was that voice again, soft and sad. "Haven't you?"

She shook her head, shutting down the question and the voice that threatened to seep past the barrier she'd constructed long ago. Life had dealt her too many disappointments, especially where her husband was concerned, and she was not willing to take another chance on the unknown. "No," she said, drizzling oil in the frying pan. "I've never considered it."

11

It took less than a day for Nate to learn of Christine's late-night exploits and if the frown and brackets around his mouth were any indication, he was not pleased. He stood in the living room, hands on hips, and waited.

"I was going to tell you," Christine said, keeping her voice down so she wouldn't wake Anna, who slept in the next room. "But I didn't want to wake you last night and I was half asleep this morning when you left." Both parts were true, but her husband didn't look convinced. Or maybe it wasn't enough to appease him. Probably the latter. Nate did not like surprises or gossip, and certainly not when his wife's name was attached. She tried again. "I even wrote a note telling you where I was in case you woke up while I was gone."

"How thoughtful." He moved closer, his presence sucking most of the oxygen from the room. "Did you ever think maybe I'd take issue with my wife leaving our home in the middle of the night, driving down winding, unlit roads to a *bar*, to stop an idiot from doing something stupid?"

"Cash is not an idiot," she said quietly.

The left side of Nate's jaw twitched. Twice. "No, he's not an idiot." He paused, his dark eyes turning darker. "He's a pain in the ass, and if he ever pulls a stunt like that again, you better damn well not try to rescue him. If he wants to sleep with half the town, fine."

"Tess is my friend and she needed me."

"Anna and I need you, too. And we can't have you putting yourself in dangerous situations."

Christine sighed. "I'm sorry I didn't wake you last night and tell you. If I'd done that, you would have tried to talk me out of it, or worse, insisted on going yourself."

"That's right. I would have taken care of it."

"There's where you're wrong." She stood and faced her husband. "If you think you're getting within a football field of Natalie Servetti, think again. That woman is pure poison and I was not having her near you."

He must have heard the upset in her voice because his expression relaxed and he laid his hands on her shoulders. "You don't have anything to worry about. She's not going to come between us again."

She looked up at him, willing him to understand. "That woman would have caused the same pain for Tess and Cash that she did for us. I couldn't let that happen. Don't you see? Cash was miserable, and I'm guessing most of it had to do with Tess." Her voice dipped, softened. "I heard she was waiting for Cash when I dropped him off at his house." She smiled. "And I heard she didn't make it home last night."

Nate raised a brow. "Who told you that?"

"Pop." Her smile spread. "Not sure how he heard it, but you'd have thought someone gave him a truckload of pizzelles from the excitement in his voice. He says he has plans for those two and isn't about to stop until he hears wedding bells."

Nate shook his head. "Guess he's not settling for wedding invitations this time."

"He wants to hear the 'I do's' and he said so himself."

"Huh. He would." He eased her toward him. "I heard you were kick-ass tough in O'Reilly's last night." His dark eyes sparkled. "Stood your ground and took care of business."

Christine smiled up at him. "You're not the only Desantro who knows how to intimidate to get the job done." She leaned on tiptoe and placed a soft kiss on his mouth. "And don't forget it."

"Bossy woman." He buried his hands in her hair and deepened the kiss.

"Do you think they'll be okay?" she murmured against his lips.

"Who?"

Those dangerous hands slid down her back, cupped her butt. "Tess and Cash."

Nate sighed and pulled away. "Really, Christine? I'm already pissed at the guy; now you're going to let him interfere with our sex lives?"

She laughed. "You're not suffering in that area."

His lips twitched. "Not yet, and I want to keep it that way."

Nathan Desantro could still make her forget to breathe when he looked at her with that half smile, his dark gaze covering her. "I don't think you have anything to worry about."

That comment made the half smile spread and the dark gaze glitter. Christine was still thinking about her husband's smile and the way a single look could make her tingle as she fixed them ice tea, grabbed the mail, and headed onto the deck. Cash and Tess were on their way to their own happiness and with time and trust, their second chance would come. She handed Nate his tea and sank in the chair beside him, lifting her face to the late afternoon sun and the scent of verbena and lilacs swirling in the breeze.

"More junk mail?"

She glanced at the mail, sifted through a few bills, advertisements for car insurance and credit cards, a woodworking magazine, and a padded manila envelope from her mother. She set the others aside and opened the manila envelope. "There's something from my mother."

"Oh boy."

She reached inside the envelope and pulled out a slim white notebook with embossed roses on the cover. When she opened the notebook, she spotted four envelopes; three of them tattered and yellowed with age. The fourth was crisp and new, marked, *read first* in her mother's elegant handwriting. "They're letters." There would be a past in them, perhaps a past she didn't want to know about.

Nate touched her hand. "Do you want me to read them first? Or read them to you?"

His voice had turned gentle, his dark eyes clouded with concern. He understood that despite their painful and rocky relationship, Gloria was still her mother. He also knew at any moment Gloria's supposed kindness could turn to venom. She shook her head. "No, I'll read this one. It's marked *read first*. That's odd, don't you think?"

He shrugged. "It's your mother so who knows?"

She bit her lower lip, hesitated. "Do you want me to read it out loud?"

His smile covered her. "Sure. Go ahead."

She opened the white envelope, removed the single sheet of paper, cleared her throat, and began. "My dearest Christine, if you are reading this letter, then I am dead." Christine gasped and threw the paper aside. "Nate!"

He was out of the chair in two seconds and kneeling at her side. He pulled her against him and said, "I'm sorry, babe."

She clung to him, trying to process what she'd just read. "She's...dead."

Nate stroked her back. "I'm really sorry."

Christine sniffed. "Why would she tell me such a thing in a letter? And how did she know? Unless..." She eased from his grip and said, "You don't think she killed herself, do you?"

"No." He said the words with confidence and not a second of hesitation.

"How can you sound so certain?"

His dark eyes narrowed a fraction as though considering his words. Nate had a grim view of the world in general, including people's motives, especially her mother's. "I'm not trying to be disrespectful, but your mother loved her body too much to harm it." He leaned over and picked up the letter that had landed on the deck floor. "Let's let her tell the story. Okay?" When Christine nodded, he began to read.

If you are reading this letter, then I am dead.

Please do not think this is an attempt to elicit compassion or forgiveness from you. I know I deserve neither of those. I felt the need to be blunt in the beginning of this letter for fear you would toss it in the trash along with the notebook. THAT would be a tragedy.

I don't know the exact date of my death, but that will be easy enough for you to obtain, if you so desire. As I write this, it is December 30th and I am enjoying the warm weather of Palm Springs with my companion, Elissa Cerdi. She is young, beautiful, full of hope and promise, and so naïve. She reminds me of myself at that age, as though the world were filled with opportunity and all I had to do was look for it. I know the comparison must sound implausible, even ridiculous, given my behavior and lifestyle. But it is true, or at least it was. If you choose to read the notebook, you may learn things about me you didn't know. I learned things about me I didn't know.

You may even learn to forgive me.

But first, there is more. I was diagnosed with inoperable lung cancer last year. It was a blow, one I refused to accept, until I realized there was no beating this one. I knew I had cancer when I visited you in Magdalena. It's why I came. The doctors didn't know how long I had and since I refused all treatment, I assumed I would not see another summer. I believe I was correct on that assumption. You may check the date of my death to confirm. People think it's a horrible curse to know you are dying, that you've been given a number of days, or months, perhaps years, and the infinite timeline we believed was ours has been stripped from us, leaving us raw and exposed.

Once I understood there was no bargaining or buying my way out of this damn thing called death, I decided to stop wasting the hours I had left—hadn't I already wasted decades?—and try to get things in order. Elissa convinced me to clean out my closets and donate much of my clothing and your father's to charity. I did so, gladly. What use did I have for a closetful of evening gowns? I've begun wearing those velour lounge pants women are so fond of and I must admit they are quite comfortable. Of course, I only wear them in the house, and never if company is expected, but lately, there hasn't been anyone but Elissa.

While cleaning out your father's closet, I discovered three letters. One he'd written your Aunt Ellie many years ago. She must have given it back to him when she was dying, or maybe he found it among her belongings after her death. Oh, how I wish I had read this letter years ago, known of his feelings, known anything that might have changed the course of our destinies. But I didn't know until now, and somehow, despite how your father and I ended up, this makes it more acceptable. The second letter was written shortly after your birth, when his heart was so full of love for you that I knew I must share it. And the third was a letter I wrote him a few weeks after we became engaged. I was a lovesick young girl who thought the man she loved would love her more if she lived and breathed for him alone, giving up her work, her passions, herself—for him.

Oh, how wrong that notion proved. I had forgotten how I once felt, forgotten all of those feelings until I found these letters. They proved something to me. Your father did love me once, as much as I loved him. There is great peace in that knowledge.

I have no right to ask you to forgive me my many transgressions, but do know I left this world in peace, with thoughts of you, my dear Christine.

You might wonder why I didn't tell you of my terminal diagnosis. The answer is indeed quite simple. For once in my life I chose not to burden you, make you feel responsible, or duty-bound to 'make life better.'

Thurman Jacobs will contact you in due time. Perhaps that young man of yours would like to see Chicago and the house where you grew up. And, perhaps Lily would, too.

Love,
Mother

NATE FOLDED THE LETTER, eased it back into the envelope, and picked up the next one. He pulled Christine closer, kissed her temple. "Should I read the next one?"

She didn't want there to *be* a next one, but there was. "Yes."

DEAR ELLIE:

It's 3:45 a.m. California time and I can't sleep. I'd like to blame it on the time change, but that wouldn't be the truth. Not even close.

I've met a woman.

You're probably wondering why I don't just wait a few hours and then pick up the phone and tell you all of this. That would make the most sense, and I'm always a logical person, aren't I? The truth is, I can't wait. I must tell someone and I must do it this way, when the emotions are bouncing inside with such force, they've made me light-headed. I want you to feel this exhilaration, this joy, this boundless energy, and I want you to feel it from something other than work.

I can't wait for you to meet her. She's full of ideas and energy and possesses a keen intelligence that captivates me. Do you know she's talked of heading to London to work for a brokerage house? As happy as I am for the opportunity this would present, I've been walking around with a pit in my stomach since she gave me the news. How can I let her go? How can I live with her an ocean away for who knows how long?

The answer just hit me—I can't.

I'll be home in eight days, and then I want you to meet Gloria. She's brought me such happiness, and I plan to marry her.

Love,

Charlie

CHRISTINE LISTENED to Nate read her father's words, her heart heavy with sadness. The woman in the letter didn't sound like her mother at all. What had happened to her? Had she given up, given in, or given away too much of herself, until there was nothing left but a stranger, and an unlikeable one at that? Her father had loved her mother once, and yet that love had not survived. Had her mother's affair with Uncle Harry killed that love, or was it already dead? And if it were, how and why and when? Was it a slow, painful death filled with remorse and disillusion, or was it a quick severing of emotion, fast and final?

"Do you want time to digest what you've heard?" Nate asked, his voice warm and steady. "We can finish this later."

Her husband was trying to protect her, but the only protection lay in knowing the truth, or the truth as Gloria Blacksworth had seen it. That could prove useful, even powerful for whatever other unknowns her mother had left behind.

"No, go ahead."

He picked up the next letter and began to read.

DEAR ELLIE:

I wish you were here to share in my joy. Christine Elizabeth is all that is innocent and precious in this world. I have never known such happiness. These past several months have been difficult, but my new daughter has given me reason to believe once again in the goodness of mankind. She is a true Blacksworth from the shiny darkness of her hair to the crystal blueness of her eyes. I am truly blessed and at peace.

Love,
Charlie

HAD her father been truly pleased with her or more relieved she looked like a Blacksworth?

I'm happy, Dad, truly happy. If I've learned nothing else from yours and Mother's marriage, it's that relationships are like gardens. They require constant tending and vigilance to prevent weeds, encourage growth, and promote a bountiful harvest. I love you, Dad. I love you.

NATE SET the letter aside and reached for the final one.

DEAR CHARLES:

I miss you so. The wedding plans are progressing well, with my mother already dropping hints about a one-year anniversary baby and your father agreeing that the Blacksworth lineage must continue posthaste. I simply give them a vague smile and tell them there will be babies in due time. Your brother insists on commenting, even though he knows I'm uncomfortable with the personal nature of the subject. I think that's why he does it. Well. I will not let him ruin my thoughts of you.

I know this trip was necessary, but I miss you so. Thirteen more days until you hold me in your arms and I can tell you how much I love you.

Until then, my darling,
Gloria

CHRISTINE SWIPED a hand across her face and blinked hard. The woman in this letter was filled with love and hope and excitement, but nothing about her resembled the Gloria Blacksworth Christine had known. Nate folded the letter and stroked her back. "You should read the book," he said, his lips brushing her hair. "It might help settle things for you."

She sighed, wrapped her arms around his waist, and murmured, "Or make things worse. It could just confuse what I thought I finally figured out. I'm not ready for that, maybe I'll never be ready. Besides, how do I even know she didn't write in the book after she learned she was dying?"

He was silent for a few seconds before he said, "I thought of that."

"That's a horrible thing to think about my own mother, isn't it?"

"It's worse if it's true." He paused. "Gloria wasn't your average mother, let's not forget that. She can still pull strings and mess up lives, even from the grave."

"I know."

"Whatever you decide, I'll be here for you."

"Thank you." Nate would support her decision whatever it was. There was great comfort in that, and it gave her courage to do what she needed to, even if it was the last thing she wanted to do. "I guess we're going to Chicago."

"I figured as much. Just say when, so Jack can take over at the shop."

She eased away so she could look at his face. "You really

don't mind?" Nate didn't need to tell her he had an aversion to Chicago and her past life. He'd never been there and had shown no interest in changing that, despite the open invitations from Uncle Harry.

"Of course I mind." His dark gaze burned into her. "But you're my wife and we're in this together."

"And Lily?"

His lips twitched. "I have no idea why your mother would suggest Lily visit the house where you grew up, but there's no way that girl is letting us out of the driveway without her."

She leaned up and kissed him. "Thank you. I can't imagine life without you."

He cupped her chin with his big hand and smiled. "Then don't."

12

"Wow! Is this where you lived?" Lily had never seen a house this big in real life. It was way bigger and fancier than Mrs. Pendergrass's place. "Just you, Aunt Gloria, and Dad?"

Christine looked at Nate who made that frown face when he didn't like something and said, "Yes. I lived here, and it was only the three of us." Nate pulled up the winding driveway and parked in front of the four-car garage, still wearing that frown face.

"You had four cars?" Her sister cleared her throat and didn't answer. Why was her face getting all pink? "Christine? How many cars did you have?"

Nate turned to Lily and said in a not-happy voice, "Lily, too many questions."

"It's okay." Christine touched his arm and talked to him in the soft voice that made him touch her hair or her cheek. Or sometimes he even kissed her on the mouth. That was because Nate loved her sister. He loved Lily and Anna, too, but Christine was his wife. "You can ask me anything you want."

Nate shook his head and muttered, "You have no idea what you've just said."

Lily ignored her brother and smiled at Christine. "Is there an elevator inside? And a swimming pool?"

"What? No, of course not."

"Oh. Pop said his son's house in California is one of those fancy-dancy places with an elevator and a swimming pool."

"Sorry, no elevator and no pool."

"That's okay." Lily opened the car door and scooted out. "Uncle Harry said this house has lots of secrets in it. I'm going to see if I can find where they're hiding."

Nate said a bad word under his breath, but Lily still heard him. "Nate. No swearing or I'll tell Mom when we get back."

"Come here and carry your suitcase. The servants aren't going to wait on you."

"There are servants?"

Christine walked to the trunk of the car with Anna in her arms. "No, no servants, just us."

"And Uncle Harry, right? And Aunt Greta? And my cousins." She held out a hand and ticked their names off on her fingers. "AJ, Lizzie, and Jackson."

Nate ruffled her hair and said, "You know you aren't related to every single person you meet, right?"

She grinned. "I have lots of relatives now. Before Christine came, there was just you and Mom."

"I know, kiddo." His voice turned soft and his dark eyes got darker. "It's just that we really aren't related to everyone. Aunt Gloria isn't really—"

"Hey! Look who's here." Uncle Harry stood in the doorway, and for a second he reminded Lily of her father. Gulps of sadness made her swallow and her eyes got wet. *Oh, Daddy, I miss you so much.* Uncle Harry's eyes were the same blue as hers, the same as her dad and Christine's, Anna's and baby Jackson, too. Mom called them "Blacksworth eyes" and said a person could spot them from a mile away. Lily thought that was too far, but if her mother said it, then it must be true.

"Give me a hug, Lily girl." Uncle Harry stepped outside and Lily set down her suitcase and ran to him, flinging her body against his. "How's my girl?"

His voice was louder than her dad's and Uncle Harry said silly stuff that made her laugh. Once he showed her how far he could spit water. Lily hugged her uncle tight and said, "I missed you."

He kissed the top of her head and said, "Ditto, kiddo."

She pulled away, thinking about the new cousins she hadn't met and Uncle Harry's wife, who was now her aunt. So many people to meet and all of them family. She thought of Christine's mom who had been kind of her aunt. Sort of. Nate said she wasn't and he made that funny face like he did when he wasn't happy, but Lily still thought she was. But now the pretty lady with the sparkly jewelry was dead, and that's why they'd driven to Chicago, so they could see Christine's house and to see her mother, who was in a vase by the fireplace. How could a person fit in a vase unless it was a really big one? When Nate wasn't around, she'd ask Christine about it.

"Harry. Good to see you." Nate held out a hand and Uncle Harry shook it, then gave him a hug.

"Glad you finally made it here. Wish it were under different circumstances." He shook his head. "Damn crazy thing. Who would have guessed she was sick?"

"Do I have to get in line to see my favorite uncle?" Christine stood by Nate with Anna in her arms.

"You mean your *only* uncle." He laughed and gave Christine a big hug and then took Anna in his arms and said in a soft voice, "I'm your Uncle Harry. You sure are a beauty and quiet, too, not cranky like your old man."

"Nate's only cranky sometimes, not like before," Lily said. She peeked around Uncle Harry's shoulder and spotted a little girl with long curly blond hair. "Hi. I'm Lily." She moved toward the girl and asked, "What's your name?"

The girl grinned, flung her arms in the air and twirled three times, singing, "My name is Lizzie. Lizzie, Lizzie, *Lizzie.*"

Lily giggled. "You're silly."

Lizzie began hopping from one foot to the other. "Lily, Lily, Lily." She stopped and stared up at Lily, her brows wrinkling. "Are we cousins?"

Lily nodded. "Of course we're cousins. Christine is my sister. Uncle Harry is my uncle—"

"And who was the lady that died?" Lizzie asked in a loud whisper.

"The one who lived here?"

Lizzie nodded.

Lily leaned close and said in an equally loud whisper. "That was Aunt Gloria."

And just like that, Lily made sense out of the confusion and chaos of a blended family and even more difficult, she gave Gloria a place in that family.

CHRISTINE TOOK in her uncle's jeans and chambray double-washed shirt, definitely not the sophisticated, dapper Harry Blacksworth style she'd associated with the man. Had she ever seen him in anything as casual as jeans? His sweat outfits were only for exercise, but other than that? No, she didn't think so, and the mere fact that he stood before her, looking as out of place as Nate in a tuxedo, made the sight endearing. "Uncle Harry, you look so," Christine paused and hid a smile, "comfortable."

He attempted a frown, but it caved. "Not a word, Chrissie girl. Not a damn word." Then he stepped closer and muttered, "Next she'll have me wearing friggin' flannel and corduroy."

The "she" being Greta. Uncle Harry was all bluster these days, because they both knew he'd wear overalls and work boots if his wife asked him to do it. That's what love did to a person. "I think I'd like to see you in flannel and corduroy. Don't be surprised if your goddaughter doesn't get them for you next Christmas."

He shook his head and swore. "What the hell ever happened to style? Come to think of it, what the hell happened to *me*? Greta's got me wearing these damn jeans around the house, said she got tired of the holes I made in my trousers. How the hell was I to know a pair of gabardines wouldn't hold up on a jungle gym? The damn things cost enough."

Christine's lips twitched. "I don't think that's what the designers had in mind."

"Huh." He grinned. "Don't tell Greta, but the damn jeans are actually comfortable and I buy the high-end ones so they fit well and if paired with the right shoe, say an Italian loafer, look pretty sharp."

"No tennis shoes for you?" This time she could not keep the humor from her words.

He rolled his eyes and scowled. "Not unless I'm in the gym. I'm serious about that one. I love Greta and the kids, but I do have standards."

"You're happy, aren't you, Uncle Harry?"

"Damn straight I am." His voice dipped, turned rough. "Happier than I have a right to be." He cleared his throat and met her gaze, his blue eyes bright. "Who would have ever thought this could happen to me, huh, Chrissie girl? A wife, kids, shit, a damn two-wheeler in the garage...and who would have thought

I'd be so damned happy about it? I guess miracles really do happen."

There was much about the trip that Christine would remember with a certain nostalgia, but there was also a good deal she'd just as soon forget. It was one thing for Nate to hear about her other life, her other home, how she grew up, the privileges she enjoyed. But it was something else to sit at the long table, passing food from china that cost more than most of his men made in a week, touch the coolness of the marble in the hallway, stare out the back window at the landscaping that would be a horticulturist's haven.

Nate was silent as they lay in her old bed that first night, surrounded by her childhood and too much wealth. He hadn't said much since they'd gotten here, but she could tell by the way his gaze narrowed and his head tilted that he was taking it all in, every last cornice, every tapestry and chandelier. Was he picturing her here, thinking about how her life was and how it could have been? Was he having regrets?

The last possibility shot through her brain, burst, and sent a ripple of panic to the rest of her body. "Nate, what are you thinking?"

He stroked her back through the soft cotton of her T-shirt, his breath fanning her hair, and murmured, "I'm thinking it's a good thing I didn't see all of this before."

She lifted her head and tried to see his face in the semidarkness. "What do you mean?" Of course, she already knew what he meant, but she wanted him to say it, so she could make him see exactly how wrong he was.

He sighed and his hand stilled. "I always knew we were from different worlds, but walking into your world is a real eye-opener. If I'd done that before I touched you, we might never have happened."

Christine sucked in air and tried to keep her voice calm. "How can you say that? Do you know how much that hurts?"

"I'd never hurt you." He said this with a fierceness that spoke of truth and conviction. "I still would have been dying to touch you, and I was half in love with you the first time I saw you, but if I had come here, *seen* you in a life I couldn't begin to understand? I don't think I could have asked you to give it up."

There was fear and uncertainty laced in the breath of his words, uncomfortable and unfamiliar feelings in someone like her husband. Nate was a proud man who made commitments and choices based on integrity and doing the right thing. Fear and uncertainty had no room in his life, and yet, here they were. She kissed him on the mouth, trailed her lips along his jaw and murmured, "Even if I wanted to give it up? Even if Magdalena became my true home? You would let me leave and never know the happiness and love—" she kissed his mouth again "—and sheer joy of life with you?"

His voice turned rough. "I would want to do the right thing."

"And you have, Nathan Desantro." She sat up, slipped her fingers beneath his boxers and smiled into the semidarkness. "You most certainly have."

THE SURPRISE of the visit came the next day right before dinner. Greta and Nate were in the kitchen finishing up the last touches for the stuffed chicken-mashed potatoes-gravy-and-string bean dinner. Christine had just fed Anna and Jackson was asleep. AJ, Lizzie, and Lily were playing hide and seek in the basement. It was pretty much a day that would never have been permitted when Christine was growing up. When the doorbell rang, Harry answered it.

"Christine," he called from the foyer. "Someone to see you."

The someone was a beautiful young woman with dark hair and hazel eyes, dressed in a plain navy blouse and jeans. "Christine?" Her eyes lit up as she approached and offered a hand.

"Hello." Christine shook her hand and said, "How may I help you?"

"I'm Elissa Cerdi. I used to cook for Mrs. Blacksworth," she paused, "And then I became her companion."

"I see." But she didn't, not really. "You took care of my mother?" This was the girl her mother had referred to in her letter. Was she with Gloria when she died?

Elissa Cerdi's smile spread. "I like to think we took care of each other," she said in a soft voice. "What a wonderful woman she was, but you know that."

Well. What to say to that? "Were you the one who mailed the letters?"

The young woman's eyes glistened with tears. "She gave me very specific instructions not to mail the letters until she was gone." She sniffed, swiped at her nose. "I wanted to tell you when she was...when she was..."

"When she was near the end?"

She nodded. "But Mrs. Blacksworth wouldn't permit it. Was I wrong to listen to her?" Her voice caught, filled with grief and sadness. "Would you have wanted to say a proper good-bye to your mother?" The girl glanced at the fireplace where the bronze urn rested. "I helped her pick that out. It was so sad."

"Thank you for being there for her." Christine didn't know what she felt right now. Her mother was dead, and even though Gloria had created untold turmoil and pain, she had still been her mother. But what kind of mother hires a woman to seduce her daughter's husband? What was the real reason Gloria hadn't wanted to see Christine before she died? Oh, she'd mentioned in the letter that she hadn't wanted to cause any more inconvenience, but that didn't sound like the woman who had driven

Uncle Harry from The Presidio after her fall. Or the one who had insisted Connor Pendleton was the perfect choice for the perfect gene pool. Or the one who hired Natalie Servetti to seduce Nate, so Christine would "wake up" and get a divorce. Or the one who slept with her brother-in-law...They said people can change, but could they really? And if so, how much?

"I'm so glad to meet you." Elissa Cerdi beamed. "Mrs. Blacksworth told me all about you. And she said you married the most handsome man and you were very much in love with him and even had a baby."

Christine stared. "My mother said that?"

The girl's smile faltered, but she worked it back into place. "Well, not exactly. I was the one who said your husband must be terribly handsome because you are so beautiful, and that you must be very much in love."

"Ah. And what did my mother say to that?"

"It was toward the end and it was hard for her to speak." She blinked back tears and said in a soft voice, "But she smiled. It was just a faint tilt of her lips, but I saw it."

Or maybe the girl saw something that wasn't really there because she wanted to see it. "Was there anything else you interpreted for my mother that she didn't actually say?"

There was a split-second hesitation and then a quick nod. "There is one more thing. Maybe I shouldn't have done it, but I thought it was the right thing to do."

Christine remained calm and asked in a casual voice, "What was that?"

"The part in the letter that said Lily should come here." She chewed on her bottom lip. "I kind of wrote that."

So, Gloria had not invited Lily to Chicago. No surprise there. "Kind of?"

She shrugged. "I copied Mrs. Blacksworth's writing and wrote real light so it looked old."

"You had me fooled. You're a very good copycat."

"I'm sorry. I meant no harm. It just seemed like Lily should see where her sister grew up."

Christine nodded. "Thank you." And then, because she really was grateful and because there might be more snippets she should know that could help her determine if Gloria's professed "epiphany" were real or just another guilt trip, she said, "Would you like to stay for dinner?"

"Mrs. Blacksworth was a very kind woman." The girl's big eyes teared up. "So gentle and caring."

Harry almost spit out his drink. He wiped his mouth with his napkin and stared at Elissa Cerdi. "Are we talking about Gloria Blacksworth? Blond hair, small, spent her life making herself look young?"

"Harry." Greta shook her head and cast him a look that said, "Respect the dead, even your sister-in-law."

"Sorry," Harry mumbled. "It's just that we never really saw that side of Gloria. We were always treated to a bit harsher and unforgiving part of her."

The young woman dabbed her eyes with a tissue. "She donated much of her clothing to a center for displaced women who are forced to start over due to a divorce, or a spouse's death, and find themselves in need of a job. They don't have money to buy clothing for interviews or even to go to work. Mrs. Blacksworth was very generous."

"I'll bet all that satin and silk will come in handy at the copy machine."

"Harry. Please." This from Greta.

He shrugged but went on. "Seriously, these women are wearing thousand-dollar outfits to interview for a minimum-wage job? Am I the only one who thinks this picture is whacked?"

"It's the intention that counts, Harry." Greta sipped her wine and said in a soft voice, "That counts for a lot, even if the outcome isn't what we expect."

There was a message for him, buried somewhere within that German accent, and from the way Harry's expression softened, he understood it. "Okay, Gloria Blacksworth was a saint, how about that?"

Nate wanted to add a thought or two, but he'd keep his mouth shut. Maybe Christine needed to believe her mother had changed, but Nate wasn't buying it, not the sad letters, the "I'm dying but I don't want to bother you" routine, not even the clothing giveaway that probably had more to do with dumping last year's styles than donating to the needy.

Gloria Blacksworth's former cook-turned-companion glanced around the table, taking all of them in before saying, "She loved all of you. Every last one."

Harry sputtered. Nate coughed. Christine held her breath. But it was Lily who spoke. "And we loved her, too."

That comment carried them through the remainder of dinner and dessert and still hovered over Harry and Nate as they shared a drink later that night.

"What do you make of all this?" Harry waved a hand and arced the air.

"This? As in the crystal and chandeliers? Or this." Nate held up his glass and saluted Harry, "As in some of the finest whiskey I've ever tasted?"

They were sitting in the living room, drinking whiskey and enjoying the quietness of a house that an hour ago had been bursting with activity and noise, lots of noise. Laughter, chatter, foot stomping, running, baby fussing, and the occasional delighted shriek. It was hard to discern if the shriek had come from Lizzie or Lily. Most likely both. They'd certainly become quick buddies, which put AJ on the outs, but Harry had pulled him in with talk of golfing and a half-promise to take him to Magdalena for a visit. Did Greta know about that or had Harry just pulled it out of his parental "bag of tricks" to make the kid feel better? Nate hoped it was the first, because telling a kid something you didn't mean to carry out was a quick road to distrust and if Harry hadn't learned that yet, he would soon.

Harry pointed to Nate's glass. "That's good stuff. I'll send you a case."

"I don't need—"

"Yeah, yeah, you don't need it, and if I told you what I paid for it, you'd choke. So, when it arrives at your doorstep in a few weeks, accept it graciously." He paused. "Besides, it's Chrissie's favorite."

"Right."

Harry grinned. "I thought it would make it easier to accept if I said my niece loved it."

Nate shook his head and sipped his drink. Smooth, full, with just the right amount of burn. Maybe he would accept that case after all.

"You think this is all some kind of bullshit to get us to feel sorry for her?" Harry shook his head and sipped his whiskey. "This 'welcome to my house and remember the good times' reeks of it. I knew Gloria a hell of a long time and she never once did anything that didn't benefit her or her causes."

Nate had only seen his dead mother-in-law twice, but she'd left a trail of lies and destruction behind that almost killed his marriage. That he wasn't about to forget or forgive anytime soon. Maybe in twenty or thirty years, then again, maybe not. And he had a feeling the notebook she'd sent Christine that currently rested on the top shelf of their closet would create more havoc if and when his wife decided to read it. "She never struck me as the Mother Teresa type."

"Nope." Harry downed the rest of his drink. "Just talking about her makes me need another drink." He leaned forward, lowered his voice. "I cut way back on the drinking." He shrugged. "Keeping up with three kids is a shitload of work and this mellows me out too much. Besides, laying off the booze makes Greta happy."

Nate sighed and downed the rest of his whiskey. "The things we do for our women."

"Damn straight." Harry snatched the bottle from the coffee table and refilled Nate's glass, then his own. "If drying a dish every now and then makes them smile, why not?"

"Or making sure the toilet seat is down."

Harry nodded. "Just being polite. They think you're a friggin' prince."

"Control the belching."

"Eat the damn Brussels sprouts."

Nate laughed. "And the overcooked rolls."

"Pleasure them until—"

"Hold it." Nate pointed at Harry and said, "We are not going to discuss sex with my wife."

Harry sat up straight. "Good God, no. That's my niece we're talking about."

"Or maybe you were talking about your wife."

Harry sighed and set his drink on the table. "Greta would clobber me with that marble rolling pin of hers if she heard me talking like that. Okay, let's rewind that last part and say we're willing to do just about anything to keep our women happy."

Nate nodded and sipped his drink. "Damn straight."

"You're all right." Harry grinned and eased back in his chair. "I had my doubts about you at first, but you're good for her. I see it. And you're a hell of a lot better than that asshole Connor

Pendleton. He was more interested in getting into bed with her portfolio than with her."

Nate set his glass on the table and scratched his jaw. "Harry, what's Greta going to say when she sees you with a black eye in the morning?"

"Huh?"

He kept his voice low and calm. "Say one more thing about my wife in bed with another man and that's where this is heading." He scowled. "Fast."

"Damn, I'm sorry. I didn't mean it the way it sounded. I love Christine like she's my—" he stopped, paled.

"What?" When Harry didn't respond, Nate repeated, "Like she's your what?"

The pale bleached out the tan on Harry's face. "Daughter," he said. "Like she's my own daughter."

13

Cash pulled two beers from the fridge and made his way into the living room. Nate was in the barn checking on inventory but he'd be in for a quick beer before he headed home. He'd returned from Chicago last week and wasn't in town an hour before Cash was at his door, telling him they had a few things to settle. Cash hadn't missed the smile on Christine's face or the frown on Nate's when he led him onto the deck—to the very same spot where Nate had told him to straighten up and stop acting like a jerk. Hard to admit you're being one when you're pure miserable and bent on making everybody around you miserable, too. Even the ones you loved. Hell, especially the ones you loved. But Cash had owed him an apology and he delivered one, which, of course, wasn't good enough for Nate Desantro. He wanted to know the why, the when, and the damnable how that changed Cash's mind, even though he already knew it started and ended with Tess.

So, what the hell, Cash confessed, and when he darted around the O'Reilly's issue, just in case Christine hadn't divulged that bit of information, Nate scowled and said he'd heard all about it and it better damn well never happen again.

Then he'd slapped Cash on the back, shook his hand, and asked him what he thought of helping him out with his furniture business. That had come as a surprise, but the logic was there if you looked close enough. Nate loved to build but hated the sanding, varnishing, resanding part. As in H-A-T-E-D it. He didn't have the eye or the interest needed to complete the task, though he'd been forging through piece after piece, cursing the whole way through it. Cash had the eye and the talent. Hadn't he done refinishing work on cars back in the day? He'd sanded, painted, resanded, pinstriped, and basically created a shiny newer version of an old clunker. Nate told him if he could do that with paint and an air gun, then he could do it with stain and varnish.

Nate must have seen the interest on his face, because he skipped past the "Do you want to do this?" to "Will you be around to do this?" That was a roundabout inquiry into Cash's plans to stay in Magdalena. A month ago, he wouldn't have even considered it, but these past days and nights with Tess had made him believe they had a future together. A second chance, right here in Magdalena. He'd help Nate out, but he had bigger plans and that included Tess, both on a personal and business level.

Cash wasn't letting her get away again. They belonged together and tonight he'd tell her what he'd been hiding from her and himself for too long—he loved her. He'd always loved her, and that wasn't going to change. Maybe he was rushing things, but he'd been waiting eight years for this. Why wait a second longer to start their life together? Nate and Will wouldn't be surprised to see Tess with a diamond on her finger—not the one he'd bought her years ago, though he wanted to give that one to her as well, a symbol of a love that wouldn't die. The new ring would be bigger, bolder, with clarity, color, and whatever the hell else a person looked for when they bought a diamond. Christine could help him with that. She seemed like she'd know that kind of thing, even if her wedding ring was a simple one.

He'd ask Ramona if she still had the old engagement ring Tess had returned—okay, she'd thrown it at him, but he preferred to bury that memory. Maybe his aunt had pawned it. Or maybe she'd held onto it so she could look at it now and again and remember just how much she disliked Tess and Olivia Carrick. That would have to change, and soon.

Once he and Tess were engaged, he'd talk to her about becoming his partner on the venture he planned to start, the one he'd shared with Will yesterday that had made him lift his ball cap and scratch his head. Cash wanted to build a camp for troubled boys, right here on Will's land. The kids could come here in the summer and on vacations, learn things like basic woodworking, carpentry, plumbing, and equipment maintenance. There would be land work too: tilling, planting, and tending a garden.

There were a lot of life lessons to be gained from working together and the kids would benefit from the side-by-side respect they'd have to show each other as they performed teamwork. Knowing somebody cared about them enough to spend time teaching them a skill would make a difference. Cash was certain of it, because it had worked for him. Tess could teach them how to manage and sell the produce they grew or maybe even how to do public speaking. Whatever, didn't matter, she'd be great at it. Will and, hell, maybe even Nate, could give the older boys lessons on how to work the equipment. Cash knew what it was like to feel as though you didn't fit in anywhere. That's what had landed him in the back seat of Will's cruiser with a stiff warning. He'd teach these kids basic car mechanics and maybe Nate would give a cooking class 101. Hah, that would be interesting, but if anybody could pull it off, Nate could.

JJ hadn't been strong enough to get out of the self-destruction mode and it had killed him. The boy who had shot Cash in Philly was seventeen years old, a kid with a rap sheet since he was thirteen. Cash didn't much believe in divine intervention but if these troubled kids kept getting thrown in his path and had become the cause of life-changing events, maybe it was time to redirect as many kids as he could. Maybe that would save a life, maybe it would save a dream, too.

Cash and Tess could start over and they could help these kids start over, too. Will wasn't letting up on him about Philly and the "rest of the story," as he called it. The man was too damn smart and had been in law enforcement too damn long to believe Cash's story about taking time off and exploring other opportunities outside of being a policeman. Will Carrick wanted the *details* of what led Cash to make that decision, and apparently getting a bullet in the chest and shoulder wasn't reason enough. He was right, of course, but the man usually was about things like character and motive. Okay, he'd tell him the whole story, not the watered-down crap he'd been throwing at him.

Before he had time to consider how he was going to tell Will the truth, the screen door clanged open and Nate called from the kitchen, "Got that beer ready?"

"Yup."

Nate made his way into the living room, snatched his beer, and eased into a chair. "I'm going to have to install a few more fans in the barn before summer kicks in." He took a long pull on his beer and wiped his forehead with the back of his hand. "Too damn close out there."

Summers in Magdalena were hot and sticky and people found relief with fans, dips in the lake outside town, and lots of water—or other beverages. "I could help you."

Nate's gaze narrowed a fraction. "You're serious about staying here, aren't you?"

Cash hedged. "If the pieces all fit, then yeah, I'm dead serious."

"Hmm." Nate studied his beer a second, then slid a glance at Cash and smiled. "I'm guessing the big piece is Tess. Will she stay? Will she marry your sorry ass, give you a kid or two and a casserole every Tuesday?"

"Go to hell." Cash grinned. "I hadn't thought about the casserole part. Which one would you recommend?"

Nate shrugged. "Couldn't say. My wife's not much of a cook."

"I'm guessing she makes up for it in other areas."

The smile faded. Nate Desantro did not like anyone insinuating *anything* sexual about his wife, even if the insinuation wasn't meant to be sexual. "She does."

"Good." He drifted back on safe ground before his buddy flattened him with a scowl. "Tess was a decent cook, but I have no idea if she can even boil an egg anymore."

"Won't matter."

The man was knee-deep in love with his wife. Who would have thought? Cash knew that feeling even if he'd denied it for too long. "Good to know."

Nate nodded. "Glad to help." His lips twitched. "Should I dig out a suit? Or is this going to be a jeans and T-shirt ceremony?"

The man was awfully certain there would be a marriage. Well, good, Cash needed that bit of reassurance. He and Tess hadn't said the words yet, but "I love you" had been smothered in every kiss, every minute of their lovemaking. Hadn't it? All they needed to do was put sound to feeling and spit out the words. He'd say, "I love you, Tess Carrick. I've never stopped loving you. Will you share your life with me? Will you be my wife?" And she'd throw her arms around his neck, tear up, and sob, "I love you, Daniel Casherdon! Yes, I will share my life with you. Yes, I will marry you."

Simple. Easy. Sweat beaded along his forehead, trickled down his temples. "Damn but it's hot in here."

Nate smiled. "That's not the heat, old man, that's nerves. Take my advice, do it and be done."

"Is that what you did?"

Nate shook his head and frowned. "Hell, no. When did I ever do anything the easy way? I'm just saying, don't be a fool like I was. Say the words and get that ring on her finger so you can start breathing again."

"There's a lot to figure out." Like would she be willing to stay in Magdalena, or would she want a job that took her all over the world like the last one? And when the kids came, what then? And Cash would have to confess the real reason he'd resigned from the force...and...

"Just do it," Nate said, with a knowing look.

"Okay." Cash took a long pull on his beer. Nate was right. It was time to suck it up and tell Tess he loved her and wanted a life with her. And damn, Nate was right about doing it so he could take a full breath again. The guy really was head over heels for his wife. Who would have thought Nate Desantro would be giving him relationship advice?

He'd like to say he and Nate strategized about how and when Cash would spill the truth and pop the question, and even where he might take Tess on their honeymoon, but that didn't happen. Instead, his old partner from Philly, Ben Reed, took that exact moment to barrel up the driveway in his shiny new sports car, spewing gravel and a whole lot of dread. And he wasn't alone.

Paige Reed eased out of the sports car: long, toned, blond, sexy as hell. She was a dancer, traveled with a dance group around the country. She was also Ben's cousin, and some called her Cash's almost-girlfriend.

Cash didn't see it that way. Unfortunately, Ben and Paige did, and that was probably what they were doing outside his door right now. Checking in and checking up on him because he hadn't answered the last eighty-nine phone calls she'd made or the texts. Did she really not get it? She might be Ben's cousin and she might be beautiful, intelligent, with the longest legs he'd ever seen, and she might be able to bend her body in *and* out of bed like a contortionist, but there was a problem. A huge, insurmountable problem that had become a mountain these last several weeks.

She wasn't Tess. Nobody was. And now that he'd touched Tess again, tasted her, listened to her soft breathing while she slept, he didn't want anybody else. He'd never wanted anybody else, and the women who had filled his bed had been nothing but an excuse and a miserable attempt to forget the woman he loved. Cousin or not, Ben should not have brought her here.

"Who's that?" Nate leaned forward and peered at the couple.

Cash set his beer on the table and eased himself from the recliner. "My old partner." He paused and added, "And his cousin." How the hell had they found him? He'd only mentioned Magdalena to Paige twice, when she wouldn't leave him alone about hometown memories and family, as if he were going to share the truth.

"Huh."

That sound meant something, like Nate had already deduced the cousin was more than a cousin. But how? Cash hadn't even looked at him. He had to stay calm and get rid of them as soon as possible. Certainly, before Tess returned from the grocery store.

Cash opened the door and forced a smile. "What a surprise. Ben." Pause. "Paige."

Ben grinned and held out a hand. "Good to see you, man. I had a helluva time finding this place. You could have saved me a lot of grief if you'd just returned my cousin's phone calls. You know how she gets all emotional when she doesn't hear from you. Pictures that pretty face with a scratch on it."

"Ben! Stop tormenting him." Paige stepped inside the door and smiled up at Cash. "And I do not get emotional," her voice dipped. "I get concerned." She stroked his cheek and kissed him softly on the mouth. "Hello, Daniel."

The only other person who called him that was Tess. He'd told Paige his name was Cash, but she'd ignored him and continued calling him Daniel, saying she loved the sound of it on her lips. Whatever. It didn't do anything for him to hear her say it, not like when Tess called him by that name—usually when they were in bed. She'd called him that last night and the sound of her voice saying his name was still embedded in his heart.

"Paige." His lips stretched into a tight smile. "What a surprise."

She leaned into him, pressing her body against his, fingers stroking the hair curling along the back of his neck. "I've missed you." A breathy sigh. "So much."

He'd always thought she was an actor as well as a dancer, but she'd denied it. Still, she could be an actor, majoring in drama. Cash eased her hands from around his neck and pulled away. "I'd like to introduce you to my friend, Nate Desantro."

Nate stood, nodded, and held out a hand to Paige, and then Ben. "Pleased to meet you," he said, avoiding Cash's gaze. Oh, but Nate was taking it all in, Cash could tell by the quiet stance, the alertness, the cautious speech. He didn't know what to make of these people, especially Paige Reed. Well, neither did Cash. Paige had been alluring and sexy and didn't mind his moods or his silence. She traveled weeks at a time with her dance group and called him when she was in town.

It had worked well for them for almost two years, until she broke her ankle and couldn't travel. She'd just started back when Cash was shot. Maybe it was his near-death experience or maybe it was because her friends had started having babies, but Paige had become clingy, in an "I can't breathe" way. The spark they'd shared fizzled and Cash found himself avoiding her. Or maybe it wasn't Paige at all. Maybe when he'd been lying in the hospital fighting for his life, he'd realized that while she was an alluring woman, she wasn't *his* woman. *She wasn't Tess.*

"I'm so glad to meet you." Paige clasped Nate's hand and said, "I don't know anything about this town or Cash's family. He's never wanted to talk about it, like he's wanted for a crime or has a wife and kids stashed away here."

How about an ex-fiancée who is about to become a fiancée and a dead almost brother-in-law?

Nate coughed and cleared his throat. "You'd be surprised what goes on in small towns like these."

Nate should know. His wife's father had kept a secret family hidden here for fourteen years.

Paige's green eyes lit up. "Do tell. I love secrets."

"I'm not the one to ask," Nate said, shaking his head. "I prefer to keep my head down and ignore the gossip."

"Oh. Well, that's sad." She clasped Cash's arm and looked up at him. "I intend to find out every little detail about you while I'm here."

She'd find a mountain of details about him the second she entered town. Eight years ago, tragedy tore Cash Casherdon and Tess Carrick apart, but the love never died. Now, they were going to get a second chance, and nothing could stop them this time. Yeah, she wouldn't like that detail.

"There's not much to tell," Nate said, sliding a look his way. "He was a hoodlum but he could sure tune a Chevy V8, and he was a good cop. But," he shrugged his broad shoulders, "bright lights, big city called him, and he left our tiny dot on the map for bigger and better things."

Paige nodded. "I want to see where you grew up, where you went to school, where you—"

"No." She wasn't seeing anything but the sign leading out of Magdalena. "Nate and I are working on a project right now that requires a lot of hours. I don't have time to show you around." He toned down the irritation in his voice and said, "Sorry."

"That's my cousin you're talking to," Ben said, challenge in his voice. "Not some second-hand rug you plan to wipe your feet on."

Nate stepped in and tried to save Cash. "It's been a long several days. My fault for pushing him before he was ready. It's just," he shrugged and looked at Cash, "he's finally found something that makes him feel alive again and I want him to go for it and hold nothing back."

He was talking about proposing to Tess.

"I think that's a great idea," Paige said. "You should go for it, Daniel. Go after what you want."

You have no idea what you're saying.

Ben crossed his arms over his chest and studied Cash. "There's still respect when it comes to a woman, especially if the woman's my cousin. Now, I'm all for a challenge, but you have to know the obstacles and the chances of success. Have you considered these?"

Oh, he'd spent years considering *and* denying them. "To the point of overkill." *Wasn't that the truth?*

"Then go for it." His buddy grinned. "And don't accept no for an answer."

"That's what I've been telling him." Nate nodded at Ben and Paige. "It's been nice meeting you but if you'll excuse me, I have a wife and baby waiting for me."

"Your wife's a lucky lady," Paige said, smiling at him.

"I'm the lucky one." Nate turned to Cash and held out a hand. "See you soon." He paused, and his lips twitched before he finished with, "Daniel."

Cash watched him go, wishing he could hop in Nate's truck and leave Ben and Paige here. Hell, he'd let them stay at the cabin a few days and he'd head to Ramona's. Of course, he'd have to confess to Tess, but once he told her he loved her, wanted to marry her, and spend the rest of his life with her, why would she be upset about a woman who thought she was his girlfriend?

On second thought, maybe he ought to get a ring on her finger, even the old one, and *then* he'd tell her about Paige. The woman had never been his girlfriend even though she might have thought in some small part of her brain that sharing a bed and the shower constituted girlfriend. It didn't and she should have understood that because he'd never said the word *love* unless he was referring to her marinara sauce or those dancer's legs.

"Where are you staying?" He had to know the plan so he could figure out his own plan, which would not be with Paige.

Ben cleared his throat and said, "I've got a place in town." He paused and said, "It's called Heart Sent."

"Mimi Pendergrass owns the place. Great lady, fantastic cordon bleu." Cash turned to Paige whose neck and cheeks had turned the palest pink. "And you?"

She let out a half-laugh and touched his hand. "I thought I'd stay with you."

"Uh—"

"Okay, I'm outta here while you two lovebirds figure it out." Ben gave his cousin a peck on the cheek and said, "I spotted a diner that advertised homemade apple tarts. Think I'll check it out. See you two later."

Damn. Now what? The sooner he set Paige straight, as in whatever might or might not have existed between them was over, the better.

"Is your shoulder bothering you? You look like you're in pain." She ran a hand along his left shoulder. "I could massage it for you."

"I'm fine." He didn't want to hurt Paige, but she deserved the truth. "How about we sit down and talk? Do you want something to drink? Wine? Beer? Tea?" Did he have tea? Hadn't Tess left a box in the cupboard? Thinking about her squeezed his chest, stole his breath. Every second Paige spent here without Tess knowing jeopardized what they shared.

Cash sank into the recliner, but instead of Paige sitting in the chair next to him, she slung her long legs over the recliner and shimmied into his lap. "Paige? What are you doing?"

She turned on her side, snuggled her head against his chest, and flung an arm around his waist. "This feels so good." She sighed, let out a long breath. "So very good."

Cash tensed. *Now what?* "Paige—"

"Shhh." She began unbuttoning his shirt. He tried to stop her but she batted his hand away. "I know why you've been avoiding me, and it's okay."

She knew? No, she absolutely did not know.

"Ben said you went through some tough stuff." She paused and thank God, those nimble fingers stilled. "He said that after the shooting, you hated everything, even yourself. He told me you wouldn't see anybody, and your aunt was the only one allowed to visit. That's why I stayed away, but Ben convinced me to come after you."

Damn you, Ben Reed.

"He said you needed to feel alive again and I could do that."

"He said that?" What the hell did Ben know about feeling alive? He was still making himself miserable because his wife left him—three years ago. Yeah, he knew as much about feeling alive as a dead man did. Nothing.

"In so many words." The fingers started again, this time sliding along his belly, landing on his crotch. "He said finding the right woman makes a man feel alive." She stroked his crotch. "I think I can make you feel alive." She ran her tongue along his jaw and whispered, "What do you think?"

Cash was too busy trying to still Paige's wandering hand that he didn't hear the car pull in the drive, didn't even know someone was standing outside the door until he looked up and spotted Tess watching him, two bags of groceries in her arms, her face the color of paste. "Tess!"

"What?" Paige scrambled to her feet as Cash pushed out of the chair and ran outside.

"Tess! Wait!"

But it was too late. The woman he loved was gone.

14

I t took less than fifty minutes for the town to start buzzing about Cash Casherdon and Tess Carrick and the *woman* who came between them.

Did you hear a woman visited him?

She called him "Daniel," can you believe that? A stranger, no less.

How do you know she's a stranger? Maybe she's not, maybe she's part of another life Tess knows nothing about...

Charlie Blacksworth did it, why not Cash?

Who does she think she is, waltzing in here with her brother?

Speaking of waltzing, I heard she was a dancer.

What kind of dancer?

You never know what kind now, do you?

You can't tell what goes on in the city.

Wasn't the man with her a cousin, not a brother?

Who knows? Who cares? What was she doing here and why now, when Cash and Tess were seconds from a wedding announcement?

Says who?

Wanda Cummings spotted him going in the jeweler's the other day. How's that for proof?

Now what?

Now what, indeed?

Christine had been on her way out of the office when Bree called, saying something "absolutely, unbelievably horrible" had happened and could she meet her and Gina at Lina's Café in ten minutes? How could she ignore that request? She called Miriam to let her know she'd be late picking up Anna and had just ordered an ice tea when Bree and Gina burst into the diner, faces flushed, voices animated as they headed toward her.

Bree stopped at the counter and said, "Hi, Phyllis. When you get a sec, we'll have an ice tea and a raspberry lemonade, extra lemon. Thanks!" Then she made her way to Christine's booth and slid in beside Gina. "Oh, my goodness, this is so horrible." Bree snatched a menu and fanned herself. "I simply cannot believe it. We have to do something." She looked at Christine, her eyes wide, lips pinched. "This could be disastrous."

"Bree. Take a breath." Christine held her gaze. "Now somebody tell me what's going on."

Gina sighed and drummed her fingers on the Formica table. She seemed almost as upset as Bree, which was a stretch, since Gina rarely showed emotion and Bree always showed emotion. "Some woman showed up at Cash's today and Tess saw her."

"A woman? Who?" And it better not be Natalie Servetti or Christine might have to consider a petition to run the woman out of town.

Bree stuck her nose in the air and uttered, "Her name is Paige."

Gina rolled her eyes at Bree's theatrics and added, "She's the cousin of the guy who was Cash's partner in Philly."

They didn't say girlfriend or former girlfriend, but common sense tagged her as one or the other. "Why is she here?" And then, "So that's what Nate meant when I asked him how Cash was and he said, 'a storm's brewing.'"

"He said that?" Bree leaned forward and whispered in a loud

voice. "Was he there? Did he see *her*? And why didn't he tell you?"

Both women stared at Christine, waiting. "I don't know. Nate doesn't gossip."

"This is not gossip," Bree said in a firm voice. "This is called intervention. We're helping a friend, and if I see that woman strutting around town, I will yank every last hair out of her blond head."

"Bree." Gina placed a hand on her friend's arm. "That sounds like the hormones talking."

Bree patted her belly and sniffed. "That's true, but I'd still want to do it, hormones or not."

"We know." Gina turned to Christine and said, "That's all the information we have. Nothing else about exactly why they're here, how long they're staying, and what the woman was doing crawling all over Cash's lap and unbuttoning his shirt."

"And she had a hand on his crotch," Bree whispered. "Damn that woman. And damn Cash for getting into such a fix."

"Wait. How do you know all of this if it just happened? Did Tess tell you?" Christine couldn't imagine Tess hanging around long enough to get a report on the intimacies of the relationship Cash shared with the woman named Paige.

"Her uncle called me." A faint smile flitted over Bree's full lips. "He was at Olivia's when Tess showed up, half hysterical and covered in tears and grief. Will being at Mrs. Carrick's so much is another story, one I'm still trying to figure out. Anyway, he knows how close Tess and I are and he wanted me to be the first to know."

Gina slid her a look. "He called me, too, but I was with a patient and couldn't take the call."

Bree ignored this and shook her head. "This is eight years all over again. They came so close and then, poof, it all blew up." She swiped at her eyes, careful to avoid the blue eyeliner. "Is this going to be like one of those tragedies we had to read in high school where the couple never ends up together?"

"Absolutely not." Gina said this with a ferocity that dared anyone challenge her. "We're going to get rid of that woman *and* her cousin."

"And exactly how do we get rid of them?" Christine sipped her ice tea and waited.

Gina's lips curved into a faint smile. "I plan to find out where they're staying and confront them."

"And if she's staying at Cash's?" Bree asked. "What then? Will you barge right in and give her a piece of your mind?"

"I'll do what needs to be done," Gina said in a quiet voice. "Tess and Cash have suffered their share of misery and they deserve a second chance. Who better to help them than us?"

Christine agreed but there was something that hadn't been addressed and while nobody wanted to acknowledge it, someone had to say it out loud. "What if the woman really was his girlfriend? What if she thought she had a right to be with him?" When Bree's lips flattened and Gina's eyes narrowed, she held up a hand and said, "I'm on your side. I want Tess and Cash together, too. Remember, I'm the one who almost lost her husband because of Natalie Servetti's antics."

"Whore," Bree muttered.

Gina looked at her and added, "Skank whore."

They all laughed and spent the next few minutes devising and revising strategies to get rid of the opposition, namely the woman named Paige, who may or may not have been involved with Cash and who may or may not still be involved with him... or think she was...

When the tall, dark stranger walked into Lina's, Christine spotted him first. Strangers in this town were an intrigue, like the warm, decadent center of a chocolate lava cake, and they made people curious. When she lived in Chicago, strangers were everywhere: in elevators, restaurants, streets, highways, the gym. She'd never wondered about them, where they were going, what they did for a living, if they had children, a sick parent, a rescue dog? It hadn't mattered because the unspoken rule was to mind your own business—ignore, block out, don't care.

But this town wasn't like that and because she'd been here a while, she wasn't like that any longer either. Oh, there were still people she didn't know, but a lot of them knew her and if they didn't, they weren't shy about inquiring and offering up a name and a handshake. Nate called those people busybodies, said he didn't like them prying into his personal affairs, but the truth was, he didn't much like anybody prying, except Christine. She could "pry away" and he'd answer, even if he didn't want to.

So, who was the guy in the Harley T-shirt and jeans who was heading toward them? Christine zeroed in on the eyes. They met hers and he nodded his dark head and smiled. "Excuse me." Before she could think about the intelligence of her actions, she slid out of the booth and blocked the man's path. "Are you new in town?" He had to be the cousin. The broad shoulders, thick neck, self-assured stance, all spoke of police. This man had to be Cash's former partner.

"Just passing through." His smile deepened and he extended a hand. "Ben Reed."

Christine shook his hand and said, "Christine Desantro."

"Desantro? I just met a Desantro a little while ago." He paused. "Nate, I think."

"That's my husband."

He nodded. "Lucky man."

"Yes, he is," Bree said, scooting toward the edge of the booth. "And he's good friends with Cash Casherdon. Are you his old partner?"

Ben Reed turned and pinned his blue gaze on Bree. "I am."

"Hmph." She eyed him. "Where's your cousin?"

That gaze narrowed. "How do you know about my cousin?"

Bree lifted a brow and offered a silky response. "We make it our job to find these kinds of things out."

The man merely stared, then looked from Bree, to Gina, and finally to Christine. "Is somebody going to tell me what's going on?"

"I'll tell you." Surprisingly, this came from Gina.

Ben Reed's gaze swung to her and just as surprising was his next question. Big, bold, unafraid. "How about you start from the beginning and tell me why I feel you'd like to boot us out of town in the back of a garbage truck."

"Because we would," Bree said, and this time her smile was real.

"Because Cash is in love with our best friend," Gina said, ignoring Bree. "He's always been in love with her. Did he tell you how he ended up in Philly? Why Tess broke off the engagement three days before the wedding?" Her voice grew louder, her eyes darker. "How he begged her to work things out, but she wouldn't?" Pause. "Or couldn't?" She studied him, contempt spreading over her face. "Of course not. You don't even know who Tess is, but Cash has never forgotten her and he's never gotten over her. They belong together and they have a shot at a second chance, or did, until your cousin showed up."

"Hey, don't pin this on my cousin. She was with Cash for almost two years."

"Was she?" Gina asked. "Or was she merely filling in?"

Ben Reed's jaw twitched. "You're talking about my cousin."

"We mean no disrespect," Bree said, emotion simmering in her words. "It's just that Cash and Tess belong together, like ham and Swiss on rye."

"What?"

"Okay, then, peanut butter and jelly."

Oh, Bree. Christine stepped in before Cash's partner thought they were all crazy. "What Bree means is that Tess and Cash belong together because they're two parts of a whole."

Bree nodded. "That's what I said. Peanut butter and —"

"Destiny," Gina blurted out. "Destiny brought them back together."

"Destiny?" He rubbed his jaw, zeroed in on them and said matter-of-factly, "And here I thought it was two bullet holes that sent him back here."

HE HAD to talk to her. *Now.* Cash barreled down the road in Will's old truck, ignoring the potholes and definitely the speed limit. The image of Tess staring at him from the other side of the screen door pounded his brain. There'd been shock, disbelief, and pain flittering across that beautiful face seconds before she turned and ran.

Damn. He pressed the accelerator, desperate to reach Olivia Carrick's house so he could talk to Tess, make her understand that what she'd seen had not been what she thought. Hell, what had it been—a woman's attempts to rekindle a relationship that had never been about more than filling a physical need? Paige might want to believe it had been about more than sex, but it hadn't. Not for him. She deserved a man who could commit, but he wasn't that man. The only woman he'd ever been able to commit to was Tess. She owned his heart, lived in his soul, and he had to tell her that before she shut down and pushed him away so hard he'd never find his way back again.

He pulled into Olivia Carrick's driveway behind Tess's car and eased out of the truck, ignoring Edith Finnegan, who had stopped watering her violets and raised a pink-gloved hand to shield her eyes as she followed Cash. *Damn busybody.* He climbed the steps but before he could ring the bell, Will opened the door.

"Cash." He stepped onto the front porch, closing the door behind him.

"I have to see her." He didn't even try to hide the panic in his voice.

Will laid a hand on his shoulder, his expression softening. "She needs some time."

Cash shrugged off Will's hand and stepped back. "I have to see her, Will. *Now*. I have to explain." Over two hundred pounds of muscle and determination blocked Cash from the front door, but it was the respect for the man that kept him from trying to break through.

"She's devastated, son." He shook his head and sighed. "Damn but we did not see this coming. When your woman sees you with someone else, that burns her brain like a branding iron and it's near impossible to erase."

Desperation surged through his body, spurted out in sound. "I can erase it. Just let me see her."

Will shook his head. "Can't do that. Not yet. Olivia's with her now, which is difficult enough to believe seeing as the woman isn't keen on shows of emotion." His voice dipped. "But she's learning."

Cash planted his hands on his hips and stared at Will. "I'm not letting her run away like last time. I won't do it, Will." He sucked in air, spat out, "Not again."

"Good. Fight for her. You two love each other and you belong together."

"How about you tell her that?"

"I plan to." Will's blue eyes held Cash's. "But how about you make damn sure there are no more women slipping onto your lap *or* your bed before you come calling again?"

Cash left the Carricks' but he was damn well not giving up.

He had to make Tess understand he loved her, had always loved her, and he'd start with her old engagement ring. The jeweler was sizing the new one, but it wouldn't be ready for three more days. Tess might be gone by then, just like last time. In all of his years doing police work, logic beat out panic every time. Too bad it didn't work in his personal life. When he reached Ramona's, he had one goal in mind: find the ring and head straight back to the Carricks' with an apology and a proposal. He should have stopped to realize a man didn't apologize to his almost-fiancée for witnessing a woman crawling around on his lap and then present her with a ring and a pledge of "till death do us part." It would have made more sense to spread it out instead of jumbling it all together, but Cash didn't have time and right now, common sense was not anywhere nearby.

He tore into the house and straight to Ramona's bedroom. It was dark and cramped with record albums and an old stereo. There were magazines in one corner, scraps of fabric on a chair, and books. Lots and lots of books. A handmade jewelry box rested on top of an old walnut dresser along with an arrange-ment of red silk roses in a glass vase. Cash had made the jewelry box for her in high school shop class. Why had she kept it? He'd scored a *B-* but it was really *C* work. The shop teacher told him he'd received extra points because he'd never seen a shine like that or felt wood so smooth. Cash flipped the box open, fingered around earrings and necklaces, but Tess's engagement ring wasn't there. Next, he rummaged through the dresser drawers, but still nothing. He didn't like poking around in his aunt's belongings, but he wasn't going to call and ask about the ring now, not when the town probably already knew what had happened. Ramona would have a thought or three, and he really did not want a lecture.

The nightstand would be an odd place to keep a diamond ring, but his choices were dwindling and so was time. Cash opened the nightstand and rummaged through a few papers, pens, a book. He spotted the jewelry case from Howard's, grabbed it, and flipped it open. Tess's engagement ring winked at him, small in comparison to the one he'd recently chosen, but still beautiful. A symbol of hope, dreams, and love. Cash snapped the case shut and shoved it in his jeans pocket. As he closed the drawer, his gaze landed on a piece of paper with Tess's name on it. He eased it from the drawer and unfolded it. Tess's scrawl covered the page, and it was written to him, with a date on it of almost eight years ago.

What the hell was going on and why hadn't either of them told him about it?

He sat on the edge of the bed and began to read.

15

The banging woke Tess from a half-sleep. Her head ached and she'd cried so many tears, her eyes were swollen and her nose hurt. If only she could rewind the last twelve hours and forget what she saw...but the image of the beautiful blond on Cash's lap would not go away. Had she really thought he'd been pining for her all these years, so caught up in his grief that he'd never been able to move on? Never been able to find comfort and commitment with another woman? Just because she'd made a few attempts that ended once the word *long-term* spilled out did not mean he'd buried himself in work and shunned relationships as she had. Or maybe it wasn't even a relationship. Maybe it was simply a way to pass time. When Cash had touched her a few nights ago, the years apart had slipped away and it was almost as if they'd never been apart, but they had. Eight years was a long time.

"Tess?" The banging had stopped, replaced with her mother's soft voice on the other side of the bedroom door.

"Yes?"

"Cash is here. He says it's urgent."

"I don't want to see him." *I can't see him.* "Tell him I'm asleep."

Seconds later, the door burst open, followed by the brilliance of the overhead light. "Mom, what's going on?"

"Get up." Cash stood at the end of her bed, eyes narrowed, jaw clenched. "We need to talk."

Her mother interrupted. "Cash, I don't think this is a good time. I don't want to have to call your uncle, but I will."

He ignored Olivia and threw something at Tess. It was a letter—*the letter*.

"Still not want to talk?"

She glanced at her mother. "It's okay. He can stay."

Olivia was not convinced it was a good idea. "Are you sure?"

"Yes." Pause. "Can you close the door?"

When they were alone, he moved closer, his breathing harsh and unsteady, his expression fierce. "How could you not tell me you were carrying my baby?"

There was anger and pain in his voice. "I...I should have." She sat up and scooted toward the head of the bed, out of his reach. "By the time I found out I was pregnant, you were gone and I was at Riki's."

"Oh, that's a good one. I'll bet she gave you some great advice." His jaw clenched, unclenched, before he spit out, "Is she the one who suggested the abortion?"

Tess looked away. It would be easy to blame everything on her unstable sister, but it wouldn't be the truth. "It was my idea." He looked at her as though he didn't understand what she'd just said. "I was so scared and I hated you at that moment. The last thing I wanted was a reminder of you for the rest of my life." When he remained silent, she went on. "I couldn't do it. No matter what my feelings were for you, I could not go through with it. I walked out of the clinic and went home." Her voice dipped. "The next day I lost the baby, a fallopian tube, and a lot of blood. The doctor called it an ectopic pregnancy." She paused, sipped in air. "There were complications. A high fever and days in the hospital on antibiotics. It was horrible and I couldn't tell anyone about it."

"You had your sister." His voice splintered with sarcasm and not the least bit of sympathy. "I'm sure she was a big help."

He wanted her to suffer, she understood that, but the meanness in his words was difficult to take. "Riki did what she could."

Cash shook his head. "I'm sure. So, what's the part about not being able to have kids?"

Despite his anger, his tone had shifted, settled down. "When I went for my six-week checkup, I had a lot of tenderness. They did some tests and the doctor said it was from scarring." She could still see his kind face giving her the news. "He said it could be difficult to get pregnant, and even if I did, I had an increased risk of another ectopic pregnancy."

He seemed to be thinking about what she'd just told him. "Difficult doesn't mean impossible."

She shrugged. "It's easier to think it will never happen than to hope it will and be disappointed." She'd probably just shown him more than she should have, but so what? It didn't matter now.

"I'm sorry you had to go through that."

She glanced up. His eyes were on her, studying her face. "Thank you." He deserved to hear the rest of the truth. "I came back because your aunt threatened to tell my mother about the pregnancy if I didn't." She glanced at the letter on the bed and said, "I wrote that letter because I owed you the truth. It was returned several weeks after I sent it." She paused, pushed out the next words. "I had no idea your aunt read it and kept a copy."

Cash ran a hand through his hair, blew out a long breath. "So, you had no intention of coming back here because of me."

It wasn't even a question. She shrugged. "Not at the time."

"And she wanted you here, why?" He pinned her with eyes full of hurt, anger, and disbelief.

"To...make you care about life again."

"Huh. And how were you supposed to do that?" He rubbed his jaw. "Sleep with me?"

"No!" Then a softer, "No, that was not part of the deal. She was worried about you, about how you didn't seem to care about anything. I think she was desperate to help you. I guess she thought I might give you hope again."

He shook his head and swore under his breath. "Oh, you've done more than that, haven't you, Tess? You gave me hope, made me really start to believe in second chances, and then you ripped it apart."

"There's no reason for you to believe me or trust me, but I *was* going to tell you about the baby." She drew in a deep breath, held his gaze, and said, "And what I almost did, and that I might not be able to get pregnant. I didn't know how, but I knew I had to do it." Her voice cracked, split apart. "And I knew once I told you, we'd be done."

She waited for him to tell her she could take her good intentions and go to hell. But he didn't. He said nothing. And then he was gone.

"OH, WILL, THIS IS SO SAD."

"All we can do now is hope Tess and Cash are strong enough to fight through this."

"I feel so helpless." Olivia placed a banana-nut muffin on the plate and handed it to him. Ramona Casherdon had given her the recipe years ago, when they were still on speaking terms. She said the key to a good banana-nut muffin was the sour cream, and she'd been right. That was the last thing she'd been right about.

Will eased the paper wrapper off and bit into the muffin. "You sure do know how to bake a good muffin. These are delicious."

Olivia smiled and sipped her coffee. She should just say thank you and let it go, but she didn't want *that* woman somehow hearing about the muffins and accusing Olivia of calling the recipe her own. "Thank you," she managed, "but I only followed the recipe." She slid her gaze to the metal cooling rack and the muffins lined up like plump soldiers in two straight lines. "Ramona Casherdon gave me the recipe."

He paused, his hand halfway to his mouth. "Ramona? When did she do that?"

Of course he'd sound incredulous; who wouldn't? The town knew she and Cash's aunt hadn't spoken a word to each other in eight years. "Before." She brushed a few crumbs off her lap.

"Ah." He popped more muffin in his mouth and chewed.

"What?" There was an opinion wrapped in that sound and she might as well ask him about it now, because sooner or later he'd tell her anyway.

"Interesting you're still using the woman's recipes."

She shrugged. "No sense trying to find another one when this one works just fine."

"Hmm. She says the same thing about the dish towels you gave her."

"She still has those?" Olivia had gifted them to her nine years ago after they'd spent the afternoon making pumpkin rolls for The Bleeding Hearts Society bake sale.

Will nodded, a smile slipping across his face. "How about that?"

"Hmm." It was Olivia's turn to make a sound that said more than a string of sentences could. How about that, indeed? Why hadn't Ramona tossed them in the garbage or, at the very least, thrown them in a charity bag?

"Olivia? Did you ever think you and Ramona aren't that much different from each other?"

"What?" He might as well have said she was Edith Finnegan's twin. "Ramona Casherdon and I are nothing alike. How could you even say that? Seriously, Will, that is very insulting."

He shrugged, the blueness of his gaze spilling over her, into her, perhaps seeing what she did not want him to see. "You're a lot alike," he repeated, his voice soft. "You won't let anyone get close. Not even your family."

"That's not—"

"But it is. You loved my brother but you couldn't depend on him, so you had to learn to take care of yourself, take care of the kids, shield him from disappointment and the reality of being a parent and a husband. His absence hurt you, but after a while, you built a wall so nothing could get in, not even him. You didn't show your children your pain, but you didn't show them joy either."

No. *No.* "I had to be strong for all of us." What good would it have done if the children had witnessed her tears and fear?

"They never learned how to deal with problems." He paused, took a deep breath. "I'm guessing you and Tom never sat down and talked about issues and ways to handle them. How would the kids learn to deal with conflict in a positive way?"

"Oh, I can just picture Riki being positive in the face of conflict, can't you? And JJ? That boy thrived on conflict and then blamed everybody else for his problems."

His tone gentled. "And Tess?"

Olivia gripped the edge of the table and said in a firm voice, "Do not blame her breakup on me. I was dealing with my son's death and I did not have the strength for her pain, too."

"I know, and I'm not blaming you. It's just that you wouldn't let anyone help you or Tess. You kept us out and then Tess was gone."

"I never should have let her visit Riki." She sighed, worked her hands over her face. "That I regret most of all."

"Tess needs you, Olivia. She needs you to open up and show her you care, show her it's okay to be scared, okay to lean on someone else, that you don't have to always be the strong one with all the answers."

"She knows I care."

He pinned her with that gaze that saw too much. "Does she?" He pushed back his chair and stood. "You don't let anybody see that you care, Olivia. I'll bet you haven't even told her about the surgery, have you?"

When she looked away, he sighed. "I figured as much. You're going to end up alone and that's a shame, because you have a lot to give and a lifetime to share."

She sniffed and swiped a hand across her face. "I am perfectly fine."

He snatched his ball cap from the table and fitted it on his head. "Of course you are. You don't need anybody, do you?"

"What do you want from me?" Why was he ruining their friendship with cruel words and accusations?

A sad smile flitted over his lips. "I wanted your friendship. I wanted you to lean on me so I could help you through the surgery," he paused, added, "I meant the *hysterectomy*. Yes, I know. Surprised? Don't be. When a person cares about another person, the awkwardness disappears and it doesn't matter. I thought, no, I'd *hoped* that maybe in time, our friendship might grow into something else." The smile flattened and disappeared. "But I see now that you'll never let that happen. So, call me if you need your sink fixed or gutters cleaned and I'll help out. Other than that, I won't be around."

∽

IF SOMEONE HAD TOLD Olivia she'd find herself outside Ramona Casherdon's house, she would have called them delusional. And yet, here she was, a pumpkin roll in one hand and an apology in the other. When Ramona opened the door, there was a split-second of pure surprise before her expression smoothed and she said in an even tone, "Hello, Olivia." And then, "Cash isn't here."

"I'm not here to see Cash." She paused, wondering if the conversation would occur on the doorstep for passerbys to hear and speculate. "I've come to see you."

Ramona's dark eyebrows pinched together and a tiny sound slipped through her lips. She had not expected that answer and could not quite hide the surprise, maybe even shock, that flitted across her face. "Well then."

She opened the door and Olivia entered. Not much had changed in the more than eight years since Olivia had stood in this very room deciding on the cake Ramona would make for Tess's bridal shower. The room appeared darker, a bit more worn and frayed, with no bright spots. Olivia guessed it wasn't much different from its owner. "I brought you a pumpkin roll."

Ramona stared at it so long, Olivia thought she might refuse it with a nasty comment, but she didn't. Instead, she motioned to the tiny kitchen in the back and said, "I just made a pot of coffee. I'll pour you a cup."

That was Ramona's best effort at hospitality. How could Will say they were a lot alike? Olivia might not invite many people into her home, but she certainly welcomed them once they were there. She sat in one of the four white wooden chairs and set the pumpkin roll on the table.

"I never could quite get the knack of making those without the cake part tearing."

"You have to make sure it's cooled enough but not too much." Olivia shrugged. "It can be tricky."

Ramona set the coffee mug in front of Olivia and unwrapped the pumpkin roll. After all these years, she remembered Olivia preferred a drop of cream in her coffee, no sugar. She sliced two pieces and slid a plate toward her. "We've never been like other women, building up the niceties with idle chit-chat, so we can drop what we really want to say in between." She bit into a piece of pumpkin roll and studied Olivia. "Why are you here and what do you want?"

Olivia might not like idle chit-chat, but she'd learned a sprinkle here and there sweetened the truth. Apparently, Ramona Casherdon did not subscribe to sweeteners of any kind, in her coffee or her words. She wanted the straight-up truth? Fine, she'd get it. "You blackmailed Tess to get her to come back here."

Ramona met her gaze straight on. "I did."

"How cruel. How could you do that?"

Her dark eyes narrowed, her lips pinched with determination. "When someone you love is suffering, you'll do whatever is necessary to take that pain away." She paused, enunciated, "Anything. Cash gave up on living and I was not going to sit here and watch my nephew waste away with pills, drink, and regret." Her voice filled with a deadly calm. "Your daughter's name was on his lips when he was delirious with pain. She was the only one who could pull him out. What should I have done, asked her politely to return to Magdalena and make Cash whole again? I had to use you and your self-righteousness to force her to agree."

"That was a horrible thing to do." And it was equally horrible that Tess had not been able to come to her with the truth.

"The holes in your relationship with your daughter are on

you. If she'd been able to come to you, I wouldn't have had leverage, now would I?"

Olivia rubbed her temples, wishing she could block out this woman's words. How could she be so callous, so uncaring toward others? "Well, now I know, don't I? And probably most of the town knows, too."

"That's not on me. I didn't say anything."

"It doesn't matter now." She shrugged and looked at Ramona. "My daughter's heart will never heal and your nephew's refusing he has a heart."

Ramona sighed and when she spoke, there was a hint of pain in her words. "I saw all of this happening, right up to the point where Tess tells him the truth and Cash tosses her aside. I thought if he had his vindication for all the pain she caused him, he'd be able to move on." She stared at the wedge of pumpkin roll left on her plate. "I did not think he'd be in worse shape than when he was injured." When she looked at Olivia, there were tears in her eyes. "I'm the cause of that pain, and I don't know how to get rid of it." A tear slipped down her cheek, but she made no attempt to stop it, or the one that followed. "What do I know about loving like that? I could never be that exposed." She shook her head. "Might as well strip naked and jump in a pond in winter."

"That would be a sight." Olivia's voice dipped. "I'm not much good at that either, but I'm trying to be better."

Ramona eyed her. "You and Will Carrick?"

How did she know? And who else did? "Maybe."

"He's a good man." She paused. "If you don't mind sharing your thoughts, your heart," long pause, "and your bed."

Good Lord, just the thought made her jittery. "I'm working on it."

"So, when's the hysterectomy?"

"How do you know about that? Did Pop open his mouth?"

A hint of a smile flitted across her face. "He might have said something but only because he knows I've been through it."

"You had a hysterectomy? When? And why didn't I know about it?"

Ramona shot her a look. "I could have been buried six months and I'd have made certain you didn't know about it."

At least this time, the woman followed up the comment with a sly smile, which made Olivia smile, too. "Yes, I see your point."

"It was six years ago. I saw a doctor in the city. Pop and Lucy took me for the surgery, and once I got home, Lucy checked in on me every day, brought me food, newspapers, and, of course, pizzelles."

"I never knew. No one said a word."

"I said I threw out my back and couldn't work for five or six weeks. Nobody thought to question me." She smiled. "But then I could walk down the street with a giraffe and nobody but Pop would say a word."

"You have a point, Ramona." Olivia's heart grew lighter than it had been in years. "You do indeed have a point."

Her expression turned serious and filled with regret. "I want to make things right for Cash and Tess. I underestimated their love and I'm responsible for what's torn them apart."

"Cash would have found out eventually. Tess would have told him, I'm sure of it. And then they would have had a lot of decisions to make."

"What if she can't have children? I'm not sure he can accept that."

"If he loves her enough, he'll have to. There are no guarantees in this world; we both know that. We can try to catch moments with people we care about." She thought of Cash and Tess, JJ, Riki. And Will. "Because in the end, the moments are all we have."

OLIVIA CLOSED her eyes and let her fingers glide over the piano keys as sorrow and regret poured through her, drenching her heart and the cotton shirt she wore with too many tears. Song after song spilled from her soul, spread through the room in a melody of pain and loneliness.

Had Will been right? Had she become so rigid and determined to need no one that she'd pushed away those who cared about her? Pushed away Will? He was her friend, her brother-in-law, for heaven's sake. He couldn't be more than that. Could he? Why would he want to be? She wasn't twenty-five anymore, not even forty-five. She had wrinkles and stretch marks and a disposition that did not trust easily or often. But most of all, she was petrified of showing her true feelings, even to her own children, and especially not to a man like Will Carrick. And what were those feelings? Did she even know?

And what about Cash and Tess? Ramona might have blackmailed Tess, but Olivia had given her the power to do so with her judgmental ways and prejudice. She was such a hypocrite. More tears fell, more music filled the living room, seeped out of the open windows into the warm night air. That's how Tess found her a long while later, still playing, still crying.

"Mom? Are you all right?" Tess flipped on the light and rushed into the room. "Mom!"

Olivia stopped playing, turned toward her daughter, and attempted a smile. "Sorry, dear. I was lost in the music."

"What's wrong?" Tess leaned forward and hugged her. "Please tell me and don't say nothing because I know that's not true."

No, it wasn't true. She sniffed and looked up at her daughter. "I love you, dear."

Tess smiled and gave her a peck on the cheek. "I love you,

too, Mom, but now you're really scaring me. You do not say those words for no reason."

Olivia shook her head and more tears fell. "Oh, but I should have. I certainly should have."

Tess sat on the piano bench next to her mother and pulled her close. "It's okay. I know you love me."

It wasn't okay, and it had taken Will Carrick and Ramona Casherdon to show her. "You and Cash..." she stumbled, tried again, "You've got to work things out."

"I don't know, Mom. He's not exactly in a talking mood. It's not his fault. I shut him out of something he had a right to know about, and I don't think he can forgive that."

"I knew you were pregnant and I knew you miscarried, too." After all these years, she'd finally admitted it.

"What?" Tess pulled away, shock and disbelief on her face. "How?"

"A mother always knows when something isn't right. When you didn't come home after a few weeks with Riki, I knew something was up. And then she wanted the insurance card for the hospital and tried to tell me you'd suffered exhaustion and needed IVs. Heavens, that girl really does think I'm dense. I didn't need doctors' notes to figure out the basics. I didn't know about the ectopic pregnancy or that you thought about an abortion." She paused, stroked Tess's cheek. "I should have come, thought about it most nights when I couldn't sleep. But in the end, I chose not to, because we both would have had to face the miscarriage and I couldn't do it. Not so close after JJ's death. I didn't know the doctor told you that you might not be able to have children. That explains so much. Why you gave up nursing, why you withdrew from your life, how you buried that pain so deep no one could see it. Not even you."

Tess swiped at her tears. "I told myself maybe I didn't deserve to have children."

"Oh, no, child, that's not true. You'll be a wonderful mother." Olivia pulled her into her arms and held her close.

"I'll probably never be a mother at all."

"You will, you'll see. Maybe not the way you planned, but life has a way of throwing us off balance and it's up to us to set it right again." She stroked Tess's hair, murmured soothing words, and waited until the tears settled. "I know what it's like to be young and alone." She took a deep breath, forced out the words she'd only spoken out loud once. "And pregnant."

Tess met Olivia's gaze. "You were pregnant?"

"I was. Your father and I had known each other about six months." Her lips curved into a sad smile. "I was so in love with him. Then I found out I was pregnant."

"And?"

The smile faded as painful memories took over. "He said he didn't know if he wanted to get married. Imagine that? I played the organ at Sunday Mass and here I was, unmarried with a baby on the way. I didn't dare tell my parents. And then your father up and disappeared for three days. Oh, I was so petrified, but Uncle Will found him and brought him back. Next thing I knew, I was walking down the altar." More memories flooded her brain. "Three weeks after the wedding, I miscarried and I never stopped wondering if your father regretted the marriage."

"No, he wouldn't have. Dad loved you, Mom."

"He did, but he was a dreamer, always on to the next adventure. A wife and children aren't really good traveling companions, especially when the road is constantly changing." She cleared her throat and said, "Well. Now you know my dark secrets."

"Thank you for telling me." And then she asked in a gentle voice, "Is that all?"

Olivia shook her head. Might as well shed the rest of her secrets. "I have fibroids. I need a hysterectomy, and you know I don't like talking about those kinds of things, but it seems everybody already knows about it anyway." She paused. "Even your uncle."

Tess smiled. "Uncle Will knows a lot more than he's saying. I think you should listen to him, Mom."

"Oh, that man is not very happy with me right now. Said I was too closed up and unwilling to share anything, even a relationship. What on earth does that mean? And why would he say such a thing?" She rubbed her jaw and contemplated Will Carrick's words about sharing and relationships.

"Mom, you really don't know?"

"No, I really do not." But a tiny piece of her thought she might have an idea...

Tess smiled. "Uncle Will's in love with you and everybody knows it except you."

16

Olivia Carrick hadn't done anything this foolish since the time she tried to change the hose on the washing machine without turning off the water. Foolishness wasn't in her nature and yet, here she was, standing outside Will Carrick's farmhouse with a tray of chocolate chip cookies and an apology, all wrapped up and ready to deliver. She opted to knock on the heavy oak door instead of ringing the bell. If he didn't answer in two minutes, she'd leave the cookies by the door and handwrite an apology later. Right now she was exhausted from the emotional upheaval of the past few hours, but there was a part of her that was relieved and at peace. Confession was good for the soul, that's what Father Reisanski always said, but comforting another and sharing their pain? That was love.

"Olivia?" Will Carrick stood just inside his door, tall and lean, his silver reading glasses stuffed in his plaid shirt. "What are you doing here?"

She could not quite meet his gaze, so she settled on his chin and held out the cookies. "I know how much you like my chocolate chip cookies and I figured, why not make a batch tonight? It's supposed to be blasted hot tomorrow and I don't want to use the oven." She let out a laugh, her gaze shifting from his chin to his left cheek. "I hope you don't mind my stopping by at this hour. Goodness!" Her gaze shot to his. "Did I wake you?"

He shook his head and said in a quiet voice, "No." And then, "Would you like to come in?"

"Well. Just for a minute." She thrust the plate of cookies at him and said, "Here. Enjoy."

Will took the cookies and held the door open as she stepped inside. She'd been in the Carrick house several times, sat by the log fire, shared coffee and stories with Julia. But she'd never been here alone with Will after the man half-confessed to wanting more than friendship with her. And certainly not after she admitted to herself that she might want that, too. Goodness, was she crazy? No, she was petrified. And crazy.

"Olivia?" Will took her arm and led her to the comfortable plaid couch, the very same one JJ had thrown up on when he was twelve. "Sit down."

She slid onto the couch and sat very still. Next up was the apology. She'd rather make twelve dozen chocolate chip cookies than say what needed saying. "I'm sorry," she blurted out, her gaze trained on the gold-framed wedding picture of Will and Julia that sat on the end table. They were so young and full of hope and dreams, of babies, and growing old together.

Will followed her gaze. "Julia was a good woman."

Olivia nodded. "Yes, she was. She didn't have an unkind bone in her body."

"Nope. Charitable as they come."

"That's true." She could not make a fool of herself. Olivia stood and said, "Well, I am sorry for my behavior this afternoon. I hope you enjoy the cookies." She started to back away. "I put extra nuts in them because I know how you like nuts."

Will followed her to the door, but when she went to open it, he blocked it with his big hand. "How about you tell me what this is really about? I've never known you to talk this much and say absolutely nothing. What's going on?"

She inched her gaze to his. The man was much too close. "May I have my personal space?"

His lips twitched but he removed his hand from the door and stepped back. "Enough space for you?"

"Yes. Thank you." She cleared her throat. Twice. "I saw Ramona today."

"So I heard."

"Is nothing sacred?" Sometimes she almost wished she lived in a city. With strangers.

He shrugged. "Ramona told me."

"Oh." Well then, she supposed that was all right, since it came from one of the two parties having the conversation. If the culprit had been Pop Benito, she'd have marched right up to his house and seized his pizzelle maker until he swore to stop the gossip—ahem—information sharing, as he called it.

"Is there anything else?"

He asked the question like he knew there was. "About that surgery."

"The hysterectomy?"

Thank goodness the light was low or he'd see her blush. "Yes. About that." She paused and pushed on. "I'm sorry I was not more forthcoming, but it's not easy for me. I've never been the type to confide in anyone and certainly not to ask for help. It's all new to me, and really, I can take care of myself."

"That's never been in question. You're a very independent woman. I admire that." His smile made her wish the ceiling fan was on. "But leaning on another person doesn't make you weak. Letting someone share in your life is a wonderful thing." His voice dipped, turned rough. "Tom was a good man, and he loved you, but he wasn't a pillar. He couldn't handle problems or disappointment."

"No, he couldn't." Sadness engulfed her, pulled her back to years of an empty place setting at the dinner table and an even emptier bed.

"I knew you were pregnant."

"He told you?" Mortification was too mild a term for her present state.

"Didn't have much of a choice, not after I found him and made him confess."

Now was her opportunity to find out the answer she'd wondered about since Tom Carrick strode back into town and proposed. "Did he really want to marry me?"

Will touched her cheek and said, "Yes, he really did."

She blinked back tears and nodded. "Thank you."

"I want to help you, Olivia, and I want you to lean on me. I know that scares you, but I'm scared, too."

"I'm petrified. I'm...I don't know what you want from me."

He tucked a few strands of hair behind her ear. "I want to be your friend, the person you come to when you want to share something or when you're miserable. And I want you to trust me."

"But you want more."

"Eventually. I'd like to think you might want more, too." His blue eyes sparkled. "Do you think that might be possible?"

When he looked at her that way, with such open honesty and caring, anything was possible. She smiled and said in a soft voice, "It might be."

FRIENDS HELPED FRIENDS. They listened, comforted, shared, and encouraged. Tess had already lost Cash; she felt it in her soul and the only way she could get through the pain was to lean on family and friends. She'd shut them out before, but not this time. They would get her through this. Her mother had surprised her with a confession of her own and that sharing made Olivia Carrick more human, more vulnerable. Maybe not that different from her.

Gina picked up Bree and Tess and drove to Christine's, where it was private and people like Edith Finnegan were miles away. Who would have thought Nate Desantro's home would provide a safe haven? Did he even know that while he was at work, his wife was offering support and serving up the chocolate chip cookies he made last night? In his living room? With his daughter sitting on Bree's lap? Of course not. But Tess doubted he'd do more than frown, and not even a deep frown. The right partner certainly changed a person. Was her mother about to find that out with Uncle Will? A month ago, Tess would have laughed at the idea of Olivia Carrick even looking at another man, but if that man was someone as caring, considerate, and compassionate as Uncle Will? Well, anything could happen, couldn't it?

Except in Tess's case, where she'd used up her second chance and watched it explode in front of her with the letter. She almost wished Cash had continued his tirade and accusations, let the anger spew from those beautiful lips. That, she would have understood, and maybe after the hurt had died down, they could have tried to find a way to move forward. But he'd shut down right in front of her and simply walked away.

"Oh, my goodness, Tess." Bree swiped a hand across her cheek, careful to keep a firm hold on a fidgety Anna. "This is so tragic, so utterly devastating. To think we were all imagining the worst about you and there you were, pregnant, and then to lose that little soul, and a tube. Ahh. And then to learn you might never carry a baby. How did you stand it?"

"Bree." Gina shot her a look that said she should have

stopped talking four sentences ago. "You don't have to recap what happened. We know. So does Tess."

Bree placed a hand on her belly as though to protect her own female parts and the baby in her belly. "But how sad." She sniffed, sniffed again. "I simply cannot imagine."

Tess darted a glance at Anna, then looked away. Now they all knew why she'd been hesitant around the baby, never asked to hold her, and when she did look at her, it was a quick glance, then a shift to something else. She'd been carrying a lot of pain and guilt around for too many years, and her friends were determined to help her get through it.

Who knew what Cash might do? If he really loved her, then anything was possible. *Did* he love her? Enough to start over and let go of the past? They could have a good life together, maybe not the one they thought they'd have, but it could still be full and beautiful.

"And that witch of an aunt forcing you back here so you could open your heart and bleed all over again." Bree's eyes narrowed, her lips pinched. "Who did she think she was, threatening to blackmail you? And what did she think that would do to her nephew once he fell head over heels for you all over again? Huh? Then you were supposed to say 'Oh, by the way, I was carrying your child and I almost had an abortion, but I changed my mind, and then I lost the baby and then I found out I might never be able to have kids, and then—'"

"Stop." Gina shook her head and scowled. "You're giving me a headache. We don't need a play-by-play. We know Ramona's a witch." She paused, added, "But she loves Cash, as misdirected as that love might be."

Bree stuck her nose in the air and sniffed her irritation. "I know she raised him when his parents took off to God knows where, but that doesn't give her the right to manipulate other people's lives, namely Tess and Cash's."

Gina frowned, opened her mouth to argue, but Christine jumped in. "Bree does have a point. I've only met Ramona at The Bleeding Hearts meetings, but I know all about being manipulated. My mother did it to the people she 'loved' for years. It was horrible, and in the end, it worked against her."

"Thank you, Christine." Bree slid a glance at Gina. "Just because I don't have a college education does not mean my brain doesn't work. I am constantly thinking and concluding."

Gina's shot her a glance and said, "Thinking and concluding?"

"Oh, yes." Bree's smile stretched. "And I have a thing or two to say about Ramona Casherdon. That woman is no different from my mother-in-law. She didn't think about repercussions; all she cared about was making Cash feel alive again, as if people can turn their emotions on and off when they love somebody. Goes to show what that witch knows about relationships, which is nothing. I mean, could she really not see that when this whole thing blew up, it would be bad for everybody?"

Tess looked at her friends and said, "Ramona pretty much thought that once Cash knew the whole story, he wouldn't want a woman who might not be able to give him a baby. And she was certain he'd never forgive me for not telling him I was pregnant."

"Evil woman," Bree hissed.

Tess shrugged. "Doesn't matter."

"You know, I have a question." Gina rubbed her jaw, her dark gaze settling on Tess. "The doctor told you it might be difficult to get pregnant because of scarring, right? But he didn't say impossible, did he?"

Tess snatched a tissue and dabbed her eyes. "He said difficult, but I doubt most men would be willing to take that chance. And it's not exactly something you throw out over drinks."

"Maybe most men wouldn't be willing to take the chance,"

Bree said in a soft voice, honey-dipped with sympathy. "But I never thought Daniel Casherdon was like most men, and that's what this is really about, isn't it? The reason you never committed to another man wasn't because you might not be able to have children." Her voice dipped lower. "It was because of Cash. You never stopped loving him."

There were times that Bree made a lot of sense. Like now.

"That's it, isn't it, sweetheart?" Bree offered an encouraging smile. "You never stopped loving him."

Tess nodded. "You're right."

"Now what?" This from Gina. "Looks like we're at an impasse. Tess loves Cash. Cash probably loves Tess, but he's too hurt to admit it. If we don't help him see he's still in love with her, he might do something stupid."

"He might go after Natalie Servetti," Bree said in a fierce voice.

They all glared at her, but it was Gina who bit out a warning. "Do not say that woman's name again."

Bree shrugged and muttered, "She's your cousin."

Christine interrupted before Bree and Gina started attacking each other with sarcastic comments. "We've got serious issues here, like a couple that belongs together but is so hurt by the past they can't see a future together. Someone has to talk to Cash, help him see what he could have with Tess."

"It's going to take some serious eye-opening," Gina said. "Got anybody in mind?"

Christine smiled. "Of course." The smile stretched. "My husband."

Bree snickered. "Oh, I'm sure Mr. Tall and Silent will be delighted with that task."

"He's got a very soft and caring side to him," Christine said in a gentle voice.

Gina rolled her eyes. "Do not let your husband hear you

saying that about him. I think he likes the dark and dangerous persona."

"I'd ask Brody to step in and talk to Cash, but he's not big into analyzing his feelings. He says he knows what's in his heart and doesn't need to worry about how it got there, who put it there, or if it's going to stay." Her face lit up, her voice dipped. "He says it's all because of me."

"Well, then," Christine said, "That settles it. I'll talk to Nate."

WILL CARRICK OWNED a helluva lot of land and for the past five days, Cash had spent his time among the wooded areas, sometimes walking, other times sitting on a fallen tree or a large rock. He'd even discovered a pond, complete with bull frogs and blue gill. He was up and out of the cabin by 7:30 in the morning with a couple of bottles of water, an apple, and two peanut butter and jelly sandwiches. It wasn't that he was hungry, but he didn't want to do something stupid and pass out from low blood sugar. Will wouldn't find him for weeks, if and when he noticed he'd gone missing, which at the moment was unlikely since he spent so much time at Olivia Carrick's.

His aunt told him Will and Olivia "were an item." Cash guessed that meant they were together like a pair of socks or a hat and scarf. Great. He was glad for them. Somebody might as well get a happy ending. He tossed a stick in the air, watched it land several yards away. Maybe he should get a dog. Dogs were great companions: loyal, trustworthy, eager to please. They didn't possess the ability for duplicity or lies. Yup, he needed to get a dog. He'd check out the rescue center and see if he could find one, a male. Definitely, a male. Females were too much work, too unpredictable.

He'd come upon a few clearings that would be great for

target practice, if he were so inclined, which he wasn't. His gun rested in the back of a drawer with his T-shirts and underwear, a symbol of another life, one that pitted danger against adrenaline. If he hadn't been shot, he'd still be in Philly chasing bad guys and ignoring anything more important than the next shift. Ben had tried to talk to him about coming back—that was before he left in a royally pissed-off mood because of the way Cash had treated Paige. But Ben didn't know about the hesitation that gave Cash's shooter the edge, or that the reason behind the hesitation was the split-second thought that the kid looked like JJ. And Ben sure as hell didn't know JJ was his ex-fiancée's brother. Talk about a royal screw-up. That was pretty much Cash's life right now.

But didn't people say that sometimes bad things have to happen to you before you make a change? And when you're in a situation that couldn't get any worse, there's a reason for it and if you can get to the other side of that reason, you end up being grateful for the thing that almost did you in? It was probably all bullshit, but right now that's all Cash had.

He wasn't going back to Philly. He wasn't going to be a cop anymore. And he wasn't going to end up with Tess Carrick. That last acknowledgment was the one that gnawed at his gut, came to him in the middle of the night, and crushed his chest so he couldn't get a clean breath. *Shit.*

Even if Cash were willing to start over with Tess, how did you do that with lies? How did you come to a point where trust factored in without checking and rechecking facts like he'd done when he'd received a questionable tip while on the force? There was always doubt and the suspicion that self-interest played a major role in whatever "truth" spilled out. Damn it, would he never be rid of her? Would he never be able to move on and have a relationship with another woman?

When his cell phone rang, he ignored it. There wasn't

anybody he wanted to talk to, and he'd only brought the phone along in case he got lost. Other than that, it was just him, nature, and his thoughts. It was the thoughts that kept beating him down, clinging to him harder than the burrs he'd encountered a little while ago.

On "Day One" of the unraveling of lies, there'd been a bombardment of phone calls and a visit from his aunt and Will Carrick. Separately, of course, but both just as desperate to hear Cash's version of the encounter with his ex-fiancée. What was there to say? *Lies and deceit don't equal the foundation for a relationship*? Ramona had been as close to remorseful as he'd ever seen her, saying something about pure motives but wrong execution. Sure, whatever. She had surprised him when she told him she wished she'd destroyed the letter before he saw it. *And what*, he'd wanted to ask, *wait for Tess to confess to her misdeeds*? But he'd said nothing, merely shrugged and stared at her until she mumbled something, gave him a hug, and left.

What if Ramona *had* destroyed the damnable letter and he and Tess had gotten back together? Would Tess have let the lies fester between them like pus-filled wounds until one day, the poison oozed out and he learned the truth? He didn't know how that would happen, but lies had a way of bursting open when you least expected it.

His child. It had probably been too soon to tell if it was a boy or girl. He'd needed something to hang onto when he left Magdalena eight years ago, and knowing Tess was pregnant might have *forced* them to work things out, even if she did end up losing the baby. But she'd stolen his chance to know he was going to be a father. He swore once, twice, louder, until he lifted his face skyward and shouted a string of curses, all directed at the unfortunate circumstances that made up his existence.

The curses helped, but it was the release of the decibel-splitting anger and desperation amidst the quiet of nature that calmed him, cleared his head, and carved a narrow path of possibility.

There was a lot of uncertainty in his life right now, but here's what he did know: he was not leaving Magdalena. Nate had offered him work finishing furniture and if he thought Cash would be good at it—and Nate was a picky sonofabitch—then what the hell, why not? And he still wanted to work with Will on plans for the youth camp. *That* really interested him. He had a lot of ideas on what the place should look like, what it should offer, how he could work with the school to determine at-risk kids. Cash might never have kids of his own, but he could still make a mark on others, maybe save a few along the way like Will Carrick had saved him.

Rejuvenated, Cash wolfed down the peanut butter and jelly sandwiches, drank half the bottle of water, and worked his way back to the cabin, munching on his apple and making plans for the youth camp. When he reached the clearing that led to his cabin, he spotted Nate's SUV parked next to the barn. Just the person he wanted to see.

The barn doors were open, letting in fresh air and natural sunlight. Nate had his back to the door as he worked an electric sander over the sides of a bookcase and sang Led Zeppelin's "Stairway to Heaven" as it blared from the radio. The scene was too good to interrupt, especially Nate's off-key attempts to hit a few high notes. Cash waited until the song ended and the DJ started reminiscing about Led Zeppelin's greatest hits before he made his way to the long workbench.

"Hey."

Nate looked up, clearly surprised to find him there. Was it general surprise because someone had actually witnessed his singing, or was the surprise because Cash was that someone? He turned off the sander and set it on the workbench. "What's up?"

Cash shrugged, tried to maintain a straight face, but failed. "Might want to leave the high notes to someone else."

Nate laughed. "Yeah, well, I didn't know I had an audience."

Cash waited a few seconds for the "What the hell are you going to do now?" barrage, and when that didn't happen, he relaxed. "Still hating the sanding and finishing part?"

"Oh, yeah."

"Then show me where to start and I'll get going."

Two hours later, Cash had sanded the bookcase smooth enough for a high-end furniture showroom, while Nate cut out the legs for the matching desk. Damn, but it felt good to be busy. A person could only mope around so long feeling sorry for himself and then he needed to get over it and get moving. This work required concentration and would be the perfect distraction. In fact, he'd been so preoccupied these last few hours, he'd thought of nothing but the smoothness of the wood, the smell of it, the feel of it. Nate said tomorrow they'd cordon off a section of the barn for the finishing area since varnish and sanding dust didn't mix.

"How about we quit for today?" Nate set two beers on the workbench and wiped his forehead. "We'll get the fans going in another week or two before the next heat wave, but we'll have to be careful with the finishing area. Fans kick up a lot of dust."

Cash laid the sander on the bench and took a long pull on his beer. "You ever think about renting a building somewhere, get it set up for business?"

Nate shot him a look and said, "Have you been talking to my wife?"

"No, why?"

He sighed. "That's been a big point of contention for a while now. Christine wants to 'loan' me the money to rent a place, but I already took a loan from her to upgrade my equipment." He shrugged. "I like to take things slow and I've got a good setup here. Will lets me use the barn and I let him use my tools, and I help him out with projects."

"But if you had a dedicated building, imagine the production you could kick out."

Nate studied his beer, frowned. "I know. I think about it, but I'm having an issue taking my wife's money, even if she fancies it up with paperwork. It's still her money."

"A loan isn't taking. What about if *I* loaned you the money?" As soon as the question fell out of his mouth, another took hold. "Or what if I bought into the business? I've got enough money saved."

Nate met his gaze, held it. "So, you're definitely staying here?"

Cash nodded. "I'm staying." And then, "I've got this idea to start a camp for troubled kids. They'd come during school breaks and in the summer. Not sure how we'd select them or the age group, but they'd work the land, maybe learn a skill, like how to use a band saw or a jointer." He grinned. "Hell, I don't know. They'd learn about working together and that this world is not just about them and their needs. I keep thinking if we'd gotten to JJ younger, we might have saved him; same with the seventeen-year-old kid who shot me. Was there really no other alternative but to rob a convenience store and shoot a cop?"

"I think it's a great idea. Very generous."

"Yeah, well." He polished off his beer and set it on the workbench. "Will said he'd help out."

"Count me in, too. Just let me know what you need."

"Good. And I still plan to work with you, whether or not you want me to invest." He shrugged. "I actually like the sanding and varnishing part."

Nate shook his head. "Better you than me. I'll keep building and you keep sanding. As for Will and your youth camp idea, we've got to get him involved. He's got some great ideas, but he's been pretty scarce lately."

"So I've noticed." Should he tell him that Will and Olivia Carrick were "an item"? He was contemplating the thought when Nate made his decision for him.

"I heard Will and Olivia Carrick are seeing each other." He whistled under his breath. "Who would have thought?"

And there it was, the Carrick name creeping into the conversation. Cash tried to beat it down. "Never can tell, I guess. Want another beer?" He didn't wait for an answer but headed for the small fridge in the corner.

"Can't. I have to get home." He hesitated. "I'd ask you to dinner but Christine invited—" he stopped, reworked the sentence "—it might be uncomfortable for you."

Because Tess Carrick, the ex-fiancée, would be there. That's what Nate wanted to say.

"No problem. Ramona sent me chili and cornbread. I've got plenty."

Nate laughed. "I almost wish I were eating here. Christine is trying out my mother's chicken and broccoli casserole recipe, but," he paused, "she's been working on it since we got married and still hasn't quite gotten it right."

Cash saluted him with his beer. "Then I'll be thinking of you with every bite I take."

Nate shifted from one booted foot to the other, obviously uncomfortable with whatever he was about to say. Ten bucks it had the name Tess in it.

"Look, I hate this kind of stuff and I really don't want to get involved—"

"Then don't."

Nate shot him a look. "I promised my wife I'd talk to you. Nobody had more baggage than Christine and I did. My mother and her father, Lily, her damn mother. It was such a mess and I was so angry and resentful. I didn't trust her, even when I should have trusted her, I wouldn't." He stared at a the hand plane he'd just used as if reliving those moments. "It was pure torture. I wanted to hate her but I couldn't. When she was gone, I thought about her all the time and that really pissed me off. And once I touched her," his voice turned rough, "that was heaven and hell." He let out a laugh that fizzled. "Once we were married, I thought we were past the rough spots, but I had no idea it could get so much worse. I didn't think we'd survive."

Will had told Cash how Christine Desantro's mother drove into town in her fancy car and uppity attitude and paid Natalie Servetti to "fake seduce" Nate, just enough so there would be pictures to make it look real. Oh, yes, real enough to destroy their marriage, which it almost did. Christine was pregnant, too. But somehow they'd gotten past it and Will said Pop Benito had a lot to do with it. Maybe Nate *was* the only one who understood how Cash felt, and maybe the pain he talked about was still too close to the surface, like a scab that would reopen with the slightest scratch.

"That was a bad deal," Cash said. "I'm sorry."

Nate's expression turned dark, fierce. "I'd go through it a hundred times if it meant being with Christine."

"I never took you for a man who loved torture."

He touched the wedding ring on his left finger and when he spoke his voice was raw and brittle. "The real torture would be life without her."

17

The members of The Bleeding Hearts Society had gathered for their monthly meeting, but they were not thinking about Wanda Cummings's recommendation that more fertilizer was required for the droopy impatiens outside the coffee shop on Main Street. Nor were they particularly interested in Mimi Pendergrass's proposal for a new terra cotta planter by the post office. They were not even taken in with the deliciousness of Ramona Casherdon's sweet rolls or Mimi Pendergrass's signature hibiscus ice tea, the latter being a welcome relief on this extra warm summer day. No, they had other thoughts skittering through their brains, thumping in their hearts, trying desperately to sneak past their pinched lips.

What was going to happen to Cash and Tess?

When Pop Benito invited her to the meeting, Tess had almost turned him down, but then she'd realized exactly why she needed to go. There would never be a better opportunity to say what needed saying and Ramona Casherdon would be there. When else could she expect a face-to-face with the woman, even though her mother had insisted Cash's aunt had a few things to tell her. Doubtful anything Tess was interested in, but Ramona wasn't the reason Tess accepted the invitation. No, that was not it at all.

"Who's making the lavender sachets for the Flowers and Hearts sale?" Mimi glanced over her reading glasses and waited. Wanda Cummings and Bree raised their hands.

Of course, Bree had a question and a comment. She always did. "I was thinking maybe the thread should be lavender, too, since we're making *lavender* sachets." She smiled at the group. "You know, in keeping with the theme."

"Uh-huh." Mimi nodded. "That's a fine idea, Bree. You and Wanda work on that."

Bree lit up like a birthday candle and nodded.

"Now, on to the basil, oregano, and parsley. We need twenty pots planted by next Sunday so they'll be well past the shocky state by sale time." Mimi pointed to Pop. "You're in charge of these." She winked. "And don't forget to say your special prayers or whatever it is you do to get that basil of yours to grow like the Amazon jungle."

Pop laughed and saluted her. "Will do." He turned to Tess and said in a loud whisper, "You can help."

How did he even know if she would be here at the end of summer, when The Bleeding Hearts Society held their annual sales event, if she didn't know herself? Right now, she had no idea where she'd be, but before she left this building, she had to clear the air. Tess wished Christine had been able to attend today. She'd had her own share of grief with this town and the man she loved and was a source of comfort and reassurance to Tess. Unfortunately, Anna had a doctor's appointment, which left Bree, and while Bree was a good friend and meant well, she'd never known the heartache of losing the man you loved.

When Mimi paused to let Wanda Cummings, The Bleeding Hearts secretary, catch up with her notes, Tess stood and cleared throat. "Mimi, would you mind if I spoke a moment?"

A hush swirled about the room faster than a midsummer thunderstorm. Wanda Cummings set down her pen. Bree gasped. Some members stopped nibbling their sweet rolls. Others gulped down their hibiscus tea. Ramona Casherdon grew very still and Pop fidgeted in his chair. No one spoke until finally, Mimi Pendergrass removed her green polka-dotted reading glasses and said, "Why, of course, dear. You go right on ahead and take as much time as you need."

Tess nodded. "Thank you." She looked around the room, her gaze darting over Cash's aunt, settling on Bree, who offered a smile of encouragement. "I've been running from my life for eight years: hopping planes, overscheduling, moving so fast I didn't have time to think. Or feel. I sold lipstick and made a lot of money doing it. I'd probably still be selling it if my company hadn't been sold and I'd gotten the boot." She took in the surprised looks and continued. "It's the best thing that could have happened to me because it forced me to think about my life."

She took a deep breath and pushed out the words she'd kept inside for too long. "You all know what happened eight years ago, and you also know how it split the town, pitting one person against another. Even relatives couldn't agree on what was right and what wasn't. I was the cause of much of that grief, not Cash, even though I blamed him. I should have stayed despite my grief over losing my brother, but I didn't." Her voice dipped, turned raw. "And I lost more than a fiancé. I lost hope and a chance for what I wanted most: a family with the man I loved. You all know I ran away from this town, but you don't know what I did, and that's what I want to tell you."

"Tess!" Bree's eyes were bright, her face shocked. "You don't have to do this." Her eyes grew brighter. "Please. Don't."

Tess offered a faint smile and said, "Thanks, Bree, but I do. I should have done this a long time ago." She fixed her gaze on

Ramona. "I took off to my sister's, and you can all guess how that turned out. I love Riki, but she's not good at big-picture things," she paused. "Or consequences."

"I don't see how your confession will benefit anyone but provide fodder for town gossip." This from Ramona Casherdon who locked gazes with Tess.

Ramona didn't want her to continue? Now that was truly bizarre. The woman should have been spattering testimony to Tess's horrible character and dirty secrets. So, why wasn't she? Why did she look almost compassionate? Tess skipped past Ramona and honed in on Bree's belly until her vision blurred. "When I was at Riki's, I found out I was pregnant. I didn't know what to do and even thought about an abortion." She paused to let the words sink into the listeners' heads. "I went to the clinic but I couldn't go through with it." She blinked, blinked again and kept her gaze on the pink cotton stretching over Bree's rounded belly. "The next day I lost the baby. The doctors said it was an ectopic pregnancy. There were complications and I spent days in the hospital, feverish and so sick."

Tess cleared her throat, pushed out the last painful bits of confession. "When I went for my checkup, I was still having trouble. Pain, tenderness. It seems there was scarring and..." *Say it. Just say it.* "The doctor said I might never be able to get pregnant. So. Now you know. And I'm sure you figured out by now that Cash knew nothing about any of this until last week." She tried to smile, but her lips wobbled and fell flat. "I think you've all guessed about me long enough. Still, I wanted you to hear the truth." She nodded and eased into her chair.

Pop scratched his head and nodded. "Where's that leave you and Cash?"

"Yes, where does that leave the two of you?" Wanda Cummings scooted her ample figure forward in her chair and leaned toward Tess.

What to say to that? "Cash and I aren't...he doesn't..."

"He has to!" Bree's words burst into the room in a rush of hope and anguish. "He still loves you, I know he does. We have got to find a way to make him see how much he needs you."

Pop slapped his hand on the table and said, "Dang right we do. I promised Lucy there'd be a wedding and on my wife's favorite roses, there's going to be one."

Tess darted a glance at Ramona, held her gaze. "I don't think that's going to happen."

"I heard he's planning to stay here, set up shop with Nate Desantro," Wanda Cummings murmured. "Isn't that what you told me, Pop?"

Pop and his tales. Apparently he knew how to spread news faster than the *Magdalena Press.* He scratched his head again and appeared very interested in dissecting a piece of sweet roll. "I might have said something along those lines, but there's always room for misinterpretation."

"I know what you said." Wanda stuck her pointy chin in the air and challenged Pop to dispute her words.

He shrugged. "So you know. That ain't the problem now, is it? The problem is getting these kids together when hurt and pride is standing in the way. Like my Lucy always said, 'Even love that blooms eternal runs into patches of crabgrass.' And there you have it." He picked up a piece of sweet roll, popped it in his mouth.

"My." Mimi Pendergrass shook her head, making the redball earrings she wore bob and dance. "I think you've got The Society's support." She slid a sideways glance at Cash's aunt, who remained still and silent. "Or at least most of them. Answer a question for me, Tess. I know it might be a tad embarrassing but you've shared more today than most people do in twenty years. So, I'm going to ask you straight out. Do you love Cash? Do you want another chance with him?"

Love him? She loved him so much it hurt when she breathed. Did she want another chance? Well, that was like asking Pop if he had an obsession with pizzelles. Tess opened her mouth to speak, but emotion suffocated the words, so she simply nodded.

"Well then," Mimi Pendergrass picked up a pen and turned all business, "what are we going to do about that? Anyone have a plan?"

Tess stared at Mimi, not sure she'd heard right. The Bleeding Hearts Society was going to formulate a plan to get her and Cash back together?

Wanda Cummings let out her thoughts in a gush. "We can invite him here and take turns telling him why he and Tess should give it another go. And I'll give testimony to the joys of being married to the same person for," she paused and laughed, "too many years to remember."

"Thank you, Wanda." Mimi jotted down a few notes. "We'll take that recommendation under advisement. Anyone else?"

Bree raised her hand and when Mimi nodded, she said, "I have old pictures of Tess and Cash. Do you think it would help for him to see them? Maybe he'd remember how happy he was?" She paused, her voice dipped. "How happy he could be again?"

No, he will not want to see those pictures or those memories.

Ramona Casherdon's voice split into Tess's thoughts. "I have something to say." The woman met Tess's gaze, held it. Then she did something Tess was certain she'd never witnessed before: she smiled. "Tess, I want you to marry my nephew." The smile stretched. "You belong together and I'm sorry it took me so many years to realize it."

"Hallelujah!" Pop stood and raised his arms above his head. "Those are the sweetest words I've heard in a long time. Thank you, Ramona." He placed his bony hands on the table, spread his fingers wide, and leaned forward. "We're gonna get this boy and we're gonna get him good."

"Pop?" Mimi's voice said she was clearly confused with Pop's agenda.

"Letters, Mimi. Letters. The whole town's gonna write the boy letters on why he and Tess belong together and they're gonna share their own love stories. Short and sweet." He grinned, swept a hand around the table, "Or long and lusty."

And that was how The Bleeding Hearts Society figured out a plan to reunite Daniel "Cash" Casherdon and Tess Carrick.

THE LETTERS BEGAN ARRIVING two days later, handwritten in blue ink, black, red, even lime green, all addressed to Daniel Casherdon, all having to do with love and starting over. And Tess.

He counted fifteen letters in the last three days, with three more today. What the hell was going on? Was everybody in Magdalena going to send him a letter, imploring him to make things right with Tess? It's not that he needed reminders of his ex-fiancée because he'd been thinking of nothing else since that day in the barn when Nate confessed that living without Christine would be the real torture. Damn, that was serious stuff that could emasculate a guy if it got in the wrong hands. Except Nate didn't seem to care who knew how he felt about his wife. Maybe because he'd almost lost her.

Well, Cash *had* lost Tess, no "almost" about it. But what if they could make it right, get that "second chance" with each other? The most peaceful moments he'd experienced in years were the times when she'd stayed with him in the cabin, sharing a meal, conversation, a bed. Paige had called twice, saying she forgave him for being so harsh with her and offering to visit whenever he liked, for however long he liked. She didn't mention the fact that he'd run out the door calling another woman's name. Apparently, she'd categorized that behavior under the "harsh" category and had forgiven him that, too.

Tess would not have been so generous. She'd probably have pulled out his gun and aimed it at his crotch, threatening to pull the trigger if he looked sideways at a woman. Paige was more about seduction and bending a man to her ways, while Tess had always been about confrontation and talking first, seduction and bending later. But the time she most needed to confront and talk had been after JJ's death, and yet, she'd run away.

Cash grabbed a letter and tore it open. What would this one say? Who would it be from? He knew all of the senders, or at least recognized the family names. Some were heartfelt; others humorous; still others quoted poems, lyrics, and Scripture. When he received the first batch of letters, he'd almost tossed them in the trash. But then he opened one, and then another, and continued on until he'd read all of them. The sentiments stayed with him as he put a coat of varnish on a rocker or buffed out a row of spindles. These people had good hearts and they cared, rare qualities in today's society. He unfolded a letter and read.

Dear Cash:

You and Nate have been friends a long time, despite an eight-year hiatus. That boy was going down a bad path of misery, bursting with enough anger and resentment to fill a pond. But then, miracle of miracles, Christine walked into his life. Now how's that for trouble? You see them now all lovey-dovey, but don't go thinking it was all rosy for them because it was more thorns than petals. But then one day they really looked at each other, really talked, and really fell in love. I'm sure you know the other near-disaster that happened after they were married.

Almost tore poor Nate apart. But they worked through it and their love is stronger than steel.

You and Tess belong together, like Nate and Christine. Give love a chance. We're all cheering for you.

Fondly,
Betty Rafferty

CASH SET that one aside and reached for another.

CASH:

Lucy and I had our share of struggles, but we never let the crabgrass strangle us. Grab onto Tess's hand and pull her out of the weeds. You two belong together, barefoot in a field of clover.

And as my Lucy used to say, "Be happy with the life you got, not the one you didn't get."

Pop Benito

THE THIRD LETTER was not a letter at all, but a photograph of Tess, Gina, and Bree, laughing into the camera, arms flung around each other's waists. His gaze zeroed in on Tess and the gown she wore: her wedding gown. Had they taken this the night he'd shot JJ? Maybe at the exact moment the boy drew his last breath? Cash stared at the photo so hard and long his eyes hurt, then he flipped it over and looked on the back. *You and Tess need to smile again. Gina.*

"Hello. Hello."

Cash turned to find a young girl standing on the other side of the screen door with a shoebox in her hands. She was small-built with thick black hair and glasses. "Hi." He tossed the picture of Tess, Gina, and Bree on the table and made his way toward the girl. "Can I help you?"

"I'm Lily." She smiled up at him as he opened the door and thrust the box toward him. "These are from Pop. He said they are supposed to sweeten you up." The smile spread. "He's silly."

So, this was Lily Desantro, Nate's sister. Christine's, too. He only seen her once or twice, when she was a baby. "Come on in, Lily. I'm Cash."

"I know." She glanced around the family room and kitchen. "Do you have a clock?"

"On the microwave. Why?"

She headed toward the kitchen and the digital display on the microwave. "Four-o-five. Nate said I can only stay five minutes and then I have to go find him in the barn because he doesn't want me to bug you."

Cash laughed. "You aren't bugging me."

Her blue eyes grew shiny behind her thick glasses. "Can you ask him if I can stay longer? I don't want to ask because he'll get all frowny."

"Okay, I'll ask. Now how about we see what Pop sent that's supposed to sweeten me up?" He lifted the shoebox and peeked inside even though he had a pretty good idea what was in there. Sure enough, three stacks of pizzelles sat on a folded paper towel. Cash removed two pizzelles, handed one to Lily. "My favorite." He bit into one, chewed. "How about a glass of ice tea or lemonade?"

"Sure. Lemonade please." Lily scooted onto a kitchen chair and munched on her pizzelle. "Cash?"

"Huh?" He plunked a couple of ice cubes in each glass and poured the lemonade.

"I don't think you have a pig head."

He almost dropped the pitcher when she said that. Cash swung around and stared at her. "What are you talking about?"

She shrugged. "Pop said you had a pig head." She paused. "He said things could work out if you weren't a pig head. What does that mean?"

Good old Pop. He called it like he saw it. And he saw Cash as pig-headed. "You'll have to ask Pop."

Lily let out a little puff of breath, like that was not what she wanted to do. "Okay." And then, she glanced at the letters scattered on the corner of the table. "What are all those pieces of paper?"

"Just letters."

"Uh-uh." She leaned forward and located the picture of Tess, Gina, and Bree. "Not this one. Ooohhh." She pointed to the trio, her voice soft, almost reverent. "Tess. She's beautiful." She glanced up, studied him. "Pop said she was your girlfriend. You were gonna marry her and then it all went south. What did he mean, 'went south,' and why didn't you marry her?"

What the hell was Pop doing, chronicling the rise and fall of Daniel Casherdon, complete with commentaries? "You should ask Pop," he said in a quiet voice. Was every person he met going to dissect his past relationship with Tess Carrick?

"Can't you tell me, Cash?" Her eyes turned bluer, her voice softer. "And can't you fix it so it doesn't go south?" She lifted the photo and traced Tess's face. "So maybe you can still fall in love and get married. And live happily ever after."

TESS LUGGED the suitcase outside and was negotiating the porch steps when Cash barreled down the street in Will's old truck, well above the posted speed limit. He pulled in the driveway and hopped out, moving toward her with determined steps and a fierce expression on his face.

He stopped at the bottom of the steps and said in a voice raw with emotion, "Don't go. Please. I can't lose you again. Will you give us another chance? I don't want to live in the past anymore." He paused, sucked in a deep breath, and plowed on. "I need you in my life and I'll take anything you're offering. If we can't have kids, we'll adopt. If we can't adopt, we'll foster. Hell, we'll babysit Nate and Bree's kids, and who knows, maybe one day, Gina's? Or we'll get a bunch of dogs." He held his hands out to her, palms up. "Anything. Just don't leave me again."

Tess released her hand on the suitcase and moved toward him. "I'm not going anywhere." She offered him a hesitant smile. "But if you'll keep talking like that, I'll pretend I am just to hear more."

He glanced at the suitcase and the boxes stacked on the front porch. "What's all this?"

"Mom's having surgery next week and I'm delivering her suitcase to Uncle Will's so she can recover there." She cleared her throat and said, "Supposedly she's staying at his house because he only has one flight of stairs and she has two here. I'm not so sure I buy that, but I'm happy for them."

"Oh." The faintest pink crept up his neck, landed on his cheeks. "And what about the boxes?"

"JJ's." Her voice dipped. "Mom and I thought it was time to pack up his clothes. Somebody might get some use out of them."

He shoved his hands in his pockets, the pink on his neck and cheeks turning five shades deeper. "Good idea." His gaze zeroed in on the boxes.

Obviously, he was regretting the adrenaline-fueled profession of "need and can't live without you" he'd just delivered on her front lawn. Well, he wasn't getting out of the truth this time, and neither was she. Tess touched his cheek, traced the line of his jaw, stepped closer. "If I pretended I was leaving, would you tell me again how much you need me and want to be with me?"

His lips twitched. "I might." He buried his hands in her hair and eased her toward him. "Or I might just tell you I love you and have never stopped loving you."

She leaned on tiptoe, placed a soft kiss on his mouth. "I love you, Daniel Casherdon, and if you give me a chance, I will spend the rest of my life showing you just how much."

"Now that is something I could get used to." He deepened the kiss, fitting her body to his in a pledge of love and commitment. "Let's take this inside," he murmured against her lips. "To your bed...where I will undress you and taste you..." He slid a hand down her back, cupped her butt. "And pleasure you until the whole town hears you shout my name."

"Yes." She lifted her head to the sun as he trailed his tongue along the opening of her shirt. "Oh, yes."

Cash pulled back and lifted her in his arms. "If we don't go inside, we're going to give your neighbor a real show." Tess laughed and glanced toward Edith Finnegan's window. The curtain didn't move because it had been pulled wide open and there stood Edith, expression intent as she witnessed Cash and Tess pledging their hearts to one another, from this day forward. And then, miracle of all miracles, Edith Finnegan smiled.

18

Two months later
Three days before Cash and Tess's wedding

"Why don't you just ask the doctor if you're having a boy and be done with it?" Gina shook her head and gathered a length of pink tulle.

Bree ignored her and fished around for another blue Jordan almond. No one commented that she was supposed to be placing the almonds, even the blue ones, in netting and tying it with a white satin ribbon. Christine and Tess had a small mound of the Jordan almond party favors in front of them, while Bree had fewer than ten in her stack. "Brody is certain this baby is going to be his Brody Junior." She popped a blue Jordan almond in her mouth and chewed. "I think he's right this time. We changed things up a bit when I conceived and that's going to make a difference; you just wait and see."

Gina coughed and rolled her eyes. Christine smiled and Tess laughed. What would these gatherings be like without

Bree's too-honest and often too-personal comments? She and Brody were determined that baby Kinkaid number four would be a boy. But what if it weren't? Would Brody push for baby number five, six, and seven, until he had a son? At this rate, Bree would have her own basketball team in two years and a football team before she hit forty. There might not be anything left of her, but Brody would have his "brood" and maybe even a boy.

"How's your mother doing?"

Tess could always count on Christine to steer the conversation to more acceptable topics. "She's doing great. Of course, Uncle Will is spoiling her with his chicken piccata and beef burgundy. The man cooks, cleans," she paused, raised a brow, "even does toilets. And he grocery-shops and brings her fresh flowers every day. I think he irons, too."

Bree sighed. "A twilight romance. I'd be happy if Brody remembered to close the toilet lid every now and again."

What to say to that? Bree called her husband a "man's man" and maybe that was true, though Cash and Nate had other thoughts on Brody Kinkaid and his Neanderthal tactics. But Bree loved him, had always loved him, and she'd take her last breath professing that love.

"Do you think your mother will stay at Will's?" Bree set aside five blue almonds. "Maybe even get married?"

Gina interrupted before Tess could answer. "Nobody's getting married before Tess. And we're not talking about anybody getting married until after Tess and Cash tie the knot." She pinned Bree with a "do you understand?" look.

"Okay, just asking." Bree patted her very large belly and sighed. "There's a special someone out there for every person walking this earth, and I think it's wonderful when the stars bring them together."

Of course Gina was not about to let that go. "Not everyone is looking for that special someone. There are a lot of people who are perfectly happy by themselves."

Bree cast her a "You don't really mean that" look and popped another almond in her mouth.

They'd been working on the wedding checklist for the past two nights. Tess's old house was the perfect spot since no one was around to disturb the "production and assembly" table. Christine had replaced Gina as the organizer with the spreadsheets, but Gina still liked to keep the details streamlined and the production process going. Bree, on the other hand, was not a piece worker. She gabbed, stopped, popped a blue Jordan almond in her mouth, rubbed her belly, took a bathroom break. Still the same Bree. A few months ago, Tess could not have imagined she'd be sitting with her friends, working on arrangements for a wedding she thought would never happen. It had been years coming, but in three days she would marry Daniel Casherdon, the only man she ever loved.

Since the afternoon in the driveway where they'd professed their love, witnessed by the now "almost friendly" Edith Finnegan, Tess and Cash had opened up to each other and shared their dreams, their hopes, even their fears. Would there be a baby? If not, an adoption? Was Cash really okay with the not knowing? He was. Cash eventually told her the real reason he left the force in Philly, how he'd hesitated the night he was shot because the shooter reminded him of JJ. He'd never confessed that truth to anyone else but he'd needed to share it with her.

Love and trust opened up so many possibilities. Cash talked about working with Nate in the furniture business and how he'd come up with a few ideas to expand the business. He thought Tess's sales knowledge could help market their products and Nate liked the idea. So did she. He'd also shared his desire to start a youth camp for troubled kids with her help and Will's, probably Nate and Christine's too. *Your uncle might not have had kids of his own, but he's been a father and a mentor to me. I want to do the same. If he hadn't given me a chance, I'd have gone down a different road.* He'd paused, held her gaze. *And not a good one.* Once the wedding and the honeymoon to Niagara Falls were over, they'd begin mapping out serious plans for the camp. He'd even talked about a dog or two... *Rescues*, he'd said with a big grin. *Just like us.*

When the doorbell rang a half-hour later, Tess, Bree, and Gina looked at each other, mouths pinched, their eyes wide. Eight years ago, Bree had opened the door to a bloody and desperate Cash.

Christine must have sensed their fear because she pushed back her chair and said, "I'll get it." She moved toward the door and opened it. Cash stood on the other side, a big smile on his face, and he was not alone.

"Happy almost Wedding Day!" Cash, Nate, Brody, and Cash's buddy, Ben Reed, barreled through the door with a bouquet of pink and white balloons, two bottles of wine, a huge box of chocolate meltaways, and a bottle of Jack Daniel's. The latter had clearly been opened and enjoyed if the flushed faces and grins were any indication.

Brody's baritone filled the room as he sang "Truly" a cappella. Cash made his way to Tess, leaned over, and kissed her long and slow. Nate grabbed Christine's hand and led her to Olivia's piano, where he sat down and patted the seat beside him. Christine slid next to her husband and kissed him. Brody moved toward his wife and pulled her to her feet as he belted out the love ballad. Gina scratched her jaw, caught Ben Reed watching her, and turned her back to him. When Nate began playing "I Will Always Love You" they all gathered round, joining in the song of love, commitment, and forever.

Cash slung his arm around Tess's waist as they swayed to the music, her head on his shoulder, as he softly sang in her ear. Oh, yes, the men had been doing a bit of celebrating. Cash didn't sing in the shower but he was singing now; so was Nate, which was as funny as it was endearing and really should be video-taped. No one had the nerve to do it and face Nate Desantro's wrath tomorrow. So they'd commit this night to memory and pull it out years from now, faded, worn, but still capable of pulling a smile from their faces. Five songs later, Ben opened the bottles of wine and filled Olivia Carrick's juice glasses. Bree abstained, for obvious reasons. "Let's toast," Ben said, "to the future Mr. and Mrs. Daniel Casherdron; may they enjoy long nights and long lives together."

"May they create memories every day," Bree added, saluting them with her bottle of water.

"And every night." Brody whistled and cheered.

Christine raised her glass. "May they find true peace and contentment."

"And learn tolerance and patience," Nate said, with a grin, stroking the piano keys.

Gina was the last one to offer a toast. She raised her glass, looked at Cash and Tess, and said in a quiet voice filled with conviction, "It's been a long road back to each other, but you've made it because you belong together, because true love never gives up and never dies." She paused and her dark eyes grew bright. "Open your arms and your hearts and embrace the journey."

And three days later that's exactly what they did.

EPILOGUE

Pop sat on the back porch sipping an ice tea and munching on a pizzelle. In another few weeks, the night air would grow crisp and the leaves would turn from green to red, yellow, even orange. Flowers would begin to fade and wither, giving up their fanciness like an old prom dress. But this morning the scent of lavender and lemon balm drifted to him and the zinnias burst in shocks of red and pink, signs that summer had not yet left them.

He didn't sleep much last night, too many things rumbling around in his head. His belly was doing its share of rumbling, too, what with all the food he ate at the wedding. How was a person supposed to turn away from a dish of manicotti and a thick slice of roast beef? And when au gratin potatoes—not from a box either—are right next to the garlic mashed ones, well, doesn't a body need a taste of both? This body did, and this body paid for it in the middle of the night.

Pop shook his head and laughed. "Oh Lucy, it sure was tasty. And the new thing is cupcakes, fancy ones with swirly frosting. They had red velvet, triple chocolate." He scratched his jaw as a few more popped into his brain. "Vanilla, and this strawberry one that made me think of you. Things sure have changed since you and I got hitched." He sighed. "Don't make no difference if you're eating on china or a paper plate; the real test is the day-to-day living. Just wait until Tess finds out Cash picked up a dog from the rescue center. Henry's his name. Will's got him up at his place until Cash and Tess get back from Niagara Falls. Hmph. Henry."

"You should have seen me and Lily dancing. I was teaching her to do the jitterbug and she didn't do half bad." He laughed. "Oh, that girl does love to dance and you know I always did have moves. Speaking of moves, Natalie Servetti was at it again. This time she was hanging all over Cash's friend, Ben Reed. Odd thing, though, he kept looking at her cousin, Gina. Remember her? Dark hair, dark eyes, curvy. Italian with an attitude. They got matched up in the bridal party, but I think they'd make a good pair. Gotta get through some issues first; something about an ex-wife." He tapped his chin, pulled out details of Gina's past. "That poor girl never had a family who believed in her, but all it takes is the right person. The boy talked about moving here, so we'll see if he's the one." He yawned, thinking he might need a nap before Lily showed up for their checkers game.

"I'll tell you who's not impressing me right now is Brody Kinkaid. Poor Bree's about to have that baby and wasn't he bragging about going for another one if he didn't get a boy? Somebody needs to tell him to zip it or snip it. You think Nate might do that?" He scratched his jaw, considered this. "Nah. But Christine might. I'm gonna have to think on that."

He grabbed another pizzelle, took a bite, and thought about the latest bit of news that crossed his ears just yesterday. "Christine's uncle's moving to Magdalena with his brood. Building some big Hollywood-style mansion in the west end. Bought up three properties to do it. Imagine that? I'm not too keen on Charlie Blacksworth's brother rolling into this town, but you gotta give the man credit for raising someone else's kids. Still, not my first choice, but Christine sure is excited, so is Lily, and dang, even Nate and Miriam are chirping away about this guy and his family like they're royalty.

"I'm telling you, Lucy, this is going to get very interesting and I'll be right here, giving you a play-by-play." He folded his hands over his belly and closed his eyes. "Yes, indeed I certainly will."

The End

IT's the end for now, but don't worry, there'll be more heartache, betrayal, forgiveness, and redemption for the residents of Magdalena as the saga continues in *A Family Affair: Fall*, Book Four in the Truth in Lies Series! Harry's heading to Magdalena with his brood...and that should be something to witness. Gina Servetti might shy away from all things male, especially relationships, but Ben Reed is no ordinary male. Let the verbal sparring and the unwanted attraction begin.

If you'd like to be notified of my new releases, please sign up at *http://www.marycampisi.com*.

Many thanks for choosing to spend your time reading *A Family Affair: Summer*. If you enjoyed it, please consider writing a review on the site where you purchased it. And now, I must head back to Magdalena and help these characters get in and out of trouble!

LETTERS TO CASH

Letters to Cash

Here are a few of the letters Cash received as the town tried to work their magic and convince Cash that he and Tess deserved a second chance.

The heart knows what it wants. Deny that and you walk the earth in a shadow of regret. Do not live that regret one moment longer. E.F.

Look in the mirror, admit the truth, tell Tess. Easy, right? No, but damn necessary. Am I going to need a suit anytime soon? How about a tie? Nate

Family isn't about genes or sharing the same last name. It's about commitment, community, and caring. You and Tess have a lifetime to share. Do not waste another minute. Dolly Finnegan (Jack's wife)

Apparently my niece thinks I know a thing or two about relation-ships and wanted me to share some ideas with you. Hah! Christine gives this old fool too much credit. The only thing I can tell you is when you find the right woman, she'll teach you all you need to know. Harry Blacksworth

Love isn't neat and tidy like a well-organized linen drawer. It's messier than a five-year-old playing in mud, but just as sweet once you clean off the dirt. Wanda Cummings

The honeymoon suite at Heart Sent is ready and waiting. Mimi Pendergrass

Let yourself love her. She's good for you. Ramona

I've never been one to trust or love easily, but I'm taking a chance and I don't think I'll regret it. Take that chance. Olivia

Don't let fear stand in the way of true love. Will

I'm naming a burger after you and Tess. Available next week. It's called the "Take a chance on me" burger. Phyllis at Lina's Café

Cash and Tess. Forever. Love, Lily Desantro

COPYRIGHT

Copyright 2014 by Mary Campisi

A Family Affair: Summer is a work of fiction. Names, characters, and situations are all products of the author's imagination and any resemblance to real persons, locales, or events, are purely coincidental. This book is copyright protected.

Print ISBN: 978-0-9857773-7-1

ABOUT THE AUTHOR

Mary Campisi writes emotion-packed books about second chances. Whether contemporary romances, women's fiction, or Regency historicals, her books all center on belief in the beauty of that second chance. Her small town romances center around family life, friendship, and forgiveness as they explore the issues of today's contemporary women.

Mary should have known she'd become a writer when at age thirteen she began changing the ending to all the books she read. It took several years and a number of jobs, including registered nurse, receptionist in a swanky hair salon, accounts payable clerk, and practice manager in an OB/GYN office, for her to rediscover writing. Enter a mouse-less computer, a floppy disk, and a dream large enough to fill a zip drive. The rest of the story lives on in every book she writes.

When she's not working on her craft or following the lives of five adult children, Mary's digging in the dirt with her flowers and herbs, cooking, reading, walking her rescue lab mix, Cooper, or, on the perfect day, riding off into the sunset with her very own hero/husband on his Harley Ultra Limited.

If you would like to be notified when Mary has a new release, please sign up at http://www.marycampisi.-com/book/book-release-mailing-list/

Mary has published with Kensington, Carina Press, and The Wild Rose Press and she is currently working on the next book in her very popular Truth in Lies series, the A Family Affair books. This family saga is filled with heartache, betrayal, forgiveness and redemption in a small town setting.

For more information

https://www.marycampisi.com

mary@marycampisi.com

OTHER BOOKS BY MARY CAMPISI

That Second Chance Series

Book One: *Pulling Home*

Book Two: *The Way They Were*

Book Three: *Simple Riches*

Book Four: *Paradise Found*

Book Five: *Not Your Everyday Housewife*

Book Six: *The Butterfly Garden*

That Second Chance Boxed Set 1-3

That Second Chance Boxed Set 4-6

That Second Chance Complete Boxed Set 1-6

The Betrayed Trilogy

Book One: *Pieces of You*

Book Two: *Secrets of You*

Book Three: *What's Left of Her*: a novella

The Betrayed Trilogy Boxed Set

Begin Again

The Sweetest Deal

Regency Historical:

An Unlikely Husband Series

Book One - *The Seduction of Sophie Seacrest*

Book Two - *A Taste of Seduction*

Book Three - *A Touch of Seduction*, a novella

Book Four - *A Scent of Seduction*

An Unlikely Husband Boxed Set

The Model Wife Series

Book One: *The Redemption of Madeline Munrove*

Young Adult:

Pretending Normal

CPSIA information can be obtained
at www.ICGtesting.com
Printed in the USA
LVHW011705180119
604419LV00014B/319/P